HIGHER ED

TESSA McWATT

SCRIBE
Melbourne • London

Scribe Publications
18–20 Edward St, Brunswick, Victoria 3056, Australia
2 John St, Clerkenwell, London, WC1N 2ES, United Kingdom

First published in Canada by Random House Canada, 2015
Published in Australia and the UK by Scribe 2015

A portion of this novel, titled "A Taste of Marmalade," was published as a Kindle Single in September 2013.

Extract from HOWL by Allen Ginsberg. Copyright © Allen Ginsberg, 1956, used by permission of The Wylie Agency (UK) Limited.

Book design by Jennifer Lum
Typeset in Bell MT 10.5/15

Interior images: (hands) © Sergey Siz`kov / Dreamstime.com

Printed and bound in the UK by CPI Group (UK) Ltd, Croydon CR0 4YY

National Library of Australia Cataloguing-in-Publication data

McWatt, Tessa, – author.
Higher Ed / Tessa McWatt.
1. Man-woman relationships–Fiction.
813.6

9781925106763 (Australian edition)
9781925228045 (UK edition)
9781925113983 (e-book)

A CIP record for this title is available from the British Library.

scribepublications.com.au
scribepublications.co.uk

For the students

CAST

(in order of appearance)

The Administrator—Francine
The Film Professor—Robin
The Law Student—Olivia
The Civil Servant—Ed
The Waitress—Katrin

SUPPORTING PLAYERS

The Anthropology Professor—Patricia

The Film Student—Bayo

The Motorcyclist—Dario

The Driver—Rajit

The Driver's Wife—Mrs. Mahadeo

The Medical Student—Ryan

The Admirer—Nasar

The Civil Servant's Colleague—Sammy

The Civil Servant's Brother—Geoffrey

The Student Union President—Moe

The Waiter—Alejandro

The Café Manager—Claire

The BFF—Jasmine

The BFF's Mum—Jasmine's mum

The Law Student's Mum—Catherine

The Head of Quality Assurance—Lawrence

The Administrator's Brother—Scott

The Film Professor's Ex-girlfriend—Emma

The Administrator's Ex-boyfriend—John Clarke

The Law Student's Granddad—Granddad

The Law Student's Uncle—Eric

The Waitress's Mum—Beata

The Med Student's Mum—Mrs. Broughton

The Film Department Head—Richard

The Philosopher—Gilles Deleuze (as himself)

The Deceased—Anna-Maria Hunter, Keith Meyers, Jonathan Henley, Diyanat Bayar

. . . who passed through universities with radiant cool eyes hallucinating Arkan-
sas and Blake-light tragedy among the scholars of war,
who were expelled from the academies for crazy & publishing obscene odes
on the windows of the skull,
who cowered in unshaven rooms in underwear, burning their money in
wastebaskets and listening to the Terror through the wall . . .

—Allen Ginsberg, "Howl"

THE OPPOSITE

OF THIRTEEN

FRANCINE

Sayonara, sucker! Francine swipes the back of her hand across her mouth, pushes the handle, straightens up, and watches the water swirl in the bowl. Air alone will do; she can live on air. Sometimes breath puffs her up so much that she feels like she will explode.

She pushes the handle once more so that there is not a shred of pizza left in the bowl, leaves the staff washroom and returns to her office, the door clicking open but needing a hip shove before it budges. Everything in this building is swelling. She smells barf. She picks up the cup of cold tea from her desk and sips, washing it over her teeth. There are fifteen course specifications and twenty external examiners' reports on her desk, which need to be checked by her and passed back to programme leaders before she leaves today. She sits. Buck up, get yer ass in gear; pull yer finger out, as they say in this country. It's unlikely that the whole department will go, isn't it? Surely Quality Assurance and Enhancement is key to any university. She has to admit, though, that her department, like her, is a little fat. There are times when, if she wanted to, she could spend the rest of the afternoon sitting blankly in front of her screen and still get her job done.

She sees her reflection in the screen saver's swirling shapes, which dice up her features and blend them back again in hexagonals of eye, nose, mouth.

A raisin Danish and some Mentos before lunch are also now gone. It's only two in the afternoon, 1400 hours, and she's thrown up everything she's eaten so far. Excellent. She sits up straighter, pleased with herself for her conversion to the twenty-four-hour clock. Time stretches out with the higher numbers. Calories, they say, should be consumed in the early hours.

She is beautiful today.

Running her hand over her belly (okay, but . . .), her hips (a bit, sure), and along her thighs (yes, still!) doesn't change her mind. All her friends back in Philly regularly told her she had a pretty face, after all. And it's not that she doesn't want to hold on to this confidence that normally scurries off like a startled mouse; it's just that at fifty-three this big ass and slackening skin are not about to disappear.

"Men like big butts," Cindy from Philly always says, but Cindy has a black girl's perfect ramp of a rump, which men like to rest their heads on after fucking. Stop. Francine Johnson (good, honest name) will feel beautiful today, all day, she promises, or she will expire in the trying.

She does one last Google search for John Clarke. Stupid name. John-ordinary-everybody Clarke. There's the one who is the minister, there's the poet, the trader, the actor, the leader of the Church of Latter Day Saints. There's even a marathon runner named John Clarke. But there's no IT director who by now has surely procreated with the young IT star at his office, who was oh so smart and jaunty and you-would-really-like-her too—she's kind of like a guy; we talk about sports—while Francine went to England for a once-in-a-lifetime opportunity to work for her accounting firm in its new British office. There's no John-the-prick Clarke who led her on for eleven years, past the last days of her fertility, into the promise of a peaceful, childless life where adventures like the English one were just the beginning. And since the accounting firm's European demise, there has been no John Clarke, supreme asshole, cuntface, cocksucking bastard, with the guts to upload an internet page that would explain himself or just say a simple, fucking sorry.

"Sayonara, sucker," she says as she clicks onto the Guardian Soulmates icon on the desktop, entering her log-in name, ReallyYouandMe, and her password: Isoam.

No one has viewed her since her last log-in.

She has no fans.

She has five favourites.

She has no new messages.

She clicks through the favourites.

"Hear, hear!" she says, raising her mug to the screen at the fifty-five-year-old widower who describes himself as "wanting to feel beloved again." The rest are all too young for her, and they will never contact her. But their presence there, beside her profile, is better even than feeling hunger. Hunky single guys with lots of hair and good teeth—she primps her hair with her fingers, feeling the soft straightness, her most reliable feature.

She shuts down the site and turns towards the reports.

Give a damn, she urges herself, trying to waken her family's work ethic, to keep her duties from slipping. She feels suddenly sick—barfed perhaps too soon—at the idea of losing her job. Returning to the States would be one failure too many. But the announcements have made it clear: there will be a round of redundancies. They will affect every sector of the university, and every department will be scrutinized. She tries to focus on the programme report for the BA in Multimedia Studies, which her colleagues call the Mickey Mouse degree. Appreciating the historical impact of Mickey Mouse is right up her alley and she would like to see the programme stay open, but with low retention rates it seems unlikely. And the data on employability is even more damning.

How did she end up on this side of the divide? Back in the States she marched in campus demonstrations at Penn State against the local nuclear power plant. Okay, she was never arrested, but she'd been willing to be. Now she's the lock-'em-up voice of right and wrong in this university where senior managers look to her to tell them whether people a whole lot smarter than she is are teaching to regulation. She should have finished her master's and applied to the PhD programme in Landscape Ecology at Duke as she'd planned, but cranky John Clarke told her that studying more would be a waste of time and money. And she let his crankiness get to her and took a financial management diploma to be practical. But she knows what good learning is. She could teach her own programme, one that fits with national quality guidelines to boot. And her students would get jobs; they'd be relevant in tough times. She'd call her programme Environmental Containment, or a BA (Honours) in Curb Your Enthusiasm.

She needs another cup of tea. Brushing her hips to smooth down her skirt, she leaves the office.

She's beautiful today, all day, even if the atrium smells like cheese, even if the students irritate the shit out of her with the way they clump together. She waits behind a boy clump in the line-up for food.

"Alright then, Francine?" says Patricia over Francine's shoulder. She turns. Oh Patricia. Pat to friends and colleagues, Patty on the dancefloor, no doubt. Patty in front of the mirror going "Oooh, I feel love, I feel love . . ." Always asking Francine to go out with her to salsa at Ronnie Scott's on a Saturday night when they give you lessons. Patricia is late fifties, slim but buxom, with unplucked eyebrows and big hands, all of which she pulls off with enviable moxie. And she has a big smile and nice, straight teeth, which is something for an English woman her age, so Francine doesn't mind her, really.

"What do you think that smell is?" Francine asks Dancefloor Patty, who lectures in anthropology (because this gal never hid her brains so that some half-pint would love her). Francine nudges Patricia, who sparks at the touch and leans in, so that Francine has to step back.

"There's a hint of vanilla, I think," says Patricia, and, oh shit, Patricia has just sniffed her.

"I mean . . ." she waves her hand in the direction of the atrium, "out here," Francine says, and she retreats to the tight corner of her I-am-beautiful day.

"What, you mean the Starbucks smell? It's a disgrace," and Patricia shifts side to side, as though the topic has revved her engine. "The choice of this or Costa—brilliant—at twice the price of last term, to a company that pays no tax in Britain, to a company—"

"That's not what I meant . . ." Francine says. She takes another step back. Patricia comes across stern and composed, but on the right topic she's a struck match of opinion. "What are you up to these days?" Francine asks her. Wood, metal, plastic, cloth: each distinct smell comes wafting in, one after the other.

Patricia looks down at her feet and this seems to stop her hips from swaying, delivering her back to perfect composure. "It's always hectic at the beginning of a term," she says, raises a shoulder, and tilts her chin to it like a cat cleaning whiskers. The hair on Francine's arm rises: Colgate toothpaste, Dove deodorant, Aussie shampoo. There's more of this every day: the "change"—she's still goddamn changing.

"Seen anything good recently?" she asks, forcing her eyes away from Patricia's shoulder, wondering if she should ask Patricia if she thinks there will even be an anthropology department next year.

"No time," Patricia says. "Anything in mind?"

Damn it. Francine always falls into this trap, this feeling of being the one who has to follow through. "I'll see what's out there, and, yeah, we could"—she doesn't have the guts to stop there—"get together."

"Excellent," Patricia says. "Friday?"

"Yeah."

Shit.

Francine finds herself doing the thing with her silky hair that John Shitface Clarke used to tell her made his heart melt—that pulling down of her fringe in an attempt to cover her eyes. She doesn't mean to do it; it just happens. She smiles nervously as Patricia takes her in, and Patricia responds with a smile so full and ripe that the little part of Francine that keeps being the sucker is warmed.

ROBIN

He doesn't want to go mad. If this is madness he can't have it. The wind whips off the river in front of him and slaps his cheek. Robin counts the ways madness might bear down on a man: 1) he could be born mad; 2) he could slowly, over the course of years, lose the capacity to see that actions and thoughts are separate; or 3) the self might become only a threshold, a door to multiplicities. This final point is from Deleuze, whose critical theory Robin has mined for the article he must write on motion capture and animation. Deleuze has hypnotized him with *A Thousand Plateaus*, but in truth Robin is most worried about number 2.

He downs his double espresso in the Styrofoam cup, his regular mug left behind in his office this morning. This forgetfulness is surely a sign. He picks up his briefcase and makes ready to face the lecture room. He has to remember to keep his glasses high up on his nose, because Emma told him that he looks like an old man when they slide down towards the tip. Thirty-eight is the edge of old. He stands and braces himself for this second-year class in Cinema Poetics. Where is the poetry? Where are the stressed syllables and open vowels? The wind stings his chin. Father does not rhyme with much.

The river whips up again and only facts remain. Fact is, in 1963 this river froze, the Beatles sang "Please Please Me," and Fellini released *8 ½*. These are thoughts that don't require action, and this is what he's more used to, what he's certain, almost certain, he would still prefer.

In the atrium he nudges the glasses up further before he enters the lecture room. One, two, three . . . only four students are there ahead of him. Not a promising sign so early in the term. Bayo is in her seat in the front row, ready to take him on. Formaldehyde, he wants to say to her. *Formaldehyde* is not an easy word to spell—it was she who challenged his typo on the PowerPoint last week. In that need to act on her thought, Bayo revealed her madness. A mature student from Nigeria, her bosom broad, her hair long and straight from extensions—a swath of it wrapping over her forehead and across one eye like a pirate's patch—Bayo's madness is a slow-burning constant. Last term Robin caught her behind the Samuel Johnson Building setting fire to the essay he had handed back to her minutes before. Jake, Dan, and Miles also set fire to theirs, but it wasn't lunacy; they did it together in full view in the university square. Jake is from a small northern town where a bloke is not allowed to like film and art; Miles is a thin Afro-Caribbean DJ wanna-be, and so shy that he talks into his hand as though the hand were clutching a microphone; Dan used to sell drugs to celebrities: these young men aren't mad. Their actions were pure performance.

He walks to the lectern and places his briefcase on the table beside it. He takes out the pen—*I'm the pen your lover writes with*—stolen from the Epicure Café. More students stream in, and they are loud. He looks down at his Doc Martens and starts to hum.

He's fucking going to be a father.

A sheet of paper slips from his notes and floats down like a leaf. At this portent of chaos, he rushes out of the room, gripping the stolen pen, and crosses the atrium to the student union shop.

The chocolate is along the back row with bags of Haribo, Basset's Mint Imperials, Fruit Gums, Starbursts, Minstrels, and Jelly Aliens. Kit Kat is the one sane choice. He reaches for one and catches sight of familiar curly hair and wide cheekbones. Olivia is a third-year law student who took Cinema Poetics last year as an option and was the best student in the class. Her face is like Cleopatra's, her hair like Shirley Temple's, her confidence as thin but as certain as cellophane. In the second week of classes she towered over him as she asked if poets wrote only about things that are impermanent. He considered the question so thoroughly that he lost track of time, right there in front of her. Love, and water over stones, she said and brought him back. Yes. Yes, they do, he said.

Olivia catches his eye from across the aisle, but on remembering their final meeting last year, he bows his head and ducks behind the rack of greeting cards, pretending to look for a suitable card for the now confirmed autumn event. *Happy Birthday: Son, Daughter?* Oh God. He doesn't want to be a man. He wants to be a lightning bolt.

He returns to the lecture room with the Kit Kat in his breast pocket. Bayo is sitting straight, like an actor ready for a cue. She stares at him, but he bends down to pick up his notes from the floor. Image: the hands of the woman from the Epicure Café on Upper Street, the way she holds his cup as she walks towards him, the way her thumb releases the saucer as she places it before him. He arranges his notes, turns on the computer and projector, and opens the PowerPoint presentation.

"I celebrate myself and sing myself," he says, and the room goes quiet. This worked on him as an undergraduate at Warwick, and he knows it will work now. He looks over at Bayo, who appears agitated. "And what I assume, you shall assume . . . " he continues, and when the students realize he's quoting they will relax, but for now he is content to unsettle them, to confound them with the possibility that he might be saying something real. Except that Bayo has begun to wring her hands so he breaks out of his performance sooner than planned.

"Whitman refers to his book *Leaves of Grass* and the American Civil War as though they are one, making a link between them to the democratic soul, and the struggle for unification." He sees Bayo look down into her lap. "Not dissimilarly, Elsaesser and Hagener explore the reflective and reflexive potential of cinema, using the mirror and the face as a motif for understanding the self and the other . . . "

Bayo looks up again. Robin cannot push away the face of the woman in the Epicure Café, which beams like his grandmother's in a photo of her at the foot of the Eiffel Tower. A tiny stranger who smiles at him in a way that makes all things seem possible.

FRANCINE

Living on air is harder in the drizzled dullness of February, chilling at six, when Francine leaves the university. Hungry. Trying to stay that way. But sleepy as she drives west across London and the radio repeats the news of Gaza violence she heard at lunchtime. Her flat is too far away at this hour of the day. She presses the dashboard button for Kiss FM and sings along behind the wheel, because it's true, everybody wants to rule the world.

It's an hour before she nears home, turning towards Kilburn Park, then up Salusbury Road towards Willesden Lane. John Clarke would have hated Kilburn, hated its pound shops, cheap garments and kebabs. The dark brick, the crowded-front-teeth of a road that leads onto hers. John fucking Clarke would—

There's a sliding, screeching, wet bang. A body flies above the car in front of hers and glass hits her windshield. Her car smacks the back bumper of the small red sedan. Now only one sound: a low pumping vibration all around. She puts the car in park. Fuck, fuck, fuck. And opens the car door. Near the oak tree at the side of the road is a small, contorted body, face down. She has trouble breathing. She trains her eyes on the jeans, twisted

around impossibly bent legs, the black leather jacket, the motorcycle helmet, tilted up just enough to have broken the neck. The
clothes are emptied, breath having wrinkled them in its leaving.
The pumping vibe deepens: a bass line that moves up the back of
her own neck.

"I think it's a girl . . . " a voice says, and cinnamon wafts
through the fugue of voices. "Ooh, look at the legs." Francine
looks at the legs again to try to see this girl, but she is sure
this pile of clothing belongs to a man (beer, cigarettes, stale
cologne). She walks towards it: or just a boy. His bent leg shimmers like it's going to dissolve, like particles are separating to
show her the skin, twisted tendons, broken bones within.
Thank God his mother isn't here to see. Thank God it's she
who witnesses this, not his mother, who will next see him when
a sheet is pulled down to reveal a face, scrubbed and bloodless,
in the morgue.

The driver of the red sedan, over which the boy flew, is
slumped at his steering wheel, window open, his body unin-
jured and his face a stiff mask. Francine stands among the
strewn motorcycle parts. Someone is asking for an ambulance
on 999. Someone else whimpers, "He wasn't going fast." And
the driver slowly gets out of the red car. Mum, she thinks, but
doesn't know why all this mummy, mummy for the shattered
boy by the oak tree.

Sitting down on the curb, dizzy, as the others keep talking—
"It's not a girl, look"—she spots a young man running towards
them.

"Don't touch him; leave him, let me do it," the young man
yells. He tells them he's a medical student and will try to help.
His accent is Scottish. She watches his curly head as he turns the

body over and lifts the helmet's visor, then tilts and blows, one, two, three, again, one, two, three, through the broken, bloody face. Once more, harder.

The driver of the red sedan leans down to say something to the Scottish doctor. One car later and it would have been she who hit the boy. One car later and it would have been Francine who had to see his mum's face in court. Her knee begins to tremor. Fuck, fuck. She takes a deep breath. (Rubber, asphalt, and a burst of aftershave.)

"I'm sorry, I'm sorry," the med student says as he stands up. His eye is in a wink, sealed partially shut by the blood from the motorcyclist's face. Francine stands up, retches, then throws up and, from habit, stares down at it on the pavement.

She looks again at the med student's face as he wipes blood from his mouth. He catches her eye. *Cry. Cry,* she thinks. But he doesn't. It's the driver of the red sedan who begins weeping.

"I only saw him fly through the air," she's able to say to the police when they finally arrive. "I have to go," she says, adamantly, and her tongue touches a fleck of vomit on her lip. But one officer keeps asking her questions, while another questions a Filipino nanny who is worried about being deported. The med student whose name—Ryan Broughton—she listens carefully for, speaks to the third officer on the scene. The driver of the red sedan is led to the back seat of the second police vehicle. "I have to go," she says again and heads to her car before the paramedics have lifted the body into the ambulance.

Ryan Broughton catches her eye just before she climbs behind the wheel. At which stage of medical school do doctors become impassive to dead bodies? How is Ryan Broughton digesting the taste of the crushed face he sucked on? How respectfully he had turned over the ruined body. Takes just a little to be decent.

At home she dreams that every wall in her flat is painted yellow. In the middle of the night she wakes to a gush between her legs and throws back the duvet to reveal a blood-soaked mattress.

ROBIN

It's safe to leave. The atrium is in darkness; the drizzle outside will set the tone for his evening. Robin walks out of the building. The usual few students, the security guard. He looks around for the curvaceous American woman who works in QA—the body of the mature Mae West, the face of Vivien Leigh's Scarlett O'Hara. She is always staring at him, always on the verge of chatting him up, but she must have left already. Fact is that rain can fall as fast as twenty-two miles an hour, so this drizzle isn't the worst it could be, but home would be a better place just now. He takes the path towards the bus stop and waits.

Emma left two messages on his voicemail while he was teaching. She doesn't trust his reaction to the news about their baby. So she shouldn't. It's a beautiful thing, she says; it is for me, is it for you?

Deleuze: Bring something incomprehensible into the world!

In his kitchen he wipes down the white subway tiles behind the gas hob, dotted with bolognese sauce from last night. Emma's news came just after dinner; he would never normally have missed these spots. He scours the stainless steel hob itself, the wood counter, scrubs the corners, presses hard against the rings from cups, enjoying this cleaning more than anything else today. Fact is that tomatoes are not as benign as we consider them. Their Latin name means "wolf peach." Cleaning takes over from reading some days, and then he allows himself to go to bed. But he has to make two phone calls this evening, before he falls asleep with the BBC World Service at his ear. Today, the third of February, is his mother's birthday and she will have been wondering all day what might be taking him so long to call. His father will have taken her to lunch in Falmouth, possibly to Rick Stein's Fish, and now they will be reading in front of the fire, toasting each other for another day of a long, relatively happy relationship in a predominantly happy life. His brothers will have already called, from New York, from Manchester, and Robin will be the only missing element of his mother's measured happiness.

The other call will also be to Cornwall. Emma's move was right for her, and when he tells his parents the news his father will secretly wish for a granddaughter and will offer to build them a summer house in their garden that extends towards a cliff over the sea.

He turns the volume down on Emil Gilels who is playing the Beethoven piano sonata that his mother tried to learn throughout his entire childhood, her failure to do so remaining one of her only regrets. He dials Emma's number first.

"Hi, hi," he says, and listens for the right thing to say next. "Not bad, tired," he says, which is obviously wrong. "Long day, you?"

Emma describes her mother's reaction to the pregnancy in such detail that he cannot keep his eyes open. Then her sister's, then the fact of driving to the sea and walking the cliff path, the path he himself showed her. At this he perks up. He has a twinge of panic for her safety, but then the thought of his child growing up in Cornwall brings pleasure. Gorse, heather, pyramid orchids in the rolling dunes, golden samphire in the cliffs, salt marshes, slanted rain, flavoured air.

The day he and Emma broke up he said, I wish you love in the sea cliffs; I wish you everything you want. She had wanted a baby, but neither of them had really wanted each other.

"And the news from your end? How has that gone over?" she asks him. He hasn't told a soul. Emma hears this in his hesitation. Her silence shames him further.

The phone tucked under his chin, he starts to buff the stainless steel kettle, heightening the double-arched reflection of the kitchen window within it. They had come together out of inertia. Friends for years, they had turned to one another after the breakup of far more necessary and romantic connections, she to him for comfort, both of them for sex, and even that wasn't necessary. His relief at her decision to quit her job in dentistry and move from London to the southwest to teach yoga was manifest in his saying, blithely, I love you, before having sex one last time in an effort to marry theory and practice.

"How are you feeling?" he asks, wanting to take the morning sickness away for her, to make everything good for her, wanting at the same time to bury his face in the straight blond hair of the Polish waitress at Epicure and to tell her how her lack of awareness of her own beauty has loosened the tiles of his sanity.

"Still woozy in the mornings, but a bit better. Skin looks great." Her voice invites him to intimacy.

"Oh, good," is all he can say.

FRANCINE

Francine is bent over the toilet basin for the third time today, fingers deep in her throat and the omelette and toast high up in her belly, and for the third time unable to coax anything out.

This has happened before, through the years, when it stops working, when she has to find another way. Damn. She straightens up. The phone rings and makes her jump. She has already made her excuses for her third day of absence from work. There is no one else who would call.

"Patricia," she says to the woman's voice. And because Patricia has a gift for extraction, she finds herself telling her everything, from the wet bang to the crinkled jeans and finally the young doctor's face. What she doesn't tell Patricia about is the flood in the middle of the night and the disappearance of her craving for sugar. She doesn't say, that's it, last friggin' hurrah, a final shove towards change. But this change feels like a reversing, back to age thirteen, when things swirled like this, were scary like this.

"Ronnie Scott's," Patricia commands, "tonight, come on." Francine looks out her window. The plane tree's branches have recently been pruned and the knotty limbs are clothed only in translucent bark, like gauze over veins. She can see into her neighbour's front room. He has no shirt on. Nothing is opaque anymore.

"Sorry, no, can't . . . really not feeling up to it," she says, standing firm against Patricia's persistence. And to her surprise Patricia lets her off the hook with a warm wish to see her at work soon and an offer to bring around food and magazines. Francine promises she'll be back at work tomorrow and will check in with Patricia around lunchtime.

"Sure, sure," Patricia says. Yeah, like there is anything that is.

———

The next morning the atrium smells different—like Dr. Pepper in the summer. When they were teens her brother told her that Dr. Pepper was for losers. Scott knew who the losers and winners were, being so popular with other kids that he spent weekends at their homes or cottages. She'd take those opportunities to order Dr. Pepper at the A&W, her father's treat to make up for his desperate widower cooking and her loneliness without her brother at home. It was around this time that she learned the trick—the two-fingered flick on that flap at the back of the throat and whoosh—gone was the strawberry ice-cream sundae, the hot dog and French fries, the Dr. Pepper. Scott, whose annual Christmas conversation on the telephone consists of lecturing her on how she needs to think about her long-term security, will never know just how right he had been about Dr. Pepper. Maybe she should try the Atkins diet again. All that meat. She checks her butt with her hand, making a show of brushing something off her skirt—another little trick. *Plop, plop, fizz, fizz, oh what a relief it is.*

She asks for a skinny hazelnut latte, rhyming off the order comfortably now that Starbucks is on campus. She feels students behind her, their pushiness, like she's taking too much time. One of the two dark brunettes behind her glares at her and Francine finds the face hard, blunt, the first opaque thing she's seen in days. She touches her throat, sore from the failed barfing.

"Order me a cappuccino," the other woman says to her friend who says something back in a private language, then they giggle and Francine feels a lurch in her gut like she's going to release air. Nothing is solid; now even the hard mask of the woman's spite seems porous.

As she leaves with her latte, she spots that guy, the young lecturer. Robin joins the queue and Francine reaches for a napkin, a small delaying tactic. Ten years younger and she'd be following him around like a stray pet; Robin is the kind of guy she should have gone for instead of John Cuntface Clarke. Robin has eyes that squint when he's thinking, and he's always thinking when she sees him. It's not his looks—fine, but nothing special—it's something else, maybe in the way he walks. Can kindness show in a walk? Teacher of film studies and befriender of students, Robin would know the real her. He walks like he'd be a good kisser. *Annie Hall*, she wants to ask? Does he teach it? She follows him out of the atrium, leaves him behind in the square and heads back to her office.

Three days = 198 unopened e-mails.

Google is the only tolerable option.

There are three news articles for "motorcycle accident Queen's Park," and now she knows his name: Dario Martinelli, 24, of Barking. A boy. She also reads the name of the driver of the red sedan, but she can't hold it in her sights, skips over it

to find that he has been charged with dangerous driving causing death.

She searches Facebook, where Dario Martinelli's timeline
has photos, postings in Italian, and recent posts in English
about how much he loves riding his motorcycle and how the
horrendous London winter has kept him off it and wouldn't it
be great to be back in Bologna and going fast, with you, friend.
Her throat tightens. The most recent post is from Roberto
Martinelli—brother? cousin?—in Italian, but she can make
out enough to know that la famiglia grieves the loss and that
the (airless, shrunken) body will be brought home for interment. She clicks off quickly. His wrinkled clothes. He is Dario.
He has a family. Dario will have an interment, and Dario's
Facebook page will remain forever, his beloved motorbike pre-
served there in mint condition.

Dario is dead. People die every minute of every day. What's
going on with her?

She seeks the young doctor, Ryan Broughton. Finding Ryan
will help. Ryan knows what death tastes like. But she can't find
him, so she returns to Google and asks it a question. There are
countless answers: "Death tastes like blackened carbon"; "death
tastes like almonds and spoiled fruit"; "death tastes like
McGriddles", and her favourite: "it tastes like feet."

Sayonara.

OLIVIA

"Robin?" Olivia mumbles. Oi. But he won't hear; he's got those wanna-hide shoulders hunched over the row of chocolate in the far aisle. Robin. If she could steal Robin, right, she'd give him to her mum, she would, because he would make her lighten up; his words would open her. Instead there's Ed, and what is she to do with him? Right. Six days now, six days it's been since finding him. Edward of the lonely dead. Edward like a rabbit in a high-beam when he first saw her; Edward whose life's work has been to bury the unknown, unloved, unmoneyed people of Barking and Dagenham. Ed. Her dad.

Olivia makes a sound with her tongue. It's cicada-like, not the sucking of teeth that her mate Jasmine has perfected in wishing she'd been born a Jamaican. This sound is not hip, not hop. It's a sigh in reverse.

"May I have some aspirin?" she asks the cashier. One foot, then the next, back and forth, gotta slow everything down. Right. The spindly woman, who looks like she is already a mum of many even though maybe only twenty-five years old, turns to the shelves behind her and reaches for the yellow Anadin pack, turns back, slides it on the counter and waits—like a mother would—for Olivia to sort through her change for £1.20.

"Spindly," Olivia says, under her breath. The woman looks up at her with don't-mess-with-me eyes like rectangles. Olivia holds on to other words—*tattoo, milk, nicotine*—takes the box of aspirin and leaves the shop. She sees Robin retreat down the atrium. Robin's walk is like a bird's, even though she's never seen a robin walking, but he bops like something that is used to flying instead. Robin is a bebop bird. And Robin is the only bloke on the planet who has seen her cry.

Right. She weaves through the people in the atrium—the fat, the small, the smelly, the limping, the arrogant—every one of them in last-minute coffee-and-sweets-buying mode to keep them awake through class. Their choice is limited; Thames Gateway U has been branded. The dinner ladies from last year look sad in their new brown uniforms and baseball caps. The new cafeteria food is sadder than they are. *Sad and Sadder*: a Netflix blockbuster. Olivia is on the student union committee that has been lobbying the governors against outsourcing to corporations for months now, but times such as they are is all she hears. Does no one see what's happening here? Right. She lowers her eyes to avoid the faces, the sadder than sad, dumber than dumb, bleaker than bleak. Don't take it all on yourself, Robin had said. How not to? She weaves through the bodies, weaves like that girl's hair, like that man's jacket, like this boy's lies he's telling his girlfriend, and like that boy's flying Paralympic-style wheelchair. She heads towards the finance office. Maybe today the panting, pink-faced man will tell her when the last loan instalment will appear in her account. Her debt is already five times what she planned when all of this started. You can always ask for help, Robin said. If and when she becomes a solicitor will she really have chosen correctly over becoming Lara Croft instead? Right, but the law, really? The wheelchair boy is stuck—another thing she has to get sorted, so that being at this uni in a wheelchair gets easier than being a tuna in a can.

Sorry. Right. She speeds up.

Who will bury these people?

Two and a half years of law school but there are questions they have not taught her to answer. All these questions she's now in the habit of asking. She adjusts the satchel on her shoulder—books, court decisions—and pushes through. Who will bury them?

"Lonely," she says, slipped out like all the other words these days, like fish from a hand. She is going to be a rubbish lawyer.

One foot in front of the other heading out of the atrium. There's fog. Something clangs against metal, like a stay against a mast. She dips her chin into her scarf. In the square she searches for Robin. There's a man with wild hair like his, but that one walks like a zombie. Students stand in clusters in front of the Watson Building where she's headed. Smokers, listeners, worriers, huddlers. One of them could be Nasar.

Nasar's last message said: *hop u r fine. When I meet u first time it was like a dream. I like to have a friend like u trust me if u agree to start good friendship pleas text me. I really like you . . . !!! Nasar.*

The first text had been short, sharp, friendly—*hi how r u?*—but when she asked who it was and got only his name, well, what's up with that? The next two were check-ins, how are you today? This latest one is swag. Who is he and how did he get her number? The bloke she met in the student bar? The one in the kebab shop with Jasmine last week? The skinny, floppy emo from Robin's class? Skinny, floppy emo boys are not called Nasar. Jasmine thinks Olivia should have taken the Italian boy up on his offer—the short, funny man who chirpsed them up at Nico's bar. He wanted her to get on the back of his motorcycle in order to Moto and Guzzi to Bologna. Jasmine egged him on. Jasmine placed his hand on Olivia's lap. Jasmine knows shite about anything except shagging. But for Olivia shagging has been put on hold for so long, while there was shite to sort out, that even if she is secretly chuffed by being Nasar's dream to meet, oh crikey. She will ask Robin—and plan not to blubber like the last time—why, oh why love feels like a threat.

She could probably take out an injunction against Nasar, charge him with harassment under the 1998 Malicious Communications Act, because she's entitled to protection from indecent, offensive or threatening electronic communication. But, only the lonely: Nasar might just need a friend.

It's her father's fault. Six days of having to hold her tongue at home in front of Catherine, six days of thinking so much her head will burst, the image of Ed standing behind that desk, all strawless scarecrow-like and them talking all casual-like until she could see from his face that both of them were putting two and two together to make the twenty-two years of age that his daughter would be. If it hadn't been for her father she wouldn't be needing to enlist Robin, give Nasar a second thought, or do anything other than study because she needs to get a first.

Her final-year project was meant to be a simple route to a first-class degree, on account of it being straightforward while the rest of life wasn't. The law is the law, after all, and not a *Tomb Raider* game. But now even that has come unravelled, and it's like she's dubstepping to Unkle's "Only the Lonely." It started simply enough: getting more details on paupers' graves—like depth, how many, how much, how weird—and on how the council was dealing with the foxes, because this whole idea came about when she heard that foxes were ravaging paupers' graves. She got hooked and started to research the rights of untraceable, unknown deceased residents to a funeral. When Olivia called the council, the clerk corrected her use of "paupers' graves" and transferred her call to the Safeguarding Adults Team. The next day, out of nowhere, no-how, no-possible-way, she was standing in front of the funeral officer who looked too weak to do a job that might entail a bit of digging and lifting coffins. And then he started to look at her all funny, like the fall-down-on-his-knees scarecrow of Oz. When she asked Edward Reynolds if he knew a certain Catherine Mason, one time of Romford Road, the look on his face made the whole entire room a Rubik's cube, the colours lining up, like for the first time ever.

Her friend Jasmine says "Ah, Jeezus" when things like this happen. Jasmine's mother is a born-again, on account of her husband moving out seven years ago, but when Jasmine says *Jeezus* it sounds more like something from the devil, because Jasmine is bent on showing her mother that her dad was justified. Jasmine's not her real name. Eleanor is only Jasmine because in secondary school, when her dad left and the ground dropped out of her life, she had to find something different to hold on to. So Jasmine loves this kind of thing that bonds blud and happens regular-like in their ends. "That's extra . . . " Jasmine said, first thing, when Olivia told her about the Rubik's cube moment, and she touched the side of Olivia's head. "Why did your dad leave again?" she added, now coiling the end of her own long hair around her index finger, as though the leaving of dads could be measured like curls.

"Jaz," Olivia said, "my father is a caring man," and that shut her up, but truth is that's what Olivia's mother said, over and over, "Your father is a caring man," when Olivia's questions at the age of thirteen turned to why Catherine was letting different blokes kiss her in the sitting room of the house they share with Granddad and Nan, and why there was never a bloke who stayed, and where, after all, was the one who was responsible for Olivia? Wouldn't you save kissing for someone who wouldn't be leaving? And maybe he left because you were giving it away so easily? And wouldn't it make sense to avoid that ever happening, ever?

Catherine keeps the secret of Edward the way a girl in Olivia's primary school kept a snake in a terrarium. The girl loved that snake, tended it like she could do anything the boys did, but one morning when they went into the classroom the snake was gone from the glass tank: only a circle of moulted skin was left; snake-shaped lace draped over the large rock at the far right of the terrarium. From that day on the girl was terrified of all snakes, but mostly scared that the one that got away would show up at any moment, larger, slimier, wild. When Catherine talks about Edward at a distance, she says things like this—"he cared"—but when the question of why he left crops up there's the girl-with-the-snake sound in her voice. And for Olivia there's a once-upon-a-time of a father who sang a song to himself, over and over. A simple, spiralling song that Olivia hears sometimes out of nowhere. When Catherine says these things about him and then returns to her fashion magazines and makes deadpan comments like *Innit a nightmare that some women of her age wear short shorts*, the song comes back. Tra-la-la-la-la.

Olivia walks faster.

"Robin," she says again.

Robin let her sit there and cry, not asking her to stop, not asking her to do anything, just telling her that you don't have to fix everything all by yourself.

Right.

When she arrives at the finance department, she is hot and opens her jacket. She leans over the counter trying to catch the attention of the pink-faced man she usually talks to. Her jumper rides up, her waist rubs the melamine rind of the countertop, and ahh, she catches the eye of the black-haired woman with glasses, who, oh please, this time, will not say that these things take time.

ED

It sounds like the earth's turning too fast, the planet louder than last week, and the traffic on Ripple Road hungry-hungry for getting to work, when work is the last place anybody really wants to be. Ed waits, waits, waits for the traffic that does not cease. He should go farther up to the zebra crossing near Sleepwell Bedroom Furniture, but man he'd be tempted to stop in for a lie-down rather than head to work. His toe is throbbing, stubbed last night on the damn ledge that juts up outta the floor towards his bathroom, because he was too fired up, too buzzy to stand still: there is so much to tell her.

He is going to be late, and even when he gets there he won't be able to concentrate, with only two hours' sleep last night thanks to—all night—practising there in his kitchen how to say it. A car comes close up to his foot and he has to pay attention now or he'll be mash-up to slop and never get to tell her a thing.

He hurries towards the crossing, his shoes pinching his toes, and he takes it at a pace. If she's willing to meet him again, if her mother hasn't poison-up her mind, then he will tell her that in Guyana there is fair and there is unfair, and some people does resist their coexistence and they will resist and resist until something changes or explodes, yes man. Yes, this is one of the tiny amount of the things he will tell her. Even a child who is a grown-up now needs to know things about where she is from. And who she is from, never mind the jumbies of the past. He cannot lose her again.

Miracles happen, man, miracles happen. In she walked to his offices six days ago, and there in her face was something he knew like his hand. Funny, funny feeling, that: when you know a face as a baby then all of a sudden it's there, same face, but a woman face. He has to tread softly-softly in this new world, to expect nothing, and to mention Catherine only when it feels safe to do so. How he loved that name, loved it so much he has barely said it for eighteen years. To anyone he met later called Catherine he would say, hey Cathy, or all right Kate, but never Catherine. He rubs the bald part of his head first, then runs his hand over the short dog-like pelt at the back. Man, there are miracles.

Inside Sydney House the hall is smelling better than yesterday, when that limping, overcoat-and-sandals man who sleeps on George Street in cardboard came in especially to piss and shit, as if to say, here, look after that, Safeguarding Adults Team, and he left a trail of he foulness, piss running all along the floor for so. The cleaners have done good.

What is the price of miracles?

If he loses his job just as he regains his daughter, he will consider himself one giant step ahead of the Barking and Dagenham Council, so never mind. Out of the three Protection, Funeral and Conference Officers, he is the least educated but the oldest. Sammy has the most experience and seniority, and Ralph is a specialized social work graduate, so he knows he's the one most likely for the chop, if it comes. But never mind, because even though he's losing bulk except in the belly, he's still a man with arms that could wrestle a cow like daddy did when the cow in Berbice had her foot caught up in wire and thought daddy was trying to kill she. That cow fought hard-hard, and his daddy took the cow head by the horns and bent it so, and the beast twist up and fall down to let the men hold she there and unwrap the wire slowly, slowly, for her to be released.

"Alright, Wood," says Sammy when Ed enters the Safe and Sorrow room as the two of them like to call their office. Ralph is too serious to make fun of their work and the kind of people they have to watch out for, but Sammy's all for lightening things up a little. Sammy is the real thing, though, and takes on his job like these people are family, goes into their homes and bears the smells and the sights always with a smile. Sammy is a damn good fella. Sometimes when there's not much happening in the way of advice-giving to the public or securing council flats that have been abandoned or making sure pets get sent to the shelter if the resi- dent has died or is in hospital, or when there are no care homes needing recalibrating or help with the basics, Sammy likes to lime and watch football on his brand new iPad. Sammy might be younger than Ed is, but Sammy is the main man. The two of them alone held things together for the longest time, but with the previ- ous government their budget was increased and they were allowed to hire Ralph. The three of them get along fine, never mind Ralph's damn seriousness. But now it looks like one of them is going to get shafted. And it won't be Sammy, because he's too good.

"Good, good, Sammy, You?"

"Fuck yeah, Hammers winning at last."

Sammy breathes football night and day and loves it more than his wife, who doesn't particularly seem to mind. Days are

easier with him around because Sammy is always full of hope—
even when there's nothing better to hope for than a draw.

"Whatever it takes, Sammy, whatever it takes, right? I'm
glad you're happy."

"Better than the dogs, Wood, that's all I'm saying." And it's
true, Ed does succumb to good odds at the track now and then. Ed
isn't big on sport. Besides the dogs, he can get fired up about horse
racing, but he has trouble seeing that as a sport, except for what the
horse does. If he hadn't come to London as a young man in 1974
because President Burnham had dreams of being Fidel Castro, he
might still be at the betting shop below sea level in Georgetown or
at the track a metre above sea level in Berbice, and he might still
be just watching them run instead of meeting Catherine, nearly
tripping over his own feet for those green eyes, putting up with
vexation from her dad, and getting to help Olivia grow to the point
when full sentences were coming out of her mouth.

When you tell people you used to live below sea level they
think you mad or joking, but true-true, that is where Ed moved
to as a young man from Berbice, and where houses are built on
stilts, where the whole of the town is pouring out into the sea
with the Demerara River, in the effluence of loam, gold and
sanity of an entire country. Is that the kind of thing you tell a
daughter? And if you start, do you stop? Are there ever things a
father should leave out? Olivia will need to know these facts
about her father and the kiskadee-kaieteur-foo-foo-garlic-pork
trimmings of what makes him.

"You okay, Wood?"

"Yes, Sammy, fine, fine. Just miles away."

Sammy is forty and fat with lots of hair. But he's a good man.
And that's another thing Ed has to tell Olivia: that in Guyana

black and Indian men used to have to work together in public but didn't like each other in private, but that is changing and things are better since the time he had to go back there in '85 to help his ailing daddy and ended up staying too long, when, man, it was bad and the Guyanese dollar was worthless. Blacks and Indians, like him and Sammy, they are fine-fine now.

Ed sits at his desk and turns on his computer. The requisition order for an Italian family to secure the belongings of a now deceased lodger was drawn up yesterday but the landlord was contacted only late in the evening, so this needs immediate processing. Martinelli: a good name; has its own steel band behind it. Aged twenty-four. Lord. This is the vex-he part of the job, the bad news arrows that get launched across the internet to land in who-knows-whose heart on an otherwise good day. Ed prefers the practical tasks. Before he checks the Safe and Sorrow office e-mails he fights sleep by uploading the photo he sent to himself from his home machine last night, one he found in the box beneath his bed, the one with photos of Catherine and Olivia before life bruk them up. In the scanned photo of the three-year-old Olivia, she wears a white party dress with lace and frills at the shoulders, white ankle socks and black patent leather shoes. Her face is dough-like round and slice-my-heart happy, and she holds up a T-shirt that says *I want my mummy.* Yes, girl, true-true.

"Edward," Catherine would say, her voice coming from the kitchen. "Edward," drawing out the last syllable. "Edwaard!" Then she'd tell him all the things that needed doing and fixing. "Wood," Olivia would say, trying to copy her mummy. "Wooood . . . open," as she toddled up to him with her lime-green plastic box that was a toy enough just to open, fill with stones, grass, buttons, pennies, and close again. And Wood he became.

Man, those miracles.

"You have a funeral," Sammy says, and raises his hand in the air above his keyboard before hitting send to sling the e-mail over. Ed's heart does a little hiccup; these funerals seem to be coming more regularly, and Sammy has given over most of them to him.

He checks the e-mail. The woman who needs the funeral is from Malvern Estate in Castle Green. She was forty-two, died alone, of an overdose, and the police say there is no one to bury her. So he will do it. This he is better at than knowing what to say to a grown-up daughter he last saw when she was four.

Now that he thinks of it, returning to Georgetown to attend to his family gave him good training for this very job. In Georgetown he met a man who was real bruk up at the side of the stall where his friend Sanil sold cassava and eddoe and plantain in Bourda Market. The man had been there every day he walked through the market for the five months of money-hunting that Ed had been doing to help his brother, to keep his mother in her house in Berbice because she refused to move, and this man was worse off than Ed. There were a whole lotta them worse off, but this very-very man he felt for: his hair was natty, his feet were torn up, his arms scabby, but in his face was something you could see that was quick-quick. Ed took the man home and gave him a shower and cleaned up his feet and let him sleep in his bed for twelve hours before sending him on his way. And, boy, this was the best Ed had felt since leaving London, missing his woman and his daughter. He wanted to keep the feeling, so he did this time and again with this man and others in Georgetown.

So, Carol at Rippleside Cemetery will be contacted on behalf of Anna-Marie Hunter, dead at forty-two, and there is the vicar to book, and he has to see about a place in the community plot, or whether she must be cremated. Of all the London jobs he's done—insurance, accounting, his stint in Housing—this job is the proper place for him.

And that is another thing he must tell Olivia: that after Catherine moved and told him not ever to try to find them, he learned to feel lucky for the things he didn't lose. In Guyana plenty people have nothing.

Olivia is training to be a lawyer, imagine. She already knows these things about life. Could be she got that from him? It's a notion he keeps in his cheek like a squirrel keeps winter food. When he thinks of the man in the Mazaruni River, Ed knows that the proper teaching like Olivia is getting would have helped him to know how to act, what to do in the face of a crime, no matter who committed it. She will not be like her father who was expelled for truancy and bad grades from Corentyne High School. Even so, there are things she can learn from him: he can tell her about Marabunta Creek where he played as a boy, and about orange hibiscus with red veins, about frangipani, about Gafoors Shopping Complex in Rose Hall, the town where he was born, about Bartica and the wide Essequibo River like a thick vein in his own neck. Okay, yes, he has to stop thinking or tonight he will not sleep either.

Anna-Marie Hunter is his priority now. But the most important thing about this woman's death? Man, he is ashamed to admit it, but the abiding boon to this sad event is that it will bring him Olivia again. She wants help with her research, needs it to complete her studies this year, and this, this is what a father must do.

ROBIN

These departmental meetings are more frequent, the days for his research less so. His head is filled with jargon: *research income*; *collaborative partners*; *knowledge transfer*; *impact*. These are the terms that govern all of them these days, and those who rarely showed up for meetings when he first started at this university now attend regularly. "Concepts are centres of vibrations," says Deleuze, and his more politically astute colleagues are tightly wound to the academy's tradition of knowledge for its own sake. Until a few days ago and the announcement of his fatherhood, Robin was ready to stand alongside them, to take strike action in support of the principle of excellence. But now, in this meeting called for the film department, he sits at a desk near the back of the room like a third-class student and doodles with the Polish waitress's pen on the last page of the agenda. Richard, department head, tells them that the dean is implementing the first measure of restructuring ordered by the vice-chancellor's group. Film Studies and Film and Video Practice will merge, beginning in September.

"There's an initiative towards practice-based programmes as the key to our students being better prepared for employment," Richard says, and Robin doesn't disagree or make much of this. The other theorists hum with indignation: the closing of courses will mean a streamlining of outlooks, a lack of choice and the return to the values of a polytechnic, further marginalizing the students of this underprivileged borough, when once widening participation—a university graduate in every home—was the key goal. Knowledge for its own sake.

"And this is what management think students want?" Mark, reader in cultural theory, says. "From their 'client satisfaction' surveys?" he adds, his fingers doing air quotes.

"'Key performance indicators,'" says Albert, a professor in visual theories, mirroring Mark's air quotes. They have been here before—the hardcore old guard bemoaning the MBA management-speak that has permeated the academy. Edu-business stocks, Robin has been told by Mark, have tripled on the global exchange markets over the last five years. The Epicure waitress is called Katrin. Her lips are like Emmanuelle Béart's in *Un Coeur en hiver*.

"As a result, there will be new job roles and titles, and a department structure that reflects the redefinition of how film is studied in the school," Richard says. This brings grumbling about who will decide what, how will they define "new," about the lack of consultation. "New job specifications will be posted in the coming weeks, with interviews and decisions before Easter."

Interviews? Now the room erupts. Robin resists sitting forward in his chair, the panic too obvious. "Are these new roles advertised externally?" he asks.

"No," Richard says, "but they won't replicate the posts as they currently exist. New job specifications."

"But what will distinguish the candidates—among us?" Robin asks, aware that he is the most junior in the room. Richard looks flummoxed, and the others stay silent, underscoring the challenge.

"You will take the views of the students into account, I assume?" Robin says, and sits back again.

He pictures what is growing inside Emma. Will his long nose take shape there? Or her blue eyes? He hopes for her hands, not his, but it would be a disaster if the baby were so often as sad and angry as Emma.

He can't lose his job.

"There are key performance measures," Richard finally says. "Research, teaching, community engagement—you know the deal."

"Not everything is measurable," Robin says without leaning forward, but it's loud enough to be heard at the front of the room, and Mark slaps the desktop in a right-you-are gesture of agreement, and others offer up "Exactly," rallying against Richard who was once one of them. Robin wishes he were able to talk like a poet. In school he wanted to write poems, to acknowledge his contradictions, to challenge his own reason. And his own foolishness.

—

He hides out in his office at the end of the day again. Image: a child's booster seat for his piano bench. His groin moves with the wrong kind of excitement. Everything is confused.

A polite, faint knock on his door. He can't hide the fact of the light on, so he says, "Come in." He turns towards the door to find Olivia.

"Robin, hello, sorry to bother you," she says.

It's her hair and face that make her striking: curls like tangled seaweed, open gaze, features awkwardly set. "No problem," he tells her and although he hopes desperately that he won't make her cry this time, he feels grateful for the relief a student always offers. Their needs come first from the moment they sit in the chair beside his desk and, oh, what respite not to be engaged with his own petty thoughts, indecision trying to become action. He pushes his glasses up on his nose.

"I wanted to ask your advice, or maybe your help," she says as she sits.

That was his word. You can always ask for help, he said at the end of last year, and she erupted in sobs. She had come to his office about a missed deadline, apologizing, detailing the facts of her life: the unmanageable workload in her law courses, the fact that her mother supported the whole extended family, the fact that her mother kept secrets, and, with each disclosure more intimate than the last, with him leaning forward, on the verge of comforting her, finally she said that the young men her age merely wanted her to do more than she was already doing for everyone else, and this she could not stomach. He sat back, shunting his chair a little away to the left. But when she continued about all the things that needed fixing—the university, the gender divide, immigration laws—he began to admire her for the clarity of her sense of obligation, her easy recourse to action.

"Go ahead. Ask away," he says. He notices that Olivia is carrying a hardcover book whose spine reads *Death in the Nineteenth Century*. She surveys his office, up and down the shelves and over towards the window.

"You have even more books than last year," she says. He looks up with pride at the shelf piled with film theory, cinema history, books on their sides, books standing, rows and rows of them. Poetry chapbooks and pamphlets line the window sill. He must ask the school office for another shelf.

"My one bad habit," he says.

She looks down to the book in her lap. "I was wondering if you would help me with something . . . part of my final year law project. I wanted to investigate paupers' graves," she says and looks up at him. Her brown eyes are slanted and he sees now that there might be Chinese as well as African and Caucasian blood in her. These eyes go into a squint as though she's now embarrassed about what she's just said.

"Oh yes," he says and sits forward, wanting to show enthusiasm but not yet knowing where this is going. Parenting will be like teaching—he can do this.

"Not just about the people who can't afford a burial, you know, but also about those who have no one," she says. Her enthusiasm is undercut with anxiety.

"Yes, okay."

"Well, whose responsibility is it?" Her eyes go wide with the question.

"I suppose the state's—"

"I don't mean for the burial, I mean to honour them," she says.

"I don't know. No one's, I guess," he says. His sadness meets hers and waltzes through the room. She shifts and begins to tap her foot. He finds himself wanting to tell her about his baby, about Katrin and his heart.

"My research isn't about this, exactly," she says.

"Oh?" He holds her gaze, not wanting to press her.

"But I was just wondering if in films, like, in film history, there is anything that deals with that, with how you can remember the dead, how they can be honoured."

He leans back. He is trying to grasp her vision. As a father he will have to entertain ideas more oblique than this. In the Mexican Western, *The Three Burials of Melquiades Estrada*, the quest is to honour Melquiades, to find his home, to do right by him. But that is a stretch. Then there is that romantic comedy that rebranded British cinema, but that's just—but still, yes, here is something to say.

"Well, poetry is one way it's been done in film.... " he says, leaning forward. Her face lights up. "'Fear no more the heat of the sun,'" he says, but sits back; in this territory he is merely an interloper, and Shakespeare is surely not what Olivia has in mind. But her question has him churning now. A song: everyone needs their own song. He is tempted to mention "Brokedown Palace," his secret signature tune, the song he'd like played at his own funeral. Instead he says, "But my area is really film—I use philosophy to discuss images: movement and time. Sometimes that intersects with concepts from literature, with poetry, but . . . that's not the same."

She looks disappointed.

"What are you looking for, Olivia?" he says, thinking that this young woman holds truth as a cup holds water. He himself is a sieve.

"A link, I suppose," she says, and her face looks encumbered in a way that has nothing to do with the law project. "I don't know.... "

He allows a silence to fall.

"Yes, well. Maybe it's something to keep thinking about. It sounds like you need more of a legal angle, for the dissertation," he says, annoyed at himself for not showing her that he sees where she's going with this. He is off his game. She looks disappointed again, but nods. She thanks him, and the curls at the back of her head jump as she walks to the door and leaves.

Deleuze: The shame of being a man—is there any better reason to write?

FRANCINE

Lawrence's tie has bold red stripes. Francine watches him walk through the cafeteria with their colleague, Simon, both of them holding lunch trays loaded with lasagne and bread pudding. But she smells oranges. And lavender. (*Oranges and lemons, say the bells of St. Clemens, for you and for me, from Chef Boyardee . . .*) Across the table from her, Patricia is watching her watch them, waiting for the answer to her question. How the hell can you know why you obsess on one thing and not another? The mother of the motorcyclist keeps coming up, simple, but this has not been enough of an answer for Patricia, who is tracing the path of Francine's eyes as they jump from Lawrence to the students in the queue who are doing the hokey-pokey on the spot, earphones in, all of them jangling inside themselves. Francine can almost hear the music, can almost feel the tremors in their legs. The orange smell is heightened, peeled—all of it, everything excoriated.

She looks again at Lawrence, who is not dancing inside or anywhere else. One day last week he wore a bright purple tie. Lawrence thinks he's outrageous, but Francine can see through his tie to his shirt, through his shirt to his skin, through his skin to his heart to see that it's big but broken. She knows that last year his wife told him she was having trouble seeing how they could live together in the same house for the rest of their lives. Lawrence, who heads up Quality Assurance and Enhancement, used to talk to Francine on their lunch hours, on away days, when they'd break from the group and walk and he would smoke and she'd pretend she did too. At one point in the past few years Francine thought Lawrence was starting to see her as more than a sympathy buddy, and she even started to find his fat fingers sexy. The gossip is that Lawrence had an affair with a woman at his gym, his wife moved out, and even though he's single he no longer misses her. But Francine sees through the red stripes, through all of it. Oh Larry. Lawrence is maybe like Mary Tyler Moore's Mr. Grant (*Oh Mr. Graaaaaant*). She holds back her smile and turns her attention back to Patricia.

She answers finally: "Well, what would it be like to get that call from the cops—the English cops, while you're in Italy and maybe planning to visit your son who moved to London for work?" The cafeteria hums. On his way past, Lawrence beams her a smile, which Francine returns.

"You're romanticizing it," Patricia says, and Francine sits back, wary that Patricia, who doesn't seem at all like Dancefloor Patty here in the throbbing presence of all these young people, is turning her into one of her anthropological subjects, doing psychoanalysis on the fact that Francine has been constantly sick and disoriented since the sight of Dario's bent, emptied legs.

"Explain," she says, pushing the chicken thigh on her plate through the sauce.

"You like to think you had a connection to him, because you saw him die, but this is about you, not him," Patricia says, and maybe this is a step too close to the truth or maybe it isn't.

"Maybe it was yourself you saw lying face down on the road," she says, and after a pause, "or maybe your son—a son."

"What are you talking about?" Francine puts her fork down. The Atkins diet isn't working for her and Patty should stick to the dance floor. She looks up again as Lawrence laughs with Simon. His gappy teeth look like a ten-year-old's.

"I mean," Patricia catches Francine's eye. "I mean, you seem traumatized."

Francine looks back down at her chicken. Maybe she should try the raw food diet. She could sprout her own sprouts. She won't tell Patricia that she knows the name of the driver of the red sedan—Rajit Mahadeo—and that he is charged with dangerous driving causing death. Rajit Mahadeo is a name far removed from Francine Johnson. "And how have you been, Pat?" she says, trying out familiarity.

"Fine. Busy, but this term is lighter than last, so, fine."

"Your book?"

"Mmmm. I might have lost the lust for it," Patricia says softly, and Francine wonders how one has lust for a topic like the anthropology of water ("not water itself," Patricia said when first explaining it, "the necessity of water") in the first place. At least Patricia has the lust for something.

"Shame, sounded cool," Francine says. Patricia would never say cool. Francine is merely trying to keep the kindness floating.

"I'd rather be in the garden, all year round if it weren't for winter. I'm trying orchids this year. I'm not very good," says Patricia.

This shared interest in plants is not something Francine is willing to acknowledge just yet; besides, lots of middle-aged women like to grow things. She used to grow vegetables when she lived with Auntie T, but hasn't touched a garden in decades.

Dancefloor Patty lives her passions. But there's also something delicate about her—in a horsey-woman blond-bun kind of way. Those white shirts. And blue . . . slacks . . . you'd have to call them. And Oxfords. She comes from academic stock, from a long line of philosophers and mathematicians, but she prefers people science. She writes about people as they walk towards water, as they tilt towards the sun, as they bend in fields. Francine looks at her hands now and sees that despite the desiccated skin, Patricia has girly fingers that played with dolls. Probably made them perform passion plays and tragedies. Patricia would have been a girl who put on shows, who could skip faster than all the other girls, who built ant farms.

"We'd make a good singing duo," Francine tells her.

Patricia's brow twitches, and a wrinkle at her mouth deepens.

"I mean the names—Patty and Francine—a bit fifties, don't you think? Or an ice-cream franchise . . . " Francine laughs, and this makes Patricia's face go Times Square bright. Francine looks away, looks around. Lawrence is talking with his mouth full (*Well, it's you girl and you should know it . . .*), the students across from them have plates loaded solely with chips, which she wishes she had instead of this chicken. (*Love is all around no need to fake it . . .*).

"It could have been me," Francine blurts out, turning back to Patricia.

"What?" Patricia asks in a way that sounds like she already knows.

"Not me, on the road, but me in the car. I could have been the one who hit him," Francine says, but feels stupid so she also laughs and a small bit of snot runs from her nostril to her top lip. She wipes it off and holds Patricia's gaze long enough to blush.

"I see," Patricia says softly.

"People get hit, all the time, all the time, you know, by buses, scaffolding, by lightning. It's all over the place, you know?" And Francine is surprising herself now (*You can have the town why don't you take it...*). The hair on Patricia's arm is like the peach-fuzzy down on Virginia Cooper's top lip when they were ten years old. Virginia Cooper, veterinarian's daughter, saver of fallen baby birds, who lived on her street in Philly.

"Have you spoken to your brother?" Patricia asks. Scott is the opposite of a motorcyclist—a rich, high-flying financial manager with his own driver, in NYC.

"Why would I?" Francine says, her lip starting to tremble.

Patricia doesn't shake her head at her in that way that Aunt T would when met with the same tone of voice, time after time through Francine's orphan adolescence. What was it her mother would say to her? What was it? That thing her mother said to the eleven-year-old Francine about love? That final speech she always tries to grasp the tiny thread of—to hold on to what her mother left her with. About how "love comes with . . . "? What was it that love came with? Patricia looks at her.

"My brother isn't a phone guy," Francine says.

"Do you ever wish he was?" Patricia says. Francine can't stand the compassion, the wise tone of concern, and she puts her knife and fork together on her plate, scrunches up her napkin and places it on top.

"I've got tons of work," she says before standing. "I really should get going."

—

Her office smells of banana. She clears her desk and awakens her computer.

There's a message about the restructuring plans: "Have your say" forums are to be held throughout the rest of the term. Please, God. The wide streets of Philly will feel too big, the Julys too dry and hot. Please, God. She really needs to keep this job.

She checks other mail, but can't concentrate. She clicks on to Soulmates. There's a message from bringmesunshine:

I like your profile and pic. Would love to know more about life stateside. If you're interested, please e-mail me at matthughes794@ hotmail.com.

She clicks on to bringmesunshine's profile. Oh man. She tries to be gracious. Matt is fifty-nine, describes himself as a genuine kind of guy with a childish sense of humour. He would like to find an attractive, intelligent, and sophisticated woman "because underneath the quiet, unassuming exterior lies a wheel-barrow of surprises. (OK, I've nicked that line from AA Milne, but there is some substance to it.)"

Help.

She goes back to Dario Martinelli's Facebook page. Someone has posted a YouTube video called "My friend Dario." She plays it. A jumpsuited woman, backed by bikini-ed girls in American football helmets and silver high-heeled boots dance to "my friend Dario, drives, too fast, drives, too flash . . . . doesn't care about to crash." The video has been posted by Roberto Martinelli. Such ease that a brother has with crashing and dying?

She clicks off.

Good God.

OLIVIA

Fog gone; air rusty; time tight.

Right.

She's cold. The sheepskin bits of her jacket are tattered now, the hide ripped for shite. How to afford new clothes is anybody's guess. Olivia pulls her collar up, grips her leather bag, lets her curls fall over her right eye in the very second that she spots a dark male across the square watching her walk towards the Templeton Building. Clenching her legs, she holds herself in at the place no one has entered yet—sure, yeah, the fingers of Mark from year 10, but nothing like what that bloke might have in mind. Can't be Nasar. Nasar's texts don't make her feel like she has to fend off invaders. If Jasmine knew this is what happened to her when some peng bloke took a look at her, she'd send out the fam and make some kinda virgin intervention. Olivia speeds up and heads to the doors of the atrium but stops short of going inside, waits. For what?

"Fire," she whispers.

She will try hard to get through the me-me-me of the Student Union meeting, try to remember that the May '68 geezers were really something, that some things did really change, even though a bunch of them became Tories, and then she will go home to her room, to her sites and her books. She'll never have the guts to join Anonymous, but saved on her desktop, the shortcuts to Hactivisimo, Ninja Strike Force, and Cult of the Dead Cow remind her that there are people who are not asleep at the wheel.

"Olivia, y'all right?"

She jumps; shit.

"You coming to the meeting?" It's Moe, like molasses, Moe the slowest talker in the SU or maybe the world. His face is pale, his eyes circled by shadows that might have come from once being a kid who had a lot of pressure on him to be something other than just a kid. Moe for president, Moe for a bit of caffeine, more like. Moe's American and changed his name from Moses to Moe-nearly-like-Joe when he was thirteen.

"Moe, we gotta do something with the Heston Bridge people," she says, because Moe is good with things outside of uni life, Moe is fired up internationally even if it is a slow burn, and the illegals sleeping under the bridge are bound to be rounded up soon. Slow-Moe looks at her like he's making a political calculation.

"Sure, sure, let's bring it up at the meeting," he says.

Moe is sleep-inducing, but she needs to be more like him. She should've chosen refugee law for her dissertation instead of dead people. "See you there," she says and starts to open her satchel so that he thinks she's got something important to attend to. Moe turns and plods inside. She rummages for chewing gum and waits for him to reach the automatic doors and disappear into the atrium.

She moves off; the pebble inside her Ugg boot rubs her big toe. The strumming of a guitar comes from across the square. The busker sings. She wants to stay and listen, but what if the hoodie over there is Nasar? She walks slowly. The singer hits a note that makes the hair on her arms stand up. She knows now how Robin might help.

THE TASTE

OF MARMALADE

KATRIN

This morning she has no paper for the toilet. Forgotten yesterday, no time, too tired, passed the shop, to bed. To sleep. She washes herself in the basin, on tiptoes, thigh on the sink, water splashing on the floor. Washes her hands a second, third time. Glances out of the window at the flower box, the frost that didn't come, and feels again the waiting inside. The tick-tocking of morning, watching. But she must go to work. Work takes her away from the window boxes, the waiting on the shoots in the soil, but in the café there is the man who comes every day now, to smile at her. He will never love her if she cannot even have paper for the toilet.

Outside: the crocuses, purple, white, maybe, the ones she saw last year and named Beata one, two and three, for her *mamunia*, but cannot remember which is which, along with the toilet paper. The tips, there, just beneath the dirt around the tree. This makes the hair on her arm stand up. This England sight, this not-Poland sight, this evidence that she is making her life on her own and for her *matka* when she will come in May. February in Gdansk is snow. February in London is the poking heads of purple and white.

Katrin swallows. The taste of marmalade.

In the coffee shop there is angry Claire from Tottenham and

Alejandro from Madrid and she is Katrin not from anywhere now, not from Gdansk, not from her father who left, not even from her mother who sleeps at the edge of the big bed where the pillow beside her is still dirty with her husband's hair oil.

"You take your time," Alejandro says, as she walks in, and she looks up at the clock to see that she is not yet late.

"You take the piss," she says, and they smile, because this is a sentence he himself has taught her. "Second person singular, showing improvement," he says, and her day will go well, now, here on Upper Street where the man might come back and Alejandro will make her laugh.

But Alejandro is not fun today, having a fight with his girlfriend by text, and there is a sourness from Claire: "This country is fucked. They are ripping us off." And when police sirens sound in the street: "It's all kicking off." These words make Katrin go curly inside. Claire throws slitted eyes at her and complains that Katrin is not doing enough refilling of the coffee machine. And when the man comes to the Epicure Café at the end of her shift she tries not to look unhappy.

"You need a pastry, too, sir," she tells him, holding the smile in her mouth and his coffee in her hand.

"You must call me Robin," he says, and she looks away, not because she is shy but because she loves this name. This man is one of the birds, the early morning bird, she has learned in English.

"Robin," she says and waits to see if he will take up her suggestion, but she thinks he is not really a pastry man. He has long eyelashes under his glasses. He is a man who lives through his eyes not his mouth.

"Nothing else, thanks. This is fine," he says and his long fingers, the fingers of someone who plays the piano, take hold of his coffee cup. "Did you see that film?" She does not remember the name of the German-Turkish director of this film, but its title in English, *Head-on*, is a way of speaking in this language that she must practise.

"Not yet, I will, I will," she tells him, and wishes she was not so tired at night. And there is Claire with a look like there is a snake in her throat, watching her, so Katrin moves to clean the table beside him, even though there is not dirt there, but there is the ribbon of the sun. When London first loved her it was always night time, Soho, films to help her English, and quiet bars on nights off from the loud one where she worked with Ania who went back to Poland, Ania who could not love these English men. Ania said, you are educated, they think you are cheap because you work in this bar, and they will never treat you as you deserve. Katrin would loosen the pony tail of her straight blonde hair, letting it fall towards her face to make it look less angular, more oval and English, but Ania said she would never fit in. Ania went back to Gdansk, where she is working in an office for less than one quarter of what Katrin makes in the café. Okay, so it is not anymore a bar; things are better: she works in the day.

A tall woman with a pink scarf wrapped high around her neck, covering her chin, enters Epicure. She walks like a soldier towards another woman at the back table, who stands in time for the pink woman to fall towards her and into her arms crying, like she is remembering what children do. The friend holds her tight, while the pink-scarfed woman cries and says not a word. They stand like that for a long time. Katrin watches until both of them sit down. When she looks back over at Robin he is staring at the women, before he looks at her. He nods at Katrin with a face that says, yes, sometimes things are exactly so.

Ania told Katrin's mother a lie. A lie that Ania knew was the only thing to say to her best friend's mother, because mothers are all the same. She told Beata that by the time May came and she was ready to move to her daughter in Islington, England, that the twenty-six-year-old Katrin would be married to an Englishman who would help her to find a job suited to the economics degree her daughter achieved at the University of Gdansk.

No matter. This is Robin, who teaches at a university and said her English is perfect, and this is a job in the day, and the crocuses are coming up.

FRANCINE

Almost nothing. After a whole pizza and some Doritos—a proper Saturday night feast—all that comes is a sore throat. Francine pushes at the tiny window in her bathroom, the paint chipping on the frame as she shoves it open to the cold air. She should move. This flat has done its time with her: six years, beginning with the early wailing—the wasted tears over Fuckhead on the rented bed—through the more hopeful middle period of repainting the bedroom walls, of forcing the landlord to replace the boiler, to this last stage of plumping the comfy cushions, lighting scented candles, dimming the lights: the patient waiting for someone who would change everything.

She breathes in the bronze-smelling air from outside. Traffic noises scratch the night.

Mom—what was it she'd said? *Love is . . . blah blah, Francine. Love comes with . . . blah blah.* She must remember. She walks to her living room and the couch is barely solid. Everything in the room is in *Star Trek*'s transporter room. She can't sit down.

She picks up the phone and dials.

When Scott answers his cell phone he's got his I'm-an-important-and-busy-man voice on. It's Saturday, for Christ's sake.

"Just checking in," she says.

"Hey, surprise, surprise. Whassup?" he says and oh Christ—whassup? Maybe he's just shocked that she has called again so soon after Christmas.

"Do you remember," she says, "something that Mom used to say—"

"God, Fran, really?"

Scott hasn't had a moment for their mom since she died when he was nine. Scott claims basically not to remember her, not to miss her, not to need to talk about her. But Francine knows there was something their beautiful, cancer-ridden mother said on her bed as she wheezed away her last few days in their bungalow on Minerva Street, a bed brought home by their kind-hearted dad, who is the one Francine must have got the tending plants thing from, because what she remembers most about him is the dirt on his knees from kneeling in the garden. He tended to her mother like she was the last orchid on the planet. The thing her mother said about love was said in that bungalow, and it felt like a chiming in Francine's ears, but the chiming gradually stopped, because the pulp of a teenage brain is porous. It was something that should have stayed forever. But now she can't find it, can't get back to it somehow.

"How's the winter treating you guys over there?" he says.

"Relentless, totally relentless. You?"

"Same, but at least it's sunny here—and not so goddam damp. You should come back." This is Scott's thing: to find a way to make Francine feel there's always something she's missing out on or not got quite right. And so she must stay in London if it kills her, even if, as Scott has told her time and again, the US will always be the future and England will always be the past. And damp.

She searches for something else they have in common, given that their dad, who raised them on his own for eight years, seeing her through high school and Scott through to his driver's licence, had a heart attack and left them to join his wife.

"Melissa okay?" she asks.

"Been laid off," Scott chirps, as though he's somehow pleased. Poor Melissa: no job and no kids, because her dickhead of a husband didn't want them. Ten years ago Melissa replaced a longing for children with a love for Jesus and has perpetually tried to get Francine to join her in the promise of rapture.

"Oh, I'm sorry to hear it. Any prospects?"

"Sure, sure, though the job market's tough. But, you know, she doesn't really need to work anyway. I do just fine."

Okay, that's enough. (Death tastes like Dr. Pepper.)

"She might get into charity work," he continues.

As Scott chirps on about charity being more and more important in times like these, Francine wonders whether he would be a beam-me-up Scotty if he were in this room. Would she be able to see through her little brother, or would he be an odourless, opaque mass of Scottness?

They sign off formally—Well, brother . . . Well, sister—and Francine doesn't put the phone back in its cradle properly. A few minutes later she picks it up again and books an evening out with Patricia.

ROBIN

On his route home from the tube station Epicure is a short diversion. Katrin is coming towards him as he enters, but she has her coat on, her knapsack slung over one shoulder.

"You're leaving. I was just stopping in for tea."

"It's the end of my shift—Alejandro is closing," she says and looks towards the dark-haired man at the counter who gives her a sly smile. Jealousy sketches a shape in Robin's chest.

"Are you going home?"

"Yes."

"Do you have time for tea then? We could go somewhere else."

She smiles. "Tea is not my drink, but I am learning to be English."

Her proficient English humbles his pathetic French, his effete attempts at German and Spanish. He wants to take her hand. They walk down Upper Street, something he tells himself he's doing every time he's doing it, but today he doesn't bother with the joke. Today he has the sensation of going down a tunnel. The lane behind Camden Square snakes off to a cobblestone alleyway where Moment Café is squeezed between a dress shop and an antiques dealer. The owner, Martin, has been selling records for twenty years; he added the coffee, tea, hot chocolate and pastries five years ago in order to address the rising rent, and he sells more of them now than he does records.

"This is something," Katrin says as she pulls out the barstool to sit at the high table next to the Decca wind-up gramophone. Her voice comes straight from her belly; he's never heard anything so clear. He orders tea from Martin, who brings it over to them and chats about the recording of Bach partitas that he suggested for Robin the last time he was in. Robin tries hard not to look too much at Katrin as she pours tea from the pot.

"He's gentle," Katrin says, when Martin leaves them to each other. She tells him about her Polish friend, Andrzej, who has a zipper tattoo on his arm, which gives the impression that his flesh could be unlocked if you tugged at it. Like Martin, she tells him, Andrzej is a gentle man. As she describes the rooming house where Andrzej lives with five other men, flashes in Robin's cerebral cortex convince him he knows this already, that he and Katrin have not only had this conversation before, but that they have featured together in numerous scenes accompanied by their own original soundtrack, in another time-space continuum. In *Matter and Memory*, Bergson pushes further the Cartesian split of mind and body to assert that the body is the abode of the present, while the spirit is anchored in the past, continually arriving, here, now.

"Here," he says as he offers her more tea. He lifts the petit fleurs porcelain teapot and pours. He tips it too far over, the lid tumbles off, clangs rudely off the tabletop and smashes onto the floor in two embarrassed halves. "Oh hell." He looks over at Martin who gives him a shrug. He would like to be more like Martin. He picks the two dainty pieces up, holding them together along the fracture line and making it look like nothing at all has been broken. He returns to the stool, puts the lid on the table, and as it opens again along its fissure, he turns back to her face. She has a look that says he is not a bumbling fool, that she doesn't mind if he's nervous. What if hers could be the features of his baby? He's insane, this is all insane. It's hot in here. And he is a cliché: Rath consumed by Lola in *The Blue Angel*. He is every poor bloke who ever wrote a sonnet.

"You're very funny," she says, smiling, her eyebrow hitched up.

"Funny?"

"Not funny, like the way you laugh. Funny the other way. You know: weird. Weird-funny.

"I wouldn't use weird if you're not trying to insult me . . . "

"Oh no!" She laughs. "No. I like weird." She touches his hand and he takes a breath, and is now very glad that it is hot in this café, so she won't know that the temperature of his skin has everything to do with her.

"You said you studied economics," he says, because economics has facts; facts are hard lines, real.

"Yes, but I don't like this so much now," she says.

"Why not?" he asks. She looks at her hands to consider the question, as though she must build him the answer. He knows little about Poland, and mostly through film images and phrases—shipyards; Solidarity.

"We have two kinds of university. In public universities in Poland you have only one way to look at economics. In private you have all ways open to discussion, but in state universities at first cycle—this is what we call BA—they cannot afford to teach you to challenge. Economics is not prescription, I think," she says and looks to him to see if she's right, but there could be nothing more perfect than what she has said.

"My grandfather owned a small company that made aluminium panels for prefab houses after the war," he says. Does she understand the meaning of prefab? "My father was an engineer . . . so maybe I should have made things instead of watching them."

"But it is your passion!" she says, and he feels off balance. He's embarrassed to say the things he wants to about film, but he finds his courage.

"There is a wonderful scene in three of my favourite films— an image of old people trying to recycle bottles. In one film the scene is shot in hues of blue, the other in white, and the last one in red light, for liberté, egalité, fraternité."

"But he is mocking them," she says, and of course she knows the work of Kieslowski probably as well as he does, so he nods, can't stop nodding, because there are images they share, and he is giddy with them.

Robin begins to talk on as though he is continuing the single thought they have shared for years. By the time his phone rings, he has told her everything about the year he was ten and how he built a whole village out of balsa wood, the church being the centre, the church—even though, no, no, he doesn't believe . . . it's not like they were believers—as big as the television in his parents' front room as they watched *Dad's Army* and he took strips of balsa wood and fashioned a utopia for . . . for her—he doesn't say this, of course; he doesn't say it was for her, but now that he thinks of it, it must have been for her, for who else but her has he been piecing cusps and zeniths together for all these years?

"Hi, Emma," he says softly into his mobile, but he should not have said her name, not in front of Katrin, who perhaps has not heard but who nevertheless looks away, unwittingly getting out of the way of his conversation with the mother of his child. When Emma tells him that she's done a lot of thinking and she has decided that it would be better if he moved to Cornwall with her, he turns his back on Katrin, not meaning to snub her, not wanting to do anything other than protect her from all the action-images of his life.

"Can I call you back in an hour?" he says to Emma. He hears her struggle to be gracious—of course, of course—and he rings off, looks back at Katrin, and wishes again to be a lightning bolt.

OLIVIA

"Tell me about him," Olivia says, plonking down on the bed. How can a mother lie in so long even on a Sunday? Ginger. The smell of the bed is like the herbal tea that Jasmine's mother serves over at hers while they study. The sheet has the uneven feel of her mother. She touches Catherine's pale cheek, the fold at her eyelid. Catherine doesn't like it when Olivia calls her by her name, but Catherine has never been Mummy, more like Kat Slater in *EastEnders*, less nasty, less of a slapper, but same-ish looks, same-ish secret ways about her.

"Where is he, Catherine?" Olivia says softly in her mother's ear. She will tell her she's met Edward only when she has had an answer. Catherine turns over under the sheets, blinking, looking at her daughter, through her, all the way to somewhere without secrets.

"Baby, I'm not awake."

The sleepy Catherine is the best. Olivia nuzzles into her mother's neck; powdery, plump, permanent. "Tell me about Wood."

"Oh, for God's sake," Catherine says. As she pulls the sheet up over her shoulder, Olivia smells her mother's ginger breath, all girly, while deep down Olivia has snakes and snails and puppy-dog tails.

"He didn't fight for me," Olivia says, stretching out her legs along her mother's body; silken. The melty feeling takes over her legs and then her arms. "He left. Or did you kick him out?" Nearly whispered, that last bit, on account of the eggshells in Catherine's heart.

Catherine turns over on her back and wrests her eyes open to the ceiling. "Why are you asking me this now? What's up?" she says, and turns her head to Olivia's face so that their cheeks touch.

"Nothing's up." This is whispered too.

"I don't know where he is," her mum whispers back, and they lie still; everything is soft.

Until the song Ed used to sing chimes in and there are all the things she needs to put right and, when she does, she and Catherine can move away from Granddad and Eric and take Nan with them. She'll get a first in her degree, get a job, get a flat—

"Stop shaking your foot," Catherine says, "it's shaking the whole bed."

And one thing that Olivia can't compute in all of this is how Catherine went and had a baby with a black man when her whole life she must have heard Granddad hollering Enoch Powell's rivers of blood at the telly. Her whole life she would have been made fearful of the very thing that's lying pressed up against her right now.

"You need a hubz," Olivia says.

Catherine turns her head closer and looks directly at her daughter. She brushes the curls away from Olivia's face and stares in her eyes as an optician would, looking for changes. "Do you have one?" Catherine asks, and oi, of course this is what she's wondering because this is the topic her mother loves to raise, softness or not.

"I don't need one, but you do," Olivia says sharply, turning her cheek towards her mother's mouth.

"I've got a 'hubz,' thanks," Catherine says, and argh, Catherine is talking about the swag gas man who calls himself an engineer. Even Granddad has seen through him.

"What, once-a-week William?" She feels her mum's lips swell and hears a little giggle. "He bought you dinner yet?"

"I'm getting up now," Catherine says and leaves Olivia clutching the imprint of her curves in the bed. "You get back to your studies."

Olivia pulls the sheet and blanket over her. Ginger, grapefruit and the scratchy cheap sheets her mother can't afford to toss out. She feels her idea taking shape, and Robin's role becoming clear.

KATRIN

Epicure is a place to feel proud. It serves French macarons, has specialty in panettone and Brie-wrapped phyllo, and they order from their special chefs the best wedding cake in London. Epicure mixes tart and sweet and bitter: apple and frangipane; lemon and custard; cheese and carrot; coffee and mascarpone. These new words she loves because they are nothing like the ingredients in other jobs, nothing like paper or plastic or metal.

Katrin counts the day's earnings and rolls the elastic band over the bills, twists it, doubles it over again, and puts the cash in the bag with a lock that Claire leaves for them in the evening. Epicure makes money, Katrin makes tips, and she does not have to scan bar codes like her friend Andrzej, or check that the sports food supplements are packed in each box, eighty hours a week, twelve hours a day, for £5.93 an hour. She is not in a factory. She is on Upper Street and she takes one bus to work. Her father made £400 a month for all of them. She makes this for herself in one week because Epicure gives the service charge to the server. She is proud, even though this England freedom comes with tiredness.

But tonight she is going to meet Robin for dinner. And she is clean. She is not tired.

—

To arrive. To sit. To smile. These are verbs in the intransitive form. But transitive verbs give her the trouble, because in Polish they do not only have a direct object. He sees her. She is seen by him. In Polish these are both possible. It is this form that she must stop confusing in English. Robin is sipping. He is sipping his wine, but his wine is not being sipped. Before this wine he raised a shot glass and swallowed vodka, her suggestion, because Bison was her father's drink, and they winced at the same time with the heat in their throats. But now talking in Robin's language—not only English, but the language of art and film—she is not so confident. This is the space that is opening inside her for words and pictures, and she does not want to be stupid in this. But he is kind. He looks at her as though anything she says will be a poem. She tries not to disappoint him.

"In Poland film is so poor they light it with candles, and this is what made Kieslowski so famous." She waits. He smiles, and now she can too. She sips her Spanish wine. Plum and vanilla.

"And where will you live when your mother comes?" he asks her, this fact about her remembered from weeks ago as she stood at his table, drawing her out, drawing her in.

"She will live with me, where I am." The waiter puts paella in front of her.

"It's a bedsit, right?" he says, with neither judgment nor pity.

"We have been in much smaller, it's fine." She doesn't want to talk about herself any more. "And you," she says, "you live alone?"

Behind glasses his eyes dart left towards a poster of the Alhambra. She adjusts her hair, runs her finger over her ear, before he looks at her again; something is not the same.

"I might be moving soon," he says. Her stomach bends.

"I'm coming back," she says as she stands up, not too fast, so that he will not be worried.

In the toilet she tells her face in the mirror that this is nothing, nothing. That her *matka* is coming, that she has a job in the day, that England is not Poland, that there are many fish in the lake, that this is Robin, named for something that flies, and that she must ignore this *czekam* feeling like she is the pet at the door when he is turning a key to come in.

She washes her hands.

"Are you okay?" he asks when she is back in front of his kind face.

"Yes, fine, thank you," she says and smiles.

"I'm not avoiding your question. I live alone right now," he says. The *czekam* swells and she takes a sip of wine. She must not drink too much because she will be stupid with wine.

FRANCINE

Galumphing—is that what she's doing? When she first met John he would tease her, telling her that her walk was a waddle, but then when she gained weight he started to call it a galumph. She feels her hips and tenses her thigh muscles so that she doesn't galumph along the pavement from the underground, where she has just emerged from Covent Garden tube station. Driving only on completely confident days seems to be working out for her nerves, and all this walking will work for her thighs. But right this moment she is naked in the middle of London's west end. Naked to the smells. What does soot smell like? Like damp potatoes. Naked to that woman in the hijab who has looked at Francine's legs in these stretchy trousers that expose every single bulge. Naked to the voice of the man with his head down, mumbling (*Dog Chow makes me very happy . . .*). Covent Garden station is a joke of pressing bodies, and she is exposed to them all.

It begins to rain.

She pulls her scarf tight around her, dips her chin, raises her shoulders, and looks out for the restaurant as she heads towards the Royal Opera House.

Patricia loves opera. Patricia can *Così-fan-tutte* with the best of them, and tonight they are seeing *Rigoletto*, and, when Francine asked to be briefed on the basic story and if there'd be tunes she'd recognize, Patricia corrected, "Not tunes, arias."

Of course Patricia is already at the restaurant when she arrives and this, Francine knows, is what women her age do now, what it means to be past the pause, with no time for pausing, no time to be late. You've gone all meno, Cindy used to say to her mother when she and Francine were teenagers. She never got to pause, Francine would say of her own mother. Meno-pause: the lying in wait . . . for what?

The restaurant Patricia has chosen is French, and Francine feels uneasy about the tablecloths and soft lighting because flickering up through the romantic chroma is Dario's bent leg. She pulls her chair out to take her seat across from Patricia. The knife, spoon, fork are a quivering silver (one of Dario's arms was tucked under him, the other bent back, almost curled). The plates on the table are matte white, which makes them appear almost solid, but she's not fooled, she knows that none of this really exists, and that molecules and breath and sympathy are an illusion.

"I used to come here with my ex," Patricia says, lifting up the wine list. Francine wants to block Patricia's radar, so she lifts her menu too, in front of her face. This is the first time Patricia has ever mentioned a partner, and Francine waits for a pronoun.

"We'd argue about whether it was right to eat foie gras and veal; of course, it was not what we were really arguing about. It was my way of telling him he was thoughtless, his way of telling me I thought too much."

Francine lowers her menu, feeling safer now, and looks at Patricia. "How long were you together?"

"Five years, not that long, in the scheme of things, but he was the first person I'd ever lived with. I was a late bloomer." Patricia puts the wine list down. "I'd never pinned myself down before that."

Francine would not in a million years eat foie gras, but she briefly considers it now.

"I travelled a lot—on field research trips, and he was just there, happy when I got home."

Francine might order escargots—she used to love them in her twenties when eating French food was exotic and showed you knew a thing or two about love and garlic. Love comes with . . . blah blah.

"So did you only argue when you came home?" she asks.

Patricia doesn't answer. She looks for the waiter, signals to him, and orders a bottle of Chablis. Then she looks at Francine so sternly that Francine feels she is in school again, in trouble for forgetting her gym shorts. Patricia's mouth twitches like it doesn't know what to do next. And then her face softens. The tears that might have flowed aren't coming after all. The English: they know how to do that.

"I think I just needed him to resist me, somehow, resist just being there and happy. I don't know. I'm not easy."

And in Patricia's voice is that little girl who tortured dolls, collected butterflies, made life difficult for others because it was hell to be Patricia. Francine looks down at her menu, but she has begun to perspire and has to wipe her brow.

"How about you and John. Did you fight?" Patricia asks.

I'm speaking for myself and you're perfectly welcome to speak for yourself. I take full responsibility for my own feelings and am not blaming you, but I feel angry when you don't respect my space, said John, in his gobbledy-gook, self-help jargon, so that whatever anger she might have had about him not calling her for two days was redirected back at herself and her so-called responsibility for her own feelings, which she knows now was just the Fuckface's way of shutting her out, shutting her down. So that when the day came— when she finally was able to raise her voice and yell: "Why is it always about you?"—well, he slammed a door and she ended up foetal on the floor. Only when he declared that he would never have children, even though he claimed regularly how great he'd be at it, did she finally twig that John Clarke was not the man she had imagined him to be; twig that she had known this all along; twig that John Clarke was a fuckwit. But he was her fuckwit, and she believed in sticking with things.

"No, John didn't like to fight."

"Like to fight? That's not what I asked," Patricia says with a smirk. And suddenly Francine can see through Patricia's skin, through to the blood in her veins, through to her bones. It makes her tummy rumble with hunger and makes the Chablis smell like vinegar. She sits forward in her chair, her elbows on the table, and clears her throat.

"Patricia. What is it, exactly, that you would like to hear from me?" She holds this forward tilt for two, three, four seconds, then sits back and picks up her menu, but she can feel her lip starting to tremble. Peeking over the menu she sees that Patricia is smiling, that Patricia has enjoyed Francine's defiance, and now, oh shit, she's really done it now.

—

The cup lights that line the balconies—their shimmering make the Royal Opera House appear to be on the verge of being beamed up. And it smells of . . . what? Nina Ricci, that's it. She has to hold her nose, but a little cough comes, just beneath the soft music, an aria not a tune, into the second half of *Rigoletto.* She has been struggling to stick with it and has been lulled along by the arias she recognized from Bugs Bunny cartoons, and by her memories of working on the high school production of *Oklahoma*, doing costume and makeup, sewing petticoats and bonnets, and going home singing about how the cowboys and the farmers should be friends and the elephant-eye height of the corn.

But she's sleepy. Her eyes are sliding shut. Okla, Okla, homa, homa . . . O.K.L.A.H.O.M.A. She rubs her eyes, keeps her eyebrows raised.

When she jolts awake it's the hand she feels first—Patricia's on her arm—but then she realizes that her head has dropped in Patricia's general direction, looking to be patted. Straightening up, she flushes, sweat welling like tears, and the baritone is singing like he is crying too. Patricia's face is fixed in concentration. On what? The words? Does she know Italian? The notes are sad. Patricia glances over, gives a little smile and rubs Francine's forearm just before Francine moves it away.

The next day at work, and all that week, Francine makes tea in her office and brings parcels of protein—tuna, ham, even roast beef—for lunch so that she doesn't have to appear at the Starbucks in the atrium or the Costa's in the Watson building. She doesn't answer her phone when she sees Patricia's number come up on the screen, and when Patricia leaves a voicemail message wondering how she is, Francine writes a polite text back telling her that she's incredibly busy and that all the work is keeping her mind off troubling things. She doesn't tell Patricia that it actually felt good to be tilted towards her at the opera or that she has found out that the man who killed Dario—Rajit Mahadeo—is a fifty-five-year-old night shift Quality manager at Kandhu Ltd., supplier of branded and own-labelled snack food to major UK retail centres. Rajit Mahadeo lives in Harlesden with his wife, mother-in-law, and four children aged between ten and nineteen. He was released on bail the night of the accident, having been charged with dangerous driving causing death.

The charge continues to be the disconcerting fact in the case. She saw no dangerous driving from the red sedan on that night. The others must have seen something more terrible. She should have stayed longer. Slumped over his steering wheel in tears, Rajit had not been dangerous in any way.

It could have been her.

OLIVIA

Olivia, you make heart singing. Nasar

He's probably in the queue. That's well-dred. Has he seen her? She looks behind her but sees the wheelie bloke in his Paralympic vehicle, whose name she knows for sure is Christopher. Who the fuck is Nasar? She throws the phone into her satchel. She wouldn't get in that queue in any case; she can get water from the tap in the caff and pick up a regular coffee there too. It's hard to keep her eyes open on account of how much reading she did last night so that when her tutor, Stan, looks at her and asks which EU statutes apply to jurisdiction and immunity in international law, she'll have something to say. But she's done with answering people's questions, really. All those answers have exposed her, and Nasar might be a phony name for Clive or Richard or Amir, trying to humiliate her. She's answered enough questions for a whole degree, and all it's given her is—what? No, what she needs now is continue her boycott of Costa and Starbucks, get a first on her dissertation project, and find a way to persuade Robin about her idea.

She heads down the atrium, passing another queue. How can they afford this shite, anyway? The cost of coffee in this uni has doubled since last year. Brand me with your beans. If Nasar is among these sheep, she'll never find him. And she wouldn't want to.

Head down, hands in pockets, Olivia is a panther up the stairs—oh oh oh oh, talk to me some more, Robin. But at his office on the first floor the lights are off, computer shut down.

—

Jasmine is smug-arsed and floaty. Olivia wants to pull Jasmine's hair until it comes loose at the roots. "It's fine," she says, instead of tugging. It's fine: the fact that it's been weeks since Jasmine shagged the Italian dude they met together and is only now telling Olivia about it, on account of thinking that Olivia would have been merked to know earlier.

"I know you had your eye on him," Jasmine says as she gathers up her long brown curls and makes a pile on her head, pouts like a model. Eleanor-turned-Jasmine works hard at her curls, wears Rihanna tops, and too much lipstick to make her lips look thick, all the while them being thin as shite, because Jasmine was cheated at birth, should have been born something more sexy than an Eleanor. Olivia has known her since primary school, when Eleanor was the quiet, slim but dim girl that Olivia made friends with because no one else would. Eleanor was generous, always doing things for other people, always bringing treats for Olivia, who grew to depend on her kindness, depend on her house as an escape on the days when Granddad would beer-up and go off on one. Then something happened to Eleanor in year 10, when her father started staying out all night and her mother became a Christian. Eleanor started having sex like it was her own Jesus. Her generosity turned to giving head, and giving up the inside of her, night after night, like it would change her into someone else. And so Jasmine emerged.

Jasmine sucks her teeth.

"You're always playing so hard to get, so I figured he was fair game," she says, but what does Jasmine know about fair and what does Olivia know about any game. The Italian biker would have made everything shut up for her like the seaside in winter, because she's not going to end up like Catherine with some guy riding off into the horizon, so he's better off having done Jasmine if that's what he wanted.

"He's bang tidy," Jasmine says, "and he lips like a prince." Jasmine would know. Jasmine has kissed a prince from Benin, even though both of them know that the Nigerian dude said he was from the Royal Edo people as a way to get Jasmine to open her legs. "I'm sorry," she adds, "he would have been a good one to add to your list."

Olivia nods and looks disappointed as she plays the girl with a list who might want to add yet another hubz. Jasmine admires Olivia for her brains, but also because Olivia is nearly black and surely has had it—like, lots—surely. A misconception Olivia has never tried to correct.

"We texted after, for, like, days. He called me, and once we even did it over the phone," Jasmine says. But her face goes mincy all of a sudden.

Olivia can tell there will be no studying tonight. And she is not going to get a word in about how she's going to her first funeral ever tomorrow to meet Edward Reynolds, or about how paupers' graves were a thing that people thought had disappeared with plagues and horse-drawn carriages, but that her thesis will show . . . dang, what will her thesis show? That she has a father, that her father buries these people, that maybe her father left on account of her or the shite he had to put up with in the very household she is dying to leave. And she will try to make it all better again. And then?

Olivia plants her face in the pillow on Jasmine's mother's sofa. She's always thought of this as the Born Again pillow; it's silky, packed with eiderdown. It takes the weight of her chin so tenderly—like it loves her—that she bolts up.

Right.

"I have to do some revising," she says and takes up her notebook. Jasmine gives her that look saying don't be jealous of me, it's not my fault blokes like me, but Olivia starts to make pretend notes and ignores her.

Back in the day, workhouse poor had paupers' burials, even if they had family. Coffins made of cheap wood would crack with the weight or be too small, but it's all they had. Families wanting to make coffins special put ribbon or hair or cloth over the box, and there was no affording a cart or horse; only lifting and walking would get the coffin to the plot. Olivia has sifted through letter after letter from family members asking for bodies to be exhumed from paupers' graves after the family had saved enough for a private burial. People care about these things. But do we still have rights in death? And what about a lonely death with no relatives to come claim you?

"I think I'm going now," she says to Jasmine as she closes her book.

"Look, Liv, I'm sorry, okay?" The pity in Jasmine's face is confusing because, without her knowing what for, there's lots of pity that could be heaped on a girl who hasn't got time to be touched.

"Jaz, I'm gettin' it plenty other places," Olivia says and makes a black-girl zigzag with her neck that she knows gets Jasmine's blood racing. "See you soon."

ED

Cannon-ball tree, kufa, yellow allamanda, soldier's cap, parrot beak, stinky toe: they are the flowers a child should know, would know if she was to visit she grandmother in Rose Hall. These flowers Ed's mother taught him to say when he was a child, she thinking that learning was about reciting things one after the other. But here in the chapel entrance, Olivia has her eyes on the lilies in the vase he himself bought this morning to make an impression on her, and he hopes she's thinking it is proppa good. Ed cannot take his eyes off Olivia's face because if he does it will be like losing her again, and Catherine too because Catherine is there in the girl's cat-eyes, in her straight-straight but gappy teeth. Olivia is the most beautiful thing he has ever seen.

"Please take your seats," the vicar says.

Ed is standing at the front of the chapel next to the coffin of Anna-Marie Hunter, known for her quiet and polite demeanour. Her neighbours say they didn't see much of her outside her flat for the two years she lived there: no trouble at all, just quiet and polite. Anna-Marie has no known next of kin. Anna-Marie will be cremated at 13:30. Ed will make sure this happens smoothly and quickly because he is meeting up with Olivia after. When

Neil—the vicar he regularly calls on for these funerals—is finished his few words about how life brief fa so, Ed will swing into action. It is action he was missing, back home on the river, standing doing nothing while blood spread out in the water like octopus ink. He could have said a word or two, then and there. He could have.

"'I am the resurrection and the life. He who believes in me will live, even though he dies,' says the Lord (John 11:25)," Neil says and he continues quickly, because he knows this will be the short version. Even God is going along with Anna-Marie being quiet and polite.

There are only three people, other than Ed, Neil and Olivia, to bid goodbye to this woman, and they are neighbours who have not prepared anything to say about her. The ceremony is over in no time and the neighbours leave quickly, not even talking to one another, and this is another thing that Ed must tell Olivia: that West Indian people talk to one another, even if they are strangers. *Wha gwan, gal? When last we see ya?* He wishes Olivia would talk to one of Anna-Marie's neighbours, but the girl puts her head down and looks sad when they leave the chapel.

"Wait for me in the A13—it's a caff down Ripple Road," he tells her outside when the wind blows, cold-cold, burning up he cheeks and making him hold tight to his flimsy jacket, which is the only good one he has that fits him, now that he has a paunch. He must attend to the business of Anna-Marie's remains but he desperately wants to speak to this beautiful daughter standing right here. The first time he talked to her in the staff room at the Safe and Sorrow office he was so schupity that she had to do all the talking. This time he wants to talk—to talk to her like a father.

"Will you be long?" Olivia asks, her voice like the one he has heard in his sleep.

He tells her to meet him at two o'clock, and that he hopes that is not too long for her. And it is relief like cooling rain when she agrees.

—

The A13 caff is a pitiful sight and, blast, not right for Olivia. He should have known better: this outdated box with six tables covered in plastic cloth, salt and pepper in cheap old-fashioned shakers, brown sauce for egg and chips, the signs old, the waitress old, the chairs old-old. Man, he mess up with this one. He sits down in front of her. Olivia looks up from her book.

"Hi, hi," she says and smiles, uncomfortable, but a smile in any case, so his chest fills up. "This place is nang," she says.

"Nang?"

Her face says, oh God, dotish old man.

"It's good!" she says and her fingers start tapping the table as though current is going through them at high voltage. Is *nang* a cuss word? When he was young he could cuss for Guyana. He was rass this, mudda skunthole that. If he tells her these perhaps she will be impressed, but this is wrong, not what he really wants to tell her at all.

"So, the law," he says, feeble, man, feeble, but this is where they left off first time.

"Yes, yes." Her eyes go on a tour, starting at his balding head and moving from exhibit A to B to C like she is cross-examining her origins. He lets her do her tour because it lets him do his. "How did you end up doing this job?" she says.

Nothing has been deliberate since the love that produced her. Nothing at all, so what is there to say? It's all been chaos since that day with Geoffrey at the river's edge, leading to losing Catherine and ending up just trying to keep up, a broken but decent man. One small moment in all the moments of a man's life should not stand in the way of some kind of hard-won decency.

"You know, Olivia." Okay, so that's better, saying her name is good, the name he himself chose for her. "I wasn't good at my studies, not like you. I got expelled from school . . . " He pauses to give her a moment to feel ashamed of him, but in her face there is nothing like judgment. "And, you know, when you told me you were studying law, man, that was something, and I said to myself"—he is about to say, I bring my pigs to fine market, but it's not he who has brought her up, not brought her to any market at all. "I said to myself, man, Catherine is a wonderful mum."

There, he has said it, said the name.

She nods.

His insides are twisting.

"And you know, as to how I've ended up in this job, well, it's because of lots of disruption in my past. You know I went back to Guyana, right?"

"No, I didn't. She doesn't talk about it. She just said that you had to leave us but that I was not to hate you."

Oh Jesus. She has been taught not to hate him; so she doesn't know. He takes a big breath.

"When I was about your age I came to London because I felt I was clever—more clever than I really was, mind you." The look on her face humours him, and the truth is that he doesn't know what more to say to her. Should he tell her about the politics? About how Burnham was telling people that all labour was now part of the state, along with the Berbice Bauxite Company where he got his first job when he left school? About how suddenly after independence the government couldn't afford its own labour? And the same austerity slogans the politicians shout now are what Burnham shouted then? Should he tell her that when he lost his job he was raging vex and thought he was more clever than Burnham so he and his brother left bauxite and went to the Mazaruni river where, man, there was gold, and he worked on a dredge like a real porkknocker? Would she have sympathy for him if he told her he got malaria, was too lonely, and quit gold, and while the country was starting to topple he arranged to stay with his cousin in London? And that he never had any intention of going back?

He has to simplify it. "Guyana was a place that faced a lot of hardship, after independence; a lot of hope, but a lot of trouble too." And maybe that is enough to say at this point. How much of a Guyana-lesson does the girl really need, after all? About fast money, gold, and the benefits of having a jungle to hide it? About how Geoffrey ran, and he just stood and watched? About how a whole place can go mad?

"I came to London and I had no training; it was hard then, hard for black people," he says.

Olivia nods her head; she is an educated girl.

"Then why did you stay?"

"Well . . . " Good question, good question. "I had hope for good work, Olivia." And saying her name again is another thrill. She fidgets; her hand taps the table and beneath it her leg is shaking. This girl is wound right round, and certain things set her spinning. She is like Geoffrey. Oh Jesus, she is like Geoffrey.

"I worked in different places—in the docks, but also in some shops. And I took some classes—City and Guilds," and looks at her to see if she knows about this. She nods. "And I learned accounting, then office management . . . so you see, it's still a bit of that."

"Accounting?"

"Well . . . " He laughs, and man that feels good.

"But then you went back," she says.

That's the problem, he never should have left, never should have listened to Geoffrey's nonsense. "I was cold all the time!" he says, but he knows that the girl doesn't want foolishness. "My brother had a scheme—in Bartica with a gold mine, and he was making money for so." This is enough about Geoffrey. "So I went back home. And shortly after that, my daddy died, and I had things to look after, and my mummy . . . and Guyana was harder than London, because the government bankrupt us." And he doesn't say that it's because of Burnham and Geoffrey that his daddy died, that the man's heart gave out because Burnham was stealing the country's money and Geoffrey was scheming-scheming and making bad deals and stealing money from the gold dredge on the Mazaruni River, and telling lies, making and spending so much money that one day he was driving a Jag and the next day he was taking a bus—all of that just a hint of what would happen years later, that April he left when Olivia was four.

"I stayed for three years," he says, "then I came back to London, but it was even harder to find a good job." He was older—and still black. "I did a night-time diploma in health and social care at the Barking and Dagenham College, a different kind of accounting . . . "

Olivia smiles and picks up the pen beside her notebook as if she's going to write something, but she just holds the pen and rubs the top of it. "When did you meet Mum?"

"Catherine," just to say it, because he is allowed, "came into the council office—I worked in housing then. She was so beautiful." He takes a breath. "Like you," and oh Jesus. He waits.

She smiles again. The girl is good at smiling. "Love at first sight?"

"You can be sure of that . . . for sure . . . " He nods, but even he is not convinced by the gesture. "Maybe not for her . . . Her folks didn't like black people so much."

"Still don't," Olivia says, and he wants to catch the hurt that falls from her voice. "Granddad is an angry geezer," she says, and she goes on to tell him about his former in-laws, how Catherine's brother is much the same. "Nan is ace. Mum . . . keeps to herself."

Christ. How can life come to this? Catherine had wanted to be a dancer before he went and made her pregnant and caused her to lose her shape. Now Olivia tells him how Catherine works in the box office of the Theatre Royale so she can still be close to people on the stage.

By the time they have to leave—because he has to get back to work and she has to get back to classes—he hasn't told her anything near enough. "Guyana's money is still in some Swiss bank account in the ex-president's grandchildren's name," he says. But he's left out so many of the good things—like Christmas in Rose Hall when all of the neighbours make the rounds, visit every single house of every single person they know and drink punch de crème and dance like Mother Sally, just dance, dance, dance.

"Will you ask your mother if she will see me?" he says. Olivia's cat face goes broad to bursting and maybe she thinks this is a fine idea. But then he sees different.

"Sorry, sorry. Never mind." Is that pity in his daughter's eyes? "You have so much studying to do, and your project—did this help, today?"

She studies him further, like there is an exhibit she overlooked on the first tour. Like she knows that every rope got two ends.

"I want to come to another one, to find out more—like what happens for refugees. Do you know about the men at Heston Bridge?"

He does not, and shakes his head.

"In any case, I have more research to do before I write, so will you tell me when there's another one?"

But that could be months from now, you can't predict these things, and he can't just wish for someone to die alone so that he can see his daughter. "My job is uncertain; they don't need three of us. I don't know when that will happen," he says because he would prefer to set an earlier date, like tomorrow, or eighteen years ago. But Olivia's face looks panicked.

"What?" She is bobbing again, at the knee, in her fingers. "You're going to lose your job?"

"I don't know for certain, but, you know, this is what is going on across the country," he says. Rass, man, rass.

"Oh." She looks at her notebook, picks up the pen and clicks the top over and over. She scribbles something on the page. He has let her down. "Okay, well, I'll ring you. I'll ring you," she says. She stands up and he has to let her go. He follows her to the door. Waits there to see if she will hug him or offer her hand. Is it wrong to kiss her cheek? She nods at him as if to say, yes, man, yes, it's very wrong. She turns and heads out the door of the café.

Callaloo, pepperpot, Rupununi, arapaima, Karanambu, Essequibo: words he still must say to her.

FRANCINE

Ryan Broughton is a slight, bony, young man, slouched on the velvet couch in his living room while his mother hovers just outside the door, listening, sniffing, like a wary sow. When Francine laid eyes on him again for the first time since the accident, as he floated down the stairs of his house to greet her at the door (burnt toast, bacon, toothpaste), he seemed much more slight and bony than on the evening of the accident. How in hell's name had he turned the dead weight of a body over to try to breathe life back into it? Ryan's face is pointy and pocked near his temples.

"What about tea?" his mother calls from where she is hovering.

"Mum, nothing," Ryan says. She had answered the door when Francine arrived without notice and was reluctant to let her in. Francine had paid for their phone number and address on a web directory, and the woman's Scottish brogue was burdened with suspicion. At the door she described in clipped sentences just how Ryan hadn't been able to return to his medical studies at King's College because he thought he was a failure. "He's not well," she said. "That accident has changed him." Oh God, oh God, Francine thought as she clutched the flowers she'd brought in a plastic bag: death tastes like failure.

Now Ryan shifts and pulls the zip of his hoodie up and down beside her on the couch. Francine wants to tell him that what he tried to do was the bravest thing she's ever seen. She wants to say, *I love your lips, and your breath, and the guts you must have*, but as they sit on the understuffed couch in the overstuffed living room of his mother's house, a few blocks away from Francine's flat, she is speechless. She tries though:

"You did all those things, pounding his chest . . . it was something . . . "

Ryan looks at her like she's a dumbass, but she sees the memory of the clotted blood on his lips. They stay silent and his mother pokes her head around from the kitchen again. And then Francine begins to cry. For the first time since the accident.

Ryan sits up straight with a look that says, oh hell. He waits and watches her wipe her eyes.

"He begged me to save him," he says.

"What?" She sits up as straight as he is.

"The driver, he came over to me and held on to me and begged me to save the guy." Ryan gives the couch a gentle punch.

"I'm so sorry," she says as Ryan's mother comes in and stands, hands on hips like a warning. "I wanted to give you this," Francine finally manages as Ryan's mother picks up random objects around the room—a framed photograph of a graduating Ryan, the TV remote—and she's embarrassed by what she's brought, but it's too late now. Ryan deserves a medal, a badge, whatever it is they give to heroes these days.

"Here," she says and takes the red champion anthurium out of the bag by her feet. She sees in Ryan's face that this is okay, that a living thing is an antidote to kissing death.

"That's nice," he says as he picks up the small pot and examines the waxy, almost fake-looking red petals.

"You're kind," he says.

Francine holds on to her composure. "Not anything like you," she says, and looks over to his mother. What does it take to make a good kid? When John Clarke said he didn't want children, Francine looked into his face to consider her options. They would move in together, he said, of course they would, not now, but of course they would, and they would travel for their holidays. His face said to her, I'm the best thing that has ever happened to you, kiddo, so don't push your luck. All the while John-the-liar-from-Lakawanna Clarke was considering his own options for depositing his oh-so-precious genetic coding into a more compelling vessel.

"I feel I should have stayed with you," she says. "I should have helped you. I'm so sorry."

Ryan looks up from the anthurium. He is so young, but seems so calm. "They'll need more witnesses if he doesn't plead guilty. They'll need you to testify."

She hears the trauma now, like steel-wool in his voice. "But he's not . . . " She doesn't know how to define danger. "It was an accident," she says.

"What are you talking about? Did you see how far he was flung?"

Ryan's mother sits down on the arm of the couch. She looks at Francine like she dares her to say another word that will upset her son or KAPOW!—she'll land her one.

Francine clears her throat. "Sometimes they reduce the charge," she says to Ryan's mother, but the woman is looking over at the bay window as though someone is climbing through it. The doorbell rings, and it's a relief when the woman gets up to answer it.

"If they do, they're wrong," Ryan says.

God, oh God. She folds up the bag she brought the plant in and pushes it into her coat pocket.

"Maybe if you'd stayed, you'd know that," he says.

"But he was dead," she says, and Ryan wrings his hands slowly. "But you still tried," she adds quickly.

He looks at his hands. "Of course."

"And that must be awful for you. Very painful."

His face loses its tension. He tells her that he has Rajit's phone number and that he's often thought of ringing to shout at him. And Francine wants to tell Ryan about how as a teenager she planned to become a conservationist, to save all the species and creatures she feared were becoming extinct—tigers, or even the frogs that had started to disappear from the lake that her geography teacher took the class to year after year. But her thoughts get knotted up and instead she says, "Frogs go first if the lake is polluted, so you have to watch for the frogs."

Ryan looks startled, confused. She picks up her handbag, buttons up her coat. "I'm beginning to think it's all about watching out for the frogs," she says, but Ryan's face stays the same, so she concludes, "We have to be careful."

Idiot.

"Thanks so much for seeing me," she says. "You did an amazing thing." She reaches the front door and squeezes between Ryan's mother and the *Awake* pamphlet that is being offered up by the black woman wearing a Sunday bonnet who is standing serenely at the door.

—

At work the next day she deletes the e-mail from Human Resources that contains a checklist of the elements required in the annotated job specification she is supposed to prepare in a few weeks' time so that the vice-chancellor's group can make decisions on restructuring and rationalization. She does a quick search in the *Guardian* job section and decides to branch out: environmental jobs, marketing jobs. Nothing.

She opens her deleted items box and retrieves the checklist from HR. She starts a new Word doc:

> Quality Assurance Officer:
> 1. Servicing officer to Validation Review Panels.
> 2. Advice and guidance to academic schools on QAE processes delegated to schools.
> 3. Working below my capacity, to hide my light under a bushel, to be forever sidelined and invisible, because I forgot to do all the things most other women have done by now, and have just been trying to get by on my own.

She exits without saving and reaches for her phone in her bag, to retrieve the number Ryan gave her. Deciding to work at capacity rather than below it today, she picks up the phone and calls the Mahadeo household.

—

Like Ryan, Rajit won't come to the door when Francine shows up at his house on Saturday morning three days later. Rajit, his wife tells her, is not talking to anyone, not even his favourite son.

Francine peers in from the threshold and sees someone cross the hallway, a young man, perhaps the favourite son. When the figure returns, it's back-first, as he drags a wheelchair, and a sari-ed old woman sitting in it, her legs wrapped in a blanket. There is a muscular smell of ghee and garlic. And the sad sound of daytime television.

"He is in the same clothes he was released in," his wife says.

"But he's home; he's released, right?" Francine says, watching the blanketed legs disappear across the hallway.

"Bail, madam. We have family, you know," and Francine can't tell if she means that family gave them the money or if, of course he's out on bail, his family needs him.

"And the charges?" she asks.

"My husband is not dangerous, madam. He is not good at paperwork, that is sure," Mrs. Mahadeo says, and again Francine is confused but she doesn't want to push it. She remembers what she's brought. She holds out the rubber plant. Mrs. Mahadeo stares at it then her head goes into spring-necked shaking mode, back and forth.

"Thank you, but we don't want this."

Francine draws the plant closer to her chest in gracious acceptance of the rejection.

"I'm sorry to have bothered you," she says.

"Don't be sorry, madam. You were doing what you thought was a good thing. Too much sorry sorry in this country."

Francine nods at Mrs. Mahadeo, then turns and leaves. Sayonara.

But she wants more from this visit, wants to do something for Rajit, who might merely have been looking down to check the time or change the radio station. She walks down the Harrow

Road back towards Kilburn without any idea of what doing something for him would look like.

She's hungry.

Her flat smells green. She walks to the kitchen and opens the fridge door.

Juice, cheese, salad dressing, anchovies, mustard. She pinches an anchovy from its jar and lobs it onto her tongue. She opens the Dijon mustard jar, scoops a dollop with her fingers and smears it on top of the anchovy.

She wants her mom.

"Never spit, baby, never spit—it's vile," Mom said. They had been walking down Race Street near Franklin Square in Philly, the trees yellow, red, the leaves kickable at her feet, the fountain making a dome of itself, and a great big horking gob had come out of a fat man standing on the corner of Sixth and Race. Her mother had grabbed her hand, pulled her closer as she declaimed loudly enough for the fat man to overhear her, and they'd quickly moved across the street towards the store where she would buy her daughter a new dress for going back to school. For fifth grade and all its pressures, like knowing the thing that love comes with: the other thing her mother had said to her on that day. They'd bought the dress and her mom had said it, that thing about love, for the first time, and it was less than a year later that she had repeated it, for the last time, in her hospital bed.

Now Francine needs a kind of back-to-school dress again, to wear Monday, to be seen in, because invisible is not the right choice now. She has to keep her job. "Love comes with . . . not panicking," she says to the jar of creamy French vinaigrette in her right hand.

OLIVIA

He's not Slow-Moe now. Moe is not molasses today. Too right.
Student union leader Moe has his hoodie up, a fag between his
fingers, and is walking like for once he hasn't been blazing all
night and is clear-headed in motion towards the M4 bridge
where the Bridge Men of Heston will still be sleeping. Olivia
feels the swoosh of the traffic on the M4 up above, even this
early in the morning darkness. Her knapsack is heavy, filled
with water and tins—tuna, beans, soup. Her fingers are falling-
off-cold and she shoves her hands into the coat that she's sick
of wearing, sick of patching, sick of pulling on every morning
when the end of February is supposed to be the end of winter
not the beginning. Everything is arse backwards and, shit, if
Ed loses his job like he said he might—shit. She has to think.
But her heart is racing beside the mostly racing Moe as they
hurry along Heston Road to make it to the bridge and the men
of Little Punjab below the M4 flyover before daybreak. Moe
has agreed to help her out, even though he really wants her to
help him organize #Demo, as it was her emphasis on an
ENTIRE GENERATION that was being affected, saying,
"E-E-E- entire, Moe," which he went on to adapt into the

movement's manifesto: to educate, employ, empower the young people of Britain. But Olivia has too much going on for all that. This visit is different; this is specific, contained, urgent; and she has to get right back to the library. She has to do her project, and all she thought she had to do with Ed was to help him make things pretty, the way Catherine likes them. Catherine and her lacy bras, her underpants that look like they're supposed to be on a cake. She thought that if Ed just made things a bit more frilly then Catherine would be sure to go for him again. But Catherine will not go in for a jobless bloke. Sod it. Catherine is not going to like all that death shite in any case. Catherine thinks death is for dead people. But the funeral wasn't so bad—even a few flowers in a glass vase at the front of the chapel, the priest said good stuff, and it's not like she saw a dead body or anything; it was just a box, not bad for cardboard, not something that someone could fall out of. Death isn't so scary. Catherine's got to respect that. Oh, Wood. It was his chin mostly, as he talked about gold and towns that sound like ships—his chin that she stared at because this was the bit of him that she thought she remembered: the feeling of it, the stubble along it when he pressed his face to hers or tickled her belly with it, making her squeal with his raspberries. And then she remembered his song more clearly, and the tra-la of the girl in the ring, over and over in her mind. This is fucked up.

Moe walks even faster and she spots the row of sleeping bags under the bridge. And there's an acid stench, all piss and shit and burnt wood. The traffic vibrates the ground beneath her Uggs and she stops, feeling it in her toes and all the way up her legs. There's a flutter along her shoulders with the swooshing tires overhead, and for an instant she has wings.

"We have provisions," Moe says to a groggy man at the entrance to the encampment as a few of them emerge from their sleeping bags. Olivia knows they leave the camp early and head to the carpark at the Southall Sikh temple, where sometimes they get selected for casual work. Olivia slips her heavy knapsack off her shoulders and brings it to her feet. She unzips the large compartment and takes out some of the tins, the bread, squished now, but hell, better than anything she sees around her: plastic bags of rubbish, rotting food, socks. What's with the socks? She takes out the bottles of water. They don't have long. Once the sun comes up the neighbours will be poking their heads out and adding her and Moe to their list of complaints, until that list is long enough that the Home Office and the police do something and get rid of these damn homeless, jobless illegals—even though that's not even the case for all of them. Some had visas, but they can't find work and now they can't go home or stay here either. Some were sold false papers back in India, Pakistan or Bangladesh; some stay here all day and drink and piss and shit.

A siren chirps into the underpass and now there's all kinds of stirring and moving and mumbling from beneath the blankets. A police car parks beside the camp and two officers get out and slam their doors, all TV-like, and Moe walks towards them. Moe is well-sick when it comes to talking to police, on account of his Americanness and the fact that nothing scares him. Moe would take someone like Granddad and say, *Sir, with all due respect, anti-miscegenation laws in the US were repealed on the 12th of June 1967 by Loving v. Virginia. The British created what your daughter tells me you call half-castes in every port that a cargo ship docked in across the colonized world.* And to extend the point of this long continuum of inter-everything, Moe would say, *Sir, gay marriage is becoming legal in one territory after the other. What in Abraham Lincoln's name is your problem?* Moe would point out to Granddad that his very own flesh and blood was *really, I mean, really, sir, as you can obviously see, a very simple emblem of the future.*

"You need to be moving along now, please," the officer who is barely older than Moe says to him, shooing his arms towards Moe who has gone into slow motion now, nodding and pausing with something on his mind, and taking up all the officer's patience before he says, "We're British citizens, sir, and we're helping out some people here." Moe turns to Olivia and nods, which she takes as her cue to make sure the tins and the water are handed out. She digs deeper into her sack and takes some beans, peas, and sweet-corn tins and begins to walk towards the sleeping bags.

"Miss," the other officer says. This officer is older, with one dark fucker of a unibrow. She turns towards him. "That's enough. You have to leave," and his voice is not as polite as the young dude's. She looks at Moe, but Moe is nearly smiling. She realizes that maybe Moe doesn't blaze as much as she imagined; maybe Moe appears stoned when he's in his highest power. She turns towards the men at the sleeping bags who have all been watching this as the sun comes up behind them under the lip of the bridge. She sees only heads in silhouette, at different standing, sitting, squatting heights, like a city's skyline. She looks back at the uni-brow officer and starts to move towards the sleeping bags.

"Miss!" he says, his voice closer now.

That was the truth of it right there: no one had ever picked her up but Ed, his stubble against her face as he carried her. "Pumice," she whispers and delivers the cans to the first man she reaches.

KATRIN

The snake in Claire's throat is bulging this morning. All the sunshine that Katrin collected on her shoulders from walking and not taking the 38 bus is useless now in the chill of Epicure, where Claire is filling the coffee machine and *fuck-fuck*ing at every knob or lid that resists her.

"Today is beautiful," Katrin says, to charm the snake.

"Don't get used to it—March is brutal," Claire says.

The twist in Katrin's stomach has been getting worse over the last two months. At first Claire was her friend, was her guardian against the men who came into Epicure and were not like Robin, and she was fair between Katrin and Alejandro. But now there is nothing Katrin can do right and Alejandro can do wrong.

"You didn't put the chairs up at closing. How do you expect the cleaner to do her job, for fuck's sake?" Claire says.

"I put them up," Katrin lies. The simple past tense means that the lie is not so big. She once did; she was not always doing. She walks to the back office and ties on her apron and changes her shoes to be ready for when the café opens. The exact moment that Claire started to hate her: when was it? It has something to do with Robin, so she has told Robin not to meet her in the café;

they meet at Angel tube station, or in the Green, where for one day or two this week the sun was pointed and white.

They walk; they do not sit much these days. Along the canal, through the streets around Upper Street and under trees that make her gulp at the sight of sweet white flowers over delicate green branches, and pink petals on the high bows of others. On these walks she is rewarded for *czekam*.

"I love how you smell," Robin said one day, and so she is trying every day to smell the same.

Claire wins against the machine and the coffee becomes ground. Alejandro is the one who is late today, but Claire only stands in front of him with her hands on her hips like a cowboy. He walks around her.

"Does she give breakfast at least?" Katrin says to Alejandro with eyebrows up.

"Breakfast of champions," he says, eyebrows also high. She is relieved he is here now.

"She hates me," she whispers to him and nods towards Claire now at the front table doing the accounts.

"She does," Alejandro says as he takes off his jacket and puts on the apron she holds up for him.

"Why?"

He shrugs. "I met her sister one time; she is very beautiful."

Claire laughs and they both look over to the window where she is sitting. Outside there is a man with chains looped along the bottom of his leather jacket. The man is holding a beer bottle towards his German shepherd, who is licking the opening while the man tips the beer into the dog's mouth. The dog is thirsty; it drinks and drinks. The man then lifts the bottle to his own lips and drains the remaining beer from the bottle.

"HA!" Claire says and laughs more.

Katrin runs to the door and is suddenly outside. When the man sees her, he smiles, which takes away all the words—words she might have had to express her thought that to make a dog drunk is to kill it. The man holds his beer bottle up to her like he is saying *Na zdrowie*, a cheers to the things that Katrin is not entitled to say. She goes back inside, not catching Claire's eye, but returning to the counter beside Alejandro, where she wipes the top again, going over the same spot to make it shine.

"For her sister, things probably come easy," Alejandro says.

This makes no sense. Claire goes outside to talk to the man with the German shepherd and their laughter seeps through the glass. Katrin looks at Alejandro who shrugs again, and in his shoulders he is saying, look, see, she is competing with you. Katrin carefully sets up the sugar and the stirring sticks on the small table beside the counter. In English to talk *about* something is very different from to talk *on* or *at* or *in* something. She must remember that English freedom is like the prepositions that she has difficulty to always put in the right place.

NED TIME

ROBIN

Anita Ekberg in Fellini's *La Dolce Vita*: splashing about in the Trevi Fountain, casting her spell over Marcello Mastroianni. Ekberg and Mastroianni engage in sexual foreplay to the point of eruption, the fountain showering them and then suddenly shutting off, as though spent. Deleuze cites this film as exemplary of the crystal image: the power of art through mirroring to create a moment both virtual and actual, the here and now of life. Deleuze doesn't discuss hormones, but Robin has been reading up on them and contemplating the limitations of academic discussions of art. How can poetry and science, for example, help him to understand the hormones reigning over him right now? He has snuck into his office again, third time this week, so early that no one has seen him arrive. He has read about the chemical components of the hormones possessed by a clownfish. Fact is, clownfish schools contain a hierarchy, at the top of which is the female, and when she dies the most dominant male changes sex and takes her place.

Emma arrived at his flat last night, having apologized for her unreasonable phone calls, for forcing him to think about moving to Cornwall, saying she will stay only as long as it takes for them to figure out what they will do, insisting that he is under no obligation but that they will discuss this like adults, like the friends they really are. But her mood is more fierce than before she left London—the effect of the wilds of Cornwall, the feral muliebrity of pregnancy, or merely the fact of her knowing the contents of his heart better than he does.

The knock startles him. He turns to the door. Rarely is anyone else here by 8 a.m., but when Bayo enters, her ebony face shining from perspiration as though she has run here, he is reminded that early mornings are for people whose thoughts need to be let out first thing and walked like a dog.

"Robin, this is not a bad time, is it?" she says.

"Come in."

She sits and immediately takes out papers from her large cloth bag in which she seems to carry the contents of her entire day. "I was wondering if you could look at my essay and tell me whether I'm on the right track." She hands him a sheaf of papers.

"Of course, later today, maybe. We can have a word after class." He glances at the first page: "The aim of this essay is discussing theories and films like french new wave and criticisms like textuality and spectatorship, I personally will go through the films to have the groundwork's of the theories and how the films are made in these groundwork's."

"It needs editing," she says, noting the look on his face. "I've been having a bit of trouble. Lost my disability benefit."

He looks at her with concern.

"If I go off the medication they don't give my money to me, but I have trouble to focus when I'm on it. I'm taking it again, but it takes time for the money to be put back in place, so my landlord is not happy. I have no one in this country. I've had to move twice since August. I'm not sleeping. I am sorry."

His chest goes heavy. Bayo has thoughts, actions, regrets that require medication. And this heavy feeling in his chest confirms, every time, why he teaches here, still, after three years of frustration that he has no A students—this feeling of being nothing if he's not at the centre of a real and honest struggle. Cornwall, toffs, jobs, correct grammar. And then there is this place.

"Don't worry. We'll work it out. I'll have a look, and you go and get some rest, or at least some coffee before class," he says.

When he's finished preparing for the Cinema Poetics lecture, deciding to show a clip from *The Blue Angel*, he checks his e-mail.

The job specifications have been posted on the HR website and have been e-mailed to the film lecturers. He scans the positions. There are five of them for the seven lecturers currently in the department. His shin starts to feel sore—a hiking accident in his twenties, a hairline fracture. He skims the titles: practitioner, practitioner, practitioner, technician, theorist. He reaches down and rubs his shin. They have allowed for one theorist from the three currently in his programme. The other two are more senior than he is.

Robin's father lost his first engineering job, he told all his boys when they were young, because he wasn't fierce enough to fight. But he learned from it, got a better job, and was promoted time and again, landing him at the head of the company. If Robin doesn't move to Cornwall, if Emma doesn't stay in London, if he has nothing more to do with her than send a cheque every month he is still fucked. And Katrin will not want to be with an unemployed theorist who if he had to do anything else would be writing useless poetry for her eyes only.

Their next date will be their third, so he is hesitant to ask her out. Do the Poles acknowledge the third date as pivotal? Does every Polish woman expect sex on the third date like English women do? He will tell her about the baby. She will hate him and refuse to see him again, but he will be nothing if he doesn't tell her.

Until then he will not go mad, will keep his thoughts from being actions except for those thoughts that will result in a successful application for the job he already performs.

—

The sunlight in the atrium makes spring feel like a real possibility, even though outside it is five degrees. These rare, crisp days need to be marked. He walks to the student union shop and in the queue for coffee sees the American woman from QA, who stares at him. He wants to tell her it's rude, that people don't stare like that in England, and if she wants to talk to him she should do so. Last year he received an e-mail from her informing him that he had not responded adequately to the external examiner's comments on his course evaluation. The examiner had made a wholly positive statement about his treatment of theory but noted that some of the students hadn't incorporated it as effectively as others. QA read each of these reports to monitor course improvement, and he was required to create a course improvement plan based on the fact that some students don't do as well as others. Some students don't do as well as others, he wants to say to the middle-aged Mae West. They have had one meeting together and she seemed like a pleasant enough woman—shy and yet so constituted of that shyness for it to seem almost arrogant. But that's cruel and stereotyping of her Americanness. Sorry, he would say to her if he could bear to say anything to anyone. He pays for his coffee and Kit Kat, and leaves.

—

Olivia is at his office door when he arrives back upstairs.

"Robin, me again, sorry, sorry . . . " she says, and throws the long ringlet that covers her right eye back behind her ear and tucks it in there. He opens his office door and lets them both in. As he puts his coffee and chocolate on the desk he notices after she sits down that Olivia's knee is bobbing up and down like a needle on a sewing machine and that her finger is worrying the top of her pen, back and forth, rubbing it as though for magic.

"You okay?" he says and holds up the Kit Kat, offering her some.

"Yes, yes, really," she says, declining the offer, straining to smile.

The wideness of Olivia's face obscures a clear reading of her beauty. She can be hard to look at: there is so much to take in.

"The project," Robin says, to get her started. "It might be better to approach it in terms of basic social tenets," and before he knows it, he is saying, "Does everyone have the right to be remembered somehow, and would it be meaningful, after death, to be identified with something specific? I'm not speaking in terms of legalities—that's your area—but I thought—"

"There's this man, works for Barking and Dagenham council . . . " Olivia's interruption feels like a rejection. "He looks after paupers' funerals. You know what people call them, in the papers?"

"No, I don't."

"The lonely dead," she says, her shoulders hunching. "They are mostly people without family, or if they're foreigners we don't even know who they are, they have no papers, or they are old people whose family have fucked off—they don't get funerals, not proper ones. But in my research . . . " Her knee is bobbing up and down still, her fingers wishing the pen into action. Robin sits back in his chair to try to make her feel more comfortable. "And well, you know how in Amsterdam there's a lot of drugs 'n' all?"

He nods.

"They get a lot of lonely deaths—like drug mules, like from Colombia—girls who carry drugs in their stomachs or up inside them and the drugs leak or someone kills them and they don't have real names on their passports, and nobody can find out who they are . . . or . . . " She looks at him with her wide face like an urgent, flashing sign. "And then the city has to bury them. There's this man there, a civil servant, and he looks after them. He has made it his thing to visit their homes if they had one, and he chooses music to play at their funeral. He puts flowers on the coffin and makes sure each one gets buried. With dignity."

He sits forward, "I was going to say something about music . . . in fact, about music at the funeral—" he stops himself, because he shouldn't be encouraging this tangential thinking when Olivia should be working on her dissertation, "but that's not something you can legislate; the idea of rights seems to me—"

"That kind of politics doesn't work," she says, as though that is all she needs to say to him and he will understand. And he does, but there's so much understanding developing between them that he has to draw that line, the one he must draw as a tutor—the line that says I can't go there, no matter how much I see you and agree with you: this is just my job. So he simply nods.

"This Dutch man," she says, "decided that they needed praise, like, real eulogies, even if there was no one in their lives."

Yes, this is the kind of thing he was trying to say at the beginning. "That sounds like a beautiful idea."

"And that's what I was thinking . . ." Both knees start to bob now, and she is a jackhammer to his office floor.

"Okay," he says calmly. "And coming back to the law project?"

"He got a poet to write poems for them, as their eulogies—a poem for each of the lonely dead. Somebody knows them, even if it's just in their imaginations." She sits back in the chair and her bobbing subsides.

"That is a lovely notion, Olivia. But without meaning to undercut it, have you thought about how it will inform your dissertation?"

She sits forward again. "In England's community graves, it's the same. So many people. The man at the council, he's an old man, well, not old, really, but not like you, older—and I think we need to do something." She hesitates.

"What do you mean?"

"The council is to cut its budget, and he might just be one of the people to go. But . . . " Her face becomes even wider as she looks him directly in the eyes. "If we started this new project, brought attention to it like they did in Amsterdam. If there was a poem for each of the people who dies alone, who the council has to bury, who this man has to look after, and if the council has to find the money to pay him because it's the right thing to do . . . and . . . if you could write the poems . . . "

"What?"

She sits back.

He takes her in. His grandparents died quietly, unceremoniously, his father's mother going to an early grave when his father was twelve. They were not a family for big events. He doesn't know the words to hymns; his father was adamant when he was growing up that church was nowhere for boys who needed their minds stimulated not shrunken.

"I am not a poet," he says, and she straightens up.

"You wrote that poem last year," she says, and it's true. He did use a poem of his own last term, in a moment of shameful vanity.

"That was different, that was just to make a point," he says.

"Exactly," she says. And he does not know how to respond. "You're the right person," she says firmly. "You care."

He thinks about the impact and knowledge transfer indicators he has been told he has to address in his research, and how projects should extend into the community at large, should demonstrate that there is no longer such a thing as an ivory tower. For a cynical, self-serving moment he considers a practice-based research project that combines cinema poetics and visual eulogies. He stops himself.

"I don't write poetry, really, Olivia," he says, and watches her shoulders drop. He would embarrass himself in the eyes of the avant-garde poets he loves—the Language Poets; the New Sentence poets. "Really, really, Olivia. What you're saying is great, interesting, but not for me. I can't do that." She begins to gather her things.

He searches his bookshelf and reaches up to pull out the slim volume. "You might like this," he says, as he hands it to her.

Olivia takes it and nods. "You used Ginsberg last year," she says, and nods. He winces and she smiles, thanks him, then leaps up from the chair and leaves his office.

Deleuze: What is an unconscious that no longer does anything but believe, rather than produce?

ED

Zihan restaurant—not as in Lawd bring me to the land of Zion—
is Somali and not the one he's looking for. There's a restaurant
called Pepperpot on Longbridge Road because he is sure he
passed it a year back, when he thought, man, he should be going
in. But those days he wasn't too fired up about things Guyanese.
He wasn't looking back at anything that would smell like home,
because if home hurts you have to mash it out. But don't mind
how bird vex, it can't vex with tree. So now he has to find it
because Sammy is counting on getting some pepperpot, cassava
bread, mauby or guava drink to wash it down with, after all the
bragging Ed did in the office.

   "You walk fast, mate," Sammy says, catching up with Ed on
the pavement outside the Pepperpot, which is more brukadown
than Ed remembers it. "You must be hungry to walk like that,"
and Sammy takes a fat bloke's inhalation on Longbridge Road.
Ed breathes in with him. The air is a blend of petrol and . . .
what? What is that smell? Bleakness, if that can be a smell.
Petrol and bleakness. "And why is it that you West Indians feel
like if you don't have grog—and that is your word and not
mine—with your food it ain't a meal?"

Sammy has agreed to come along to Pepperpot on the condition that he is not expected to drink rum, which he detests. Ed has brought beer—Cobra, a big bottle that he holds up like a trophy—because Sammy is a one-drink man.

"You people can drink, innit," Sammy says.

"Let's go," Ed says, and he pushes open the door to the restaurant. With a ting and a pang and a parrang braddups and a whole band playing in his head, he is back home inside this bad-lighting plastic-flowers room. Guyana maps and flags, bird of paradise, and pan playing in the tinny speakers hung up in the corners above the counter, below which take-way patties, peas and rice, and rotis are growing crusty behind the display glass. Music happens somewhere in the heart and not in the ears, true-true.

After they have ordered their food and opened the Cobra, split between them, it's time for him to ask Sammy: "Do you think a daughter should know that her uncle is in jail?" Coming right out with it is the easiest, after batting it around in his head for weeks now since Olivia found him. Straight ahead, at least with Sammy. Sammy looks at him as if to say, man, why on earth you bring this surprise 'pon me when my team is failing, like it's the worst thing he might have done the day after the Hammers have lost to Spurs.

"What you on about then?" Sammy says.

So Ed starts slowly, because this is the way the details must come while Sammy does the inevitable re-examining of the exhibits A, B, C of his face to find where there is a likeness to criminals. "I told you about Geoffrey, but I never told you he was—is—in jail."

The food arrives at the table and Sammy looks into his pepperpot like it's the dark stew of Africans who boil up white people, and maybe Indians too. He picks up his fork with purpose though, because Sammy is a good bloke.

"What happened?" Sammy asks and it takes a second before Ed realizes he's asking about Geoffrey.

"He killed a man. On a gold mine. He tried to steal, got caught, killed him: simple. So simple it's nearly ridiculous, like in a Wild West movie," Ed says.

Sammy nods and tastes his pepperpot, nods again, pleasantly surprised.

There's a long silence as Ed watches Sammy slurp up the slimy oxtail and wipe his lips with the back of his hand. Sammy is the best bloke there is, but in the silence Ed sees the man in the river, Geoffrey in the distance, running, running, and the inky blood following the path of the river like it needed a new home. He is not able to describe this to Sammy, or to explain what happened next.

"It's why Olivia's mother didn't want anything to do with me."

Sammy looks up at him like this is nonsense.

"I went back to Guyana when Geoffrey asked me to help him . . . begged me like he was dying, and when I saw him he looked so bad, but he was still boasting like a big man, and he asked me for money. How was I to get that money? He said I should borrow it from people I knew in London, from Catherine." Ed shakes his head and looks to Sammy for confirmation that he was right not to ask Catherine, but Sammy is looking at his food, moving it around on the plate. "Catherine had no money," Ed says. Nobody he knew had any. "Geoffrey and I had a big row, man, and I told him he was mad as shite. And then he stole the money he needed and he was caught in the act. He killed the man who was chasing after him, just so.

I have never understood that. Never." He should have found the money for his brother. His brother was in trouble; that's what family is for. "When I told Catherine, she said she didn't want me around, thought I had something to do with it."

"And did you?" Sammy asks him, his face as open as a net. And of course that's the question. The only reason you don't let a man see his daughter is because you think he did something wrong and because you believe all the seh-seh from other people like your knack-about father and brother.

"I followed Geoffrey that day, it's true, but I had no part in it, no part." Even to Sammy he can't tell the whole truth, because what Ed did that day—or rather didn't do—was witnessed only in his own heart, and that was the place where Catherine lived, so she might have felt it too.

"I had to pay for lawyers, help move my mum, pay her bills because it was Geoffrey who had been doing that all along —and I had no way of getting back to London. Catherine said, you stay there then."

Sammy is shaking his head now, and Ed can't tell if it's at the food or at what he's saying.

"She was wrong, too hard . . . " Sammy says. And Sammy starts with his fork and is eating at a pace, man, and Ed wants to tell him to slow down, but he watches, waiting for what is to come next, as it seems Sammy has something more to say; he just needs to fill his belly first. And then the rice and pepperpot are all gone, a swig of Cobra to wash it down, and Sammy wipes his mouth.

"When I was a teenager, my cousin burned down the community centre because they took away the sports club on Saturday afternoons. Right nutter, he was, and brought shame to

the family, but you know, he was pissed, and I didn't blame him."
Sammy releases a whoosh of air in a silent burp, covers his mouth
too late.

"But Catherine has never told Olivia about my side of the
family," Ed says.

"The past is the past, Wood."

"You think she shouldn't know?"

"Of course she should know, of course . . . but she doesn't
need to know now, not yet. You're just getting reacquainted. You
take your time on that."

Sammy has a point, but the hell in Ed's belly rumbles. And
Ed knows that while a young man wants freedom, an old man
wants only peace.

OLIVIA

Maybe it's not going to work out fine after all. She stares out of the window of the number 364 bus. Parsloes Avenue is chocka with people who must do decent jobs, what? Offices, restaurants, shops. Everyone needs an electrician, for example, like Catherine's Once-a-Week William. Everyone needs a plumber; everyone needs a barber or a salon for the weave. All of it there, necessary. And stale as shite. It's not real poetry she's looking for; it's something that will make a man seem special, the way Robin was special when he gave those lectures, the way even a small dude like him can make a whole room of barely awake wankers go oh wooo he's talking good shite here that's meaning something, like the time he did that Holy, Holy, Holy riff last year. Poetry for Ed to make a point with, even if it's just for nobody but the dead. If Ed can do that, that hushed voice thing that Robin does at the beginning of the class when no one knows he's starting the lecture, when people just think he's talking about himself, well.

What if Nasar has some of that? What if Nasar appears in front of her and has that riffing thing that makes her feel like all the world is joined up by the wind on her skin?

The 364 stops just near Jasmine's on Osborne Road. Jasmine will be a good diversion. Her house on the square is bang opposite the Dagenham Evangelical Congregational Church, which is dench for Jasmine's mum and a horror for Jaz herself.

At the door, though, she's never seen her gal so cranked. Jasmine lets her in and turns around, expecting Olivia to follow. Jaz's arms are long, her head big for the rest of her, and she walks back and forth in her living room holding that head between her flattened palms, her elbows stuck up and out like bat ears. Olivia sits on the sofa and wraps up in Jasmine's mother's pink-and-brown knitted blanket that gives her that baby-love feeling.

"He had a crash," Jaz says and it takes one, two, three long WTF moments to figure out that Jaz is talking about Dario from Bologna. Jasmine starts to explain, but Olivia can't follow, because, hell, this is something. This is one thing too much in a month that is way over much. And Jasmine is talking too fast.

"Jaz, you gotta chill."

Jasmine's pacing picks up speed. "Chill? Do you get this? He's dead, Liv, he's dead."

Olivia nods.

"He coulda been the one," Jasmine adds. And this is where Olivia has to get her head out of Jaz's wonderland, because this is the line Jaz has for every dude who rides her once and never shows up again. "It was real, this one, and now he's gone," Jasmine says with her elbows still up in the air beside her head. Olivia takes out her phone and while Jasmine paces the room she searches, finds it, and types a short but simple reply that is at least ten days late, but maybe not too late.

It's "heart sing," not "singing." Thanks.

And with that she feels lighter, what with making sure that Nasar is still alive and all. By the time she leaves Jasmine to herself to pace and be administered to by her mother with the Bible, Olivia is wondering how many more things can get in the way.

—

Eric has the TV turned up to garage-house decibels because if he fills the entire sitting room with the sound of Man United in their home stadium on a Wednesday night, then he can pretend that he's alive, and that his life is not worthless. Uncle Eric is a waster who has been living off his sister and their parents' pension for the last five years. Eric is a no-show in the game of life, let alone football. Olivia closes the door to the sitting room and heads to the kitchen with her heavy satchel. Two essays due and one exam in three weeks and nowhere to study now that staying late at uni feels like she's being caught on hidden camera footage that Nasar gets to see. She should never have texted him back. First rule of harassment cases: don't engage. Something tells her that Nasar is legit and different, but she shouldn't have. She has to be careful not to turn soft.

"Honey, it's late, have you eaten?" Catherine says, looking up from her magazine.

"Not bothered," Olivia says, but tries to control sounding cheesed off. It hasn't worked on Catherine. Her mum closes the magazine, puts her elbows on the table and her chin between her hands.

"What?" Catherine says.

When Catherine has nothing to do, no worries about bringing food home for everyone and keeping Eric full up in beer and cigarettes, nothing to dream about in her magazines, and no Once-a-Week William to be giggling for, she is a mother. Olivia has tried to resist it before, but it's tough when Catherine puts on that soft voice.

"Nothing. Got shitloads of pressure, is all," Olivia says, not looking at the big green eyes of her mother that make her look like an old version of Adele and that also make Olivia want to be picked up, even though she's taller than Catherine now. She sits down at the table. "If you ran into Wood, would you just ignore him?" She looks up at Catherine, whose eyes go squinty.

"What are you getting at?" Catherine asks.

"Nothing, just, would you?"

Olivia can tell that her mother wants to open the magazine now, her fingers itching to turn those pages so that she won't have to talk. But this time she's not going to run, maybe this time.

Olivia hears shuffling—the sound that makes the hair on her neck stand up, and if Granddad would just buy proper slippers instead of wearing the paper ones Nan got in hospital when she was ill, the shuffling would not grate on her nerves so much, but he is a stubborn old git and here he comes just as Catherine is struggling with her instinct to run, just as there might be a moment when something becomes clear.

"Olivia love, our bin was stolen again. You call the council—I'm sure it's over the road behind. They paint them over, sell them, must be." Right. Granddad hasn't combed his hair, and what's left of it is sticking up like a troll's.

"Who would they sell the bins to?" Olivia says. Catherine is back at her magazine and Granddad has won. Again. She can feel her pulse. There's thunder at her neck.

"Tendril," she says. It comes out a lot louder here at home. Because at home everyone is their own Jack-in-the-box, springing up, nattering, when the pressure is too much. Granddad's the worst, the things he has to say getting front and centre most of the time, whether they're trivial, ignorant, bigoted, or plain obnoxious. She knows that her very presence makes him the Grand Jack-in-the-box, and that her being his so-called half-caste winds him up and spins him out. Granddad also loves her, and it is this confusion in his very own cells that makes him so unpredictable, makes him blame everything and everyone else in the world instead. It's not that Granddad is such a bad man; it's just that he is the most scared of them all. He's the kind of geezer who fools you, who is clever and doesn't raise his voice except at the telly, talks like he has schooling, talks like he reads books, but deep down Granddad's ignorance is as deep as his unknowing of his own soul. Nan meanwhile has stopped hearing. Nan has taken to being sick all the time, needing to stay in bed, needing, even, to be in hospital for big bouts of delirious time when she's coughing so bad and yelling a lot and she can't hear how loud she has become. She can't hear how much she just wants Granddad to shut the fuck up and leave everybody alone and give her some peace so that she can pay attention to something other than him. Ed is not in any way like Granddad, and maybe Catherine just wasn't used to having air time of her own, so she couldn't handle it. Maybe Catherine's magazines are like Nan's deafness.

"What's everyone on about here, then?" Eric says as he enters, his belt and top button undone like he's just come out of the loo but forgot, like the stupid baby git he is. Granddad launches in about the bins, and he and Eric go on about who's stealing what, until the topics switches to Man United, because

Uncle Eric is nearly as bad as Granddad when it comes to needing to say what's on his mind.

This is where she's from; it is not who she is. She does not
have to stay here. Nan is small, doesn't take up too much room
when she's well, and Ed and Catherine will give each other space
so that no one has to fold up inside and disappear.

Who will bury these people? God bloody help her.

Her phone pings. Catherine looks up at her like she should
be told who that is. Olivia gets up from the table with her satchel
and heads upstairs.

*Thnk you for writing me. My heart sing to read you. Maybe you
meet me?*

Now she's gone and done it. But a little part of her is relieved,
and maybe even more chuffed than before, to hear from him.

KATRIN

A promenade: the English have stolen this word, but it is right. "At my university," Katrin says to Robin as they take this slow walk along the canal leaving Camden Market, "each day we met at the main fountain in the square, some classmates and I, and we would stand or sit, winter or summer, and discuss our reading. We had big, waving-arm debates, loud arguments about Malthus and market politics." She does not dare to try to translate the concepts because she will be stupid in these. And Robin knows them better than she does, but she is happy that when she talks he nods like she is not boring.

"My students meet to get high and to talk about how they can pass without doing any work," Robin says. He shakes his head. "That's not true, no, I am being harsh. Some of them are among the most inspiring people I have ever met," he says and looks at her, smiles. "But it's not like you describe. They don't have the luxury of so much debate." He takes her hand. His is warm in this not warm air and she looks at the faces of others on the canal path to see if they notice how her breathing is shallow.

It is the second time he has touched her. The first time was her chin. And that touch said *I'm so surprised by you.* And for real he said, "I had given up." They had been sitting on a bench on the canal like the one they are passing now where another couple are sitting, not talking, not touching. When she asked him what he was meaning about giving up he said there were things he'd like to tell her, but she became worried about time because she was on a break and Claire was more and more angry, and she said, no, don't tell me, not today. She has not yet found out what he had given up.

Now, more than a week after waiting for him to come into Epicure – his absence like rejection – she is content on this walk. He has asked to meet during the daytime, not evening, and this is not how she understands English men. By now they are expecting much more that Robin has asked for.

In Camden they ate lamb and spinach stew from the African stall, also sweet chocolate banana crepes, and she is a snail on this promenade, while Robin is alert with talk about his university and his wish to be more useful. "Film studies," he says, "is not what students want. They want to make movies, not interrogate how they work or what they mean; I don't make films, I'm from the old school, in which you need to know things deeply, first, before doing anything that is decent." In this sentence there is a darkness like stepping inside a cupboard. Katrin does not hold tighter to his hand, but she is more aware of its strength.

He keeps talking. Where does he want to take her with this talk?

"There's this woman," he says, and her hand loosens. Her mother will arrive in two months. She has things she must prepare. She has to get back. He holds her hand tighter and looks at her now. "I was with her, yes," he says.

"Oh, good, that's good," she says, releasing her hand, looking down at the holes on the front of her Converse trainers.

"But this is what I need to tell you."

Katrin holds the hem of his jacket and tugs him towards a bench. She has had enough walking now.

"You loved her," she says before he is even sat beside her. His face looks surprised.

"I didn't," he says, sits, pauses, then, "but I wanted to believe I could."

He is perfect in his words, always precise, and this makes her weak in front of him.

"And now?" she asks and watches as his eyes in his glasses go towards the canal, to find the right words there, in water.

"And now," he says like in a show where they are going to announce a winner and they repeat the question and make you wait, "now she is expecting a child."

She is surprised how alert she feels; her shoulders straighten; she pictures her grandmother's house by the river in Gdansk. His forehead creases with worry that she will run, so she doesn't; she doesn't want to hurt him. She wants to whisper something to him, but doesn't know what she would say.

"I want to explain it to you," he says.

She nods.

"We were friends first, and then we got together for about a year. We were never right for one another, but we stayed on, as friends, mostly. She's a year older than me, thirty-nine, and she asked me to get her pregnant. I said no, but then, when she was moving away, we had sex. I'm an idiot. I felt like nothing would ever happen for me again, so I didn't care. I'm an idiot."

The white blossoms of the tree behind Robin's head remind her how far time has come since the first days of him coming into Epicure, when shoots of daffodils had a promise. How long has he known about this baby? She is all of a sudden tired. She has worked two times her normal hours this week; she has bought a duvet for her mother. She wants to lie down with Robin, whisper to him, and fall asleep.

"Well," she says. There is nothing to say. He will be a father and fathers will live with their children, no matter what. Fathers will not leave the mothers of their children to sleep on one side of the bed forever more.

"I don't want to be with her. I want to be with you," Robin says.

She looks at his face and knows he is saying the truth. "We are very different in age." It's all she can think of—that and the fact that her *matka* will bring trinkets and books in her suitcase—unnecessary things for which there will be no space in the bedsit. She must remember to send Beata a list of things she should bring and things that should stay in Gdansk.

"No, it's nothing, the difference between us. We are exactly the same," Robin says, but stops and merely looks at her. "You're far away," he says, and this is true.

"I should go," she says. "We will talk tomorrow." She stands and puts her hand on his face. His eyes fall shut, then open wide again. "I will see you tomorrow," she assures him.

—

But the next day she is not sure of anything. And even though Alejandro has been kind as always, his joke today is about a Mexican, and it has made her uncomfortable because she is learning how racist she was in Poland. She needs London even more for all the things she has learned, for all the fingers it has pointed to her stupid ways of thinking. What will her mother do when she sees this place?

Claire is busy in the back room with accounts and supply orders, but all morning she has had her eyes on her as though someone has told her how Katrin as a child used to make monkey sounds with her friends when they saw black people on television. Katrin has a headache and her throat has become sore. Claire knows all the things she has thought and all the things she has said.

"So, it's simple: he tells her she cannot have it," Alejandro says of Robin's story with the baby, because that's what Alejandro does: finds solutions to the problems of all the people in the world. Alejandro should be a counsellor, or a judge. He has so many answers for everything. He wipes the top of the counter and straightens the napkins, moves straws to the edge of the glass top, and turns the basket of almond biscuits towards the front. Alejandro is the tidiest man Katrin has ever met. Robin, too, she has noticed, is tidy. His clothes are neat and ironed and in place; his taste is for clean lines and white spaces. The furniture shop she passes every day on Upper Street has things for Robin's kind of home. She loves this so much about him that she has to stop thinking about it. She slides the basket of almond biscuits back from the edge where Alejandro placed it.

"What?" he says.

"I don't know," she says. A customer who has finished an espresso and croissant holds her finger up for Katrin's attention. Katrin moves towards her just as Claire comes out of the back room and catches her eye. "Can we have a word?" Claire says. Katrin hunches and becomes small like a bad dog. Claire turns and walks back into the office, expecting her to follow, but Katrin must bring the customer's bill and ask Alejandro to cover while she's in the back room. When she goes into the room, Claire is already red-faced.

"I had a customer," Katrin says, and this stops Claire from saying what she had wanted to, even though she has stood up to talk.

"I thought you had more hours on your timetable than what appears to be there," Claire says.

"What do you mean?"

"If you look at the number of hours you worked in the last three weeks, it doesn't add up to what we really needed coverage for, does it?" Claire says, trying but failing in her intonation to sound kind. "We're really busy, more busy as the weather gets better, so we actually need more not less from people. You need to be able to work when we need you."

"What do you mean? I worked double hours last week."

"You covered for Alejandro's hours, but we need coverage on Sundays," Claire says, "and then at the end of the day, the early evening shift," and Claire's face is very close to Katrin's. Not angry or threatening, just close. "The business is doing well; we are opening a branch in Soho."

"I asked you for the maximum hours. You told me that was all you could give me," Katrin says. She does not know about laws in this country, how much is too much, but when Andrzej scans bar codes for too many hours the laser machine makes a stinging take place around his eyes.

"The owner might be interested in hiring another person to help."

"What does that mean?" Andrzej sends all his money back to Gdansk; he is not lucky like Katrin who can live in her own bedsit. When he visits her on Sundays his face is cold and pale.

"What do you mean what does that mean?"

"Why are you telling me that?" Heat walks up Katrin's neck.

"I just noticed, that's all. You're working fewer hours and you told me you needed hours. Times are hard but this place is doing well . . . go figure."

"I need hours." Next Sunday she has invited Andrzej to eat lunch with her, but she could work at Epicure instead.

"Then you should be working them," Claire says, one step back on her right foot.

"Is that what you wanted to say?"

Claire plays with the gold chain on her wrist, twists it, and looks back at Katrin, which brings the curling in her stomach, and the failed-exam feeling across her chest. She turns quickly and walks out of the room.

Claire will hold this too against her.

Behind the counter Alejandro is busy, with many customers before him in a queue and maybe Claire is right, she is not working enough, she is letting him down and making customers angry, but they do not look angry. He nods his head to the left, telling her to serve the customer in the front.

She makes all the coffees and rings in all the pastries and bread and salad for the next two hours and barely says a word to anyone except for very kind and helpful phrases to each of the customers. Espresso, macchiato, latte, chocolate marquis, Chantilly cream, tiramisu: English is not in so many things at Epicure. She smiles at Alejandro and he shows her with his own smile that all is fine between them.

At 8 p.m., Claire has been gone for three hours—her early day when she drives her teenager to football practice—and for three hours it is safe to believe again that Epicure is a place to feel proud. If Katrin can hold on for one year, her mother will get used to London, her savings will grow, and she can look for a job that is not with coffee.

"I have never had this kind of relation with anyone in my life," she says to Alejandro as he sweeps beneath the chairs that she lifts onto the tables. "What is wrong with me?" She wants him to tell her the truth.

"There is nothing wrong with you," he says. "She needs a good shag, that's all." Katrin doesn't like it when people say this kind of thing, but a small part of her is grateful for it.

"Maybe you could help out," she says, smiling. He gives a face like he has swallowed vinegar. "My mother will not come if I do not have a job," she adds.

When they have closed the café she feels heavy, and her tongue feels coated in butter. Her feet drag along Upper Street. Her shoulder has a pain where it meets her neck. It is not good to think too much. She takes her phone from her bag and taps a message.

Two, three, five, ten minutes and nothing from him, and the failed-exam feeling in her chest is there again. Stupid. Of course he is with the mother of his baby. You stupid. She rereads what she has said to him.

I am sorry to take so long to reply to you. I can cook you dinner so maybe we have more time to speak, and I will listen better. I will work on that for Ned time. x

Ned time? The phone she uses is not smart like it is called. It pretends to know what she wants to say, but it is as stupid as she is. She thumbs it to obey.

I mean next time.x

Before she gets to her bus stop a simple ping makes everything good again.

I like the idea of Ned time very much. Maybe that's a place where everything is as we want it to be. What about Saturday for dinner? xxx

She thumbs the screen impatiently.

Saturday is good. xxx

OLIVIA

"Darling, you used to be a child who never cried. And I used to worry that there was something wrong with you, that I had done something bad . . . " Wood says and Olivia feels all tremor-like sat here at the melamine table at the A13, on account of the fact that this man knows she's a baby who never cried and the fact that when he says *bad* Wood is like a sheep crying in the dark. This man – who is kind-hearted but a little feeble, if she is allowed to think these things about her father – held her when she fell and didn't cry, and wondered if he had done something wrong.

The A13 is familiar now, but it's like a caff out of time, all bacon grease and sticky-topped.

"Do you cry?" Right. This is a lot to ask a geezer you barely know any more. "I mean, at the funerals, ever?" What she really wants to say is please let my oddness come from somewhere legit, directly from a particular chromosome on a particular bit of sperm that created me; otherwise, I'm just a weirdo living among white people who don't get me one little bit.

Wood looks over his shoulder, Olivia turns round to follow, and there is Mary the waitress who sits and does sudoku while her punters eat their toast and drink their builders' tea. "Condensed,"

Olivia says softly. Ed doesn't hear her or doesn't let on he does, and maybe he does this kind of slippery thing too, and maybe for Ed this is normal. After a few seconds of staring at Mary, Ed looks back at Olivia.

"I used to cry a lot," he says and then smiles, "used to . . . when I couldn't get to see you. Funerals are not the same. They remind me I'm a lucky man."

Right. Right. Alice Sampson. Ed has been telling Olivia about Alice Sampson, eighty-three years old, who has just gone into a care home. Ed has been put in charge of her property, to make sure it is cleared out, to secure it and dispose of things that need disposing of. Alice. Ed says it's important to hold their names, to keep naming them, like you know them. Olivia pictures all the stuff at home—Granddad's fantasy junk that makes him believe he is better than everyone else. Right.

"What do you believe then, Wood?"

Ed's shoulder twitches like she has tickled him.

"What do you mean?"

"I mean . . . " when she was ten she found a secret shoebox in Catherine's cupboard with small scraps of paper with a few words on each, in Catherine's handwriting, as though she'd jotted down wishes and allowed them to pile up in the box instead of making them come true, " . . . what it's all about," and she waves out at the wide world.

If she tells him her idea now, makes it seem all about her project, impresses him, Barking and Dagenham Council will think he's a saint, he'll secure his job, get a promotion, Catherine will see what a man he really is.

"You all right, Olivia?" Ed asks her and touches her hand. A quick, father's touch. "You're shaking," he says.

"No, no, I'm fine, I'm thinking is all." She breathes in deeply. "Maybe we could work together. You could help me," she says, appealing to his instincts, "we could help each other," she adds, looking around and, yep, right, all melty here in the what-you-want-will-never-come café.

"Okay," Ed says, simply. "Okay," again.

Holy the solitudes of hospitals and malls! Holy the casinos filled with the millions! Holy the mysterious whispers of doubt beneath the sheets! She needs to chill. She can't tell him her plan just yet.

KATRIN

He kisses her like it's the last thing he will do in his life. Maybe she has not known kissing before. This is how they kiss in English. This is why everyone is here. He tastes of fried onions and sauerkraut from perogies she cooked for him, but there is also vodka, and one small thought comes that maybe he has drunk too much. But this kissing like the end of the world is too good to stop. His body moves if she moves. One leg for one leg, one hand for one hand, on top of her and then still if she is still. She cannot find where she ends and he begins.

And so she cries.

He pauses, caresses her cheek. "Are you all right?"

She has no words.

He slides to her side and holds her tight. She turns and he gathers her into a spoon and this feels like something that God has done.

"I'm sorry," he says, but she does not want to ask what he is sorry for in case it is something that will end this. So she makes believe and pushes everything out of the room that God did not mean to happen.

"You sing," she says, not asking but telling because he has before named Bach and Beethoven, then Bartok and Berlioz, and all the music he could think of when she played the game at dinner. Name all the music you love, she said, and only after Bartok did they notice the Bs. She slides from his arm—"Wait for me"—gets up and on her toes, crosses the cold floor, and is happy for once that the room is small. She brings the guitar.

"I sing one; you sing one." And she sits; her fingers clutch for C, then D, G—as she has learned from the book. Pick and strum. It is this song that Beata taught her on the dulcimer, but in London a guitar was £40 in Brick Lane. And she can give this kind of music to him because her mother was a girl in Warsaw and learned Czerwone Gitary's "Biały krzyż" to sing to her baby. "The translation is 'White Cross,'" she says and closes her eyes to sing to him. When she is finished she opens them and his face is like grace.

She passes him the guitar and smells their bodies in her sheets. "Do you sing?"

His fingers curl over the guitar neck and make her wet again.

He picks the strings like he knows how. And she knows this song because her mother was a girl in Warsaw when Czerwone Gitary was merely a copy of this band, and so when he sings "Blackbird singing in the dead of night, take these broken wings . . . " she does not understand how he can know her like this, or how this other B music will not make her die, right here in her own bed.

There are two more songs, more elaborate, more foreign, before he stops and looks at his wrist, but the watch was taken off in Ned time, so he picks it up from the floor and makes a face that has pain.

"I should go," he says, and the pain is now in her chest.

"Why?"

He draws her to him, pulling her down and spooning again as God decreed.

"I promised. I promised I would be there for her," he says. She does not ask then why are you here for me; she slides out from the spoon and sits up, pretends that everything is okay.

"Of course, of course," and she tells herself that she is doing this for a baby, and so it is fine. "Go quickly."

ROBIN

Her bedsit has been made beautiful. Robin touches the silk cushions on Katrin's only comfortable chair. She has dessert for their return from the Spanish restaurant, their regular now, several nights in a row.

The first night he was here she cooked a Polish dinner for him, and he touched her lips with his finger before he kissed her, and when he kissed her it was a disappearing.

Katrin has not mentioned Emma or the baby, doesn't talk or ask about them, and when he told her the bare facts before their first night together, she didn't flinch, didn't recoil, but said, simply and with force, "It's good to be a father." This is an extraordinary response. He wants to assure her that he doesn't take it lightly, that her equanimity inspires the sort of awe in him that he has previously only experienced in the presence of nature. He worries, however, that it might mean that she is not investing and that the small parts of himself that he leaves behind every time he visits her will be unsafe.

How will he manage all of this? Emma is bigger. Her face is more beautiful than it has ever looked, her cheeks flushed, but her moods more fierce. She stayed at his flat for almost a week before she reacted to his frequent evenings out, and now she has moved to a girlfriend's house, saying there is more room there, but in fact there is less room. He has told her about Katrin, but has underplayed it, sparing everyone's feelings, grappling with Deleuze's principle of courage, which consists in agreeing to flee rather than live tranquilly and hypocritically in false refuges. He hugs Katrin's green silk pillow to his chest. His guilt is adamantine.

"You are very serious, Mr. Robin," Katrin says as she approaches him on the chair. She kneels down and sits back on her heels, watching him. "You could play some guitar for me."

He shakes his head, "I'm better on the piano."

"But that I do not have!" She taps his knee. "You are a real musician," she says. He shakes his head, knowing he would perform only for her. He loosens his grip on the green cushion.

"If you could be any animal in the world, what would you be?" She smiles, encouraging him. This is a game, and his heart lifts like a child's.

"Goshawk," he says, and sees her eyebrows go up.

"What is this?"

He drops the pillow, sits forward and draws her in closer, moved by her attempt to reach him. "A bird, like an eagle, but not quite . . . "

She resists him and stays firmly planted on her heels.

"And why, why this animal? I want three words to describe it." She is still in the game. He thinks about this question, but he can't concentrate; she is so beautiful and he can't take his eyes off the small imperfection at the left side of her lip.

"It's a predator, it's free, it's beautiful." When his baby is born will Katrin agree to be part of his life; will she play games like this with his child?

She nods, taking mental notes, taking this all very seriously. "If you couldn't be a . . . what is it?"

"Goshawk . . . a northern goshawk, to be precise."

She resists a smile. "If you couldn't be this, what would you be?"

He doesn't want to play, wants only to kiss her. She looks at him as though she already knows his every thought.

"Clownfish."

"And this is a fish that lives where?"

"Warm waters: reefs, the Red Sea," he says. He does not have to go home; he can stay with her tonight.

She nods, serious again, learning something more about him. "And three reasons why you would be this fish?"

He is not going to be drawn into talking about their hermaphroditism, but she is the sea anemone to his clownfish. "Colourful, loyal, free," he says.

She nods again, taking more mental notes. "And if you could not be this bird or this fish, what would you be?"

This is hard now; he can't concentrate. He doesn't see what she's getting at. She already knows him.

"Green mamba," he says.

"What is that?"

"Snake."

"Oh dear," she says, and looks alarmed. He laughs.

"Snakes are beautiful," he says.

"I hate them," she says, and what an idiot he is to want to be a snake. But it's true. Snakes are a form of magic incarnate.

"But no, really, they are amazing, so smart. They are perfect form and content," but she doesn't look convinced. "And when are we going to have that dessert? I'm still hungry," he says, trying to divert her disappointment in him. She holds firm, puts her hands on his knees, and rubs them.

"Three words to describe snakes, then," she says.

There is nothing to consider: "Beautiful, clever, free."

She nods and adds this information to the list she is clearly making in her mind. "You are very strange," she says. And if it weren't for the look on her face he would be worried, but it's clear that she likes whatever she means by strange. "You want others to see you as a predator, free, and beautiful; you see yourself as colourful, loyal and free; but you really are beautiful, clever, and free."

His eyes fill. He grabs her shoulders and pulls her up to him. He touches the left side of her lip and then kisses her with all the life in him.

She starts to laugh, pulls away.

"What?"

She can't control her laughter and he climbs inside it, wants never to leave it. She takes a big breath in order to speak. "You want to be seen as a predator . . . " but she loses it again, and he goes with it, until they settle down with her in his arms.

"Dessert," she says, and starts to get up. He pulls her back, but finally lets her go.

"I didn't make it," Katrin says as she puts down on her small dining table a plate and two forks. "It's from Epicure—simple, but pretty, no?"

"Why is the world suddenly possessed by cupcakes and over-decorated biscuits?" he says.

"You don't like them?" she says, timidly.

"Oh, no . . . I do," he says. Idiot. He takes her by the shoulders and turns her to him. "I do." There's nothing he wants more than never to disagree with her. He kisses her and they stand in an embrace almost like dancing. Her hair smells of flowers. And it comes to him. She reminds him of Mona, that's it—Mona was a girl he knew at school in Falmouth whom he slow-danced with but never got to kiss. A girl who told him he was an anorak and that the silly things that went on in his brain should be kept in his brain. And yet he wanted to kiss her more than any girl he'd ever known. Unlike Mona, Katrin does not seem to mind hearing the things that go on in his brain. Yesterday he spoke to her for nearly an hour about afterimage—the optical illusion that takes place in the eye—and how it is easily replicated in cinema. "In a medical condition called palinopsia," he said, "you develop the capacity to perceive afterimage." Katrin looked at him and for a moment he thought that she was finally seeing his flaws. But instead she said, "When a baby is first born, it sees the world upside down."

She releases him and reaches for the plate of cupcakes. She holds one up towards him.

"Maybe for breakfast," he says. At this she puts down the cake and touches her fringe. The smell of her hair, the taste of her.

"And Emma?" she says softly.

"She's living with a friend."

Katrin pulls out a chair and sits at the table. Oh God. He sits down across from her.

"And how will it be with you and your baby?"

"I don't know yet." But this is not what he means. Deleuze: Desire stretches that far: desiring one's own annihilation or desiring the power to annihilate. "I have to get through this thing with my job." It's the job that will dictate everything, the thing that will tell him how he is to live. This is what he can count on: that he has this simple task to complete, this deliberate act of determining his future. Everything else will fall into place.

"A lot of questions for this uni to answer," she says, knowingly.

"I don't know what else to do," he admits to her.

She looks at the cupcakes on the table. "Maybe in Ned time it is not as difficult as this." She looks back at him, and he's relieved she's smiling. "During the war, when a Polish scientist asked Einstein if he thought it was possible for human beings to change, Einstein said, 'In historical time, no; in geological time, possibly; in mathematical time, absolutely.' Perhaps anything is possible in Ned time."

How is she possible? And how would life be possible without her?

FRANCINE

Lawrence is seated at the head of the boardroom table. Today his tie is orange. Orange alert: high-level threat. Francine shifts in her chocolate-coloured pencil skirt, too tight, too short, damn it. She fingers what is becoming a wide run in her pantyhose. She coughs, nervously. The four others at the table chat and tease, waiting for Lawrence, who is reading something on his Blackberry, to get on with the last item on this meeting's agenda. Sarah, Paul, Simon and Mohammad do not appear to have done any special dressing for the occasion.

"It's a good thing she went back; she was worried it would be the last time she'd see him," Sarah says.

"And it was," Paul adds. Ya, duh, you idiot. Francine notices that Paul has a stain on his collar. They are talking about Samita, who took sudden compassionate leave to go to India to see her brother. Samita is the key QA administrator, who liaises with field QA reps in each department. Francine has not until today noticed her absence.

"How old was he?" Mohammed asks.

"Young," Simon says.

"In his forties," Sarah says.

"Young," Simon says, nodding.

"Doctors can't tell you . . . they think they can tell you . . . but they can't tell you," Sarah says.

"Like the weather," Paul says, and Francine snorts, then holds back her laughter, pretending that she's coughing again (*Who can turn the world on with her smile . . .*).

"The VC group," Lawrence resumes, "has announced that the second round of redundancies won't be voluntary, like we'd thought at the beginning of the year. To be blunt with you, they're expected to be brutal." He looks at each one of them in the eye like some tribal judge, and Francine holds his gaze the longest, swallowing back what could have been another snort in less serious circumstances. She smirks but doesn't mean it and then tries to smile, but Lawrence has looked back down at his documents, then his Blackberry, checking the time.

"Any questions?" He's still looking at his phone.

That's it? Francine looks at the faces of her colleagues: Paul has started to fiddle with his nose, the fingers danger- ously close to entry. His fingers go transparent and she can see cartilage and the hands of a four-year-old boy picking his nose and eating the boogers. Sarah is smiling and Francine can see through her teeth, to the feathery canary secrets hidden behind them. The other two are blank-faced.

"It's not going to be easy going forward, but we have to assume that we're all in the firing line, so to speak," Lawrence says, and he sounds like a complete jerk. She finds herself sud- denly hot for him.

"Larry," she says as she adjusts her thighs in her chair. She has no idea why she has collapsed into cute familiarity with him. "How much warning do we get?" She's perspiring, more than a hot flash—this is like dripping sweat after running a long race.

"There's a protocol in the HR guidelines, but I'm told there'll be more time than usual. It's now March; the end of our fiscal year is July. Expect some kind of announcement in the next month or so, to take into account due notice."

Francine wipes some droplets before they slide from her eyebrows and she looks at Lawrence's tie until its orange colour separates into component yellow and red and everything about him is only the sum of its component parts laid bare.

"Any other business?" he asks. The others mumble a no, and Francine bolts out of her chair, the creases behind her knees soaking wet.

—

It's dark, everyone gone home but her. She has finally been productive. After the meeting she patted herself down with paper towel in the ladies', took off her pantyhose, retreated to her office in bare legs and boots, and stopped asking herself what her mother had said about love. Instead she thought about one of her father's favourite lines that he had tried on her as a teenager, when she didn't want a part-time job: "Take Cinderella, for example; she had a good work ethic, and she had a thing for fancy shoes . . . " She hunkered down and cleared the backlog of reports and specifications that had piled up since the beginning of February and the last breaths of Dario Martinelli.

Now she is starving; her bare legs are splotchy with cold. As she closes her office door she catches sight of Lawrence ahead of her in the corridor.

"Larry!" she calls out. He turns and smiles. His orange tie is loosened, drawn down, rousing. She swallows and thinks of her splotchy legs.

"Working late—that's not like you, Larry!"

"You don't know me then," he says and she's aware of all the things she doesn't know, one for sure being how to talk to a man who once told her that his wife never appreciated him in bed; another being how to hide her legs; and the last being why she feels that Lawrence is necessary right now.

"You have plans for dinner?" she asks.

"No, not really. Starving. Shall we?"

And suddenly she is in Philly again, in the hospital room, and her mother's mouth is dry and her lips are like snakeskin. She's not at all sure, but she thinks the thing that her mother might have said, the thing that love comes with, might have included shame.

She follows Lawrence towards the parking lot.

—

His hand is on her waist and she sucks in her gut, not moving a muscle as she gauges what her skin must feel like. The hand moves down, towards her ass, and she grabs it suddenly and does that thing she learned long ago, in another place: she kisses his hand and puts his finger in her mouth slowly, deeply.

Oh shit.

The evening started out obviously enough: the Crown Tavern on the docks, haddock and chips, from which she'd peeled away the batter and ate only the fish, a few chips, but it was the four glasses of wine and her drinking them all like water and then not feeling safe to get in her car—not knowing if Rajit pleaded not guilty of danger, not guilty of negligence, maybe pleading plain old dumb—that has brought her to this moment. This ever-so-stupid Francine who has Lawrence's finger in her mouth like a popsicle.

"Oh God," Lawrence says, and, shit, now she has to live up to the promise of this gesture.

"It's just head-count, nothing more, nothing less. You can't take it personally," Lawrence said at the Crown, well into their second bottle. "It's better to be seen to be cooperating," and he held her eyes, staring into them, but looking more like he was trying to see his own reflection.

And now with his finger in her mouth, she is desperate to be seen to be cooperating.

Dario's nose flashes into her mind. It had been driven flat to his cheeks from the impact on the road and then Ryan leaned his face over bone and blood and pried open his broken teeth and blew himself into a stranger.

"Oh God," Lawrence says again.

After glass of wine number two, he'd asked her if she would go back to the States if she lost her job. Shit no, she'd said. She didn't know what she'd do; she had options, she said, with her breath getting caught on the "p" and her mind getting stuck on an image of Scott and Melissa's spare room: the single bed with the cream-coloured satin comforter and tubular satin throw-cushions like giant butterscotch mints. The crucifix over the bed, the night table with its doily and glass of water. And now she sees that room again, the light from the window that slashes the single bed early in the morning and exposes the fingerprints and lipstick stains on the rim of the water glass.

She takes Lawrence's finger out of her mouth and licks it, rolling her tongue around it, sliding it back into her mouth.

"God," he says again.

When everything is off but her bra and underwear, his shirt unbuttoned, only his underwear and socks remaining, she looks at his belly. Then lower, to the tent-like pouch of his briefs.

Shit. She tries to back out by shuffling herself away on the bed towards the pillows, hoping he won't notice, but she sees her own thighs jiggle, and when she rests them on the duvet, the orange-peel complexion is spotlit in the track lighting overhead.

"The lights?" she says softly as she raises her knees and hugs them.

Lawrence complies then quickly takes off his shirt and whips off his socks, leaving only his briefs that look like they will rip with the force of what's inside them. Larry is packing.

When he arrives at the bed it's with a ferocious grunt as though he's already come, but she lowers her knees and allows him on top of her, and shit, yeah, there it is.

His kiss is wet; she flinches. But a kiss—it's been a long time coming, so she examines it with every inch of her tongue, tastes its haddocky tang and remembers not to probe too forcefully, to let him do some pushing forth, to allow him access to the depths of her throat, to make him think of other depths. And this seems fair enough. He has been kind to her; he has offered to protect her as best he can from the ravages of the upcoming culling; he has offered to read her job description for her; he has, bless the fat little functionary, said that she'll be the first he will give a heads-up to if he hears anything significant. And as he takes his somewhat oddly shaped—more impressive in its width than length—cock out and aims it at her, she remembers all this and starts to help him by taking down her underpants, sorry that she hasn't shaved or waxed or trimmed, but right now Larry could care less.

While he's in her she can't stop worrying if he has something that she might catch and why on earth she hasn't insisted on a condom. Then it's there: an image she hadn't realized had imprinted. The image she had not even known she'd experienced until just this second: Dario's face as his body flew across her windscreen—his visor open, the only discernible feature his white teeth bared in a silent howl.

"Ow, ow, ow," she says and pushes Lawrence up to get him to stop.

"What? You okay?" he asks, terrified he has hurt her, but she hugs him to reassure him he has not, no, not really . . . it's just . . .

"Sorry, just a second, let's . . . just . . . Stay there. Don't move," she says, "I like that," and she remembers how to be helpful and how to make it seem like everything is just right and the guy just never has to do anything but the perfect fucking he believes he's been born to do. She remembers that this is a crucial part of all of this. So she whispers: "Oh God, that feels great," and in a moment so graceful and swift that it feels like it is enacted by a petite, confident woman half her size and age, she turns over on her stomach and raises her red ass in the air like a baboon and offers it to Larry as the last thing on earth that might save her.

ROBIN

The gods are back. This day confirms it. And they are toying with him again. Since the last warm days of October, through the misery of November and his last hurrah of sex with Emma in December, and all through the dark winter, the gods said, you deserve this, you are lost in a grim forest, you are not Kurosawa's samurai, you are merely a common, irrelevant man. And now today's sun—the evil light like the cinematography in Rashomon—is their joke on him. Things were easier in the irritating shadows, the itching cold. This light, this warmth on his neck; daffodils, crocuses, a million shades of green: these will hurt without her. And those birds. God. The birds are torture. There is one tree, one supernatural tree that he must pass on his way to the tube, and this tree persecuted him this morning; this tree with branches dressed in white lace petti- coat blossom, circled by sparrows calling like fools. And the afterimage of Katrin seared into his brain: her hair, skin, the way she takes him to her. These, along with the ultrasound image of his baby, Emma's tears, and the fact that he has agreed to her request to move into his flat for the baby's birth, are torture here in the sunshine.

Today the river smells nearly like a river should. The sun makes this space behind the library feel nearly like a real shore. Robin looks around him, aware of noises near the derelict spot at the back of the Samuel Johnson building. He sees the broad back of Bayo, her weave of black hair, long down her back, her shoulders hunched over something, and then the flame opens and she drops the thing in her hand and stands back. The essay. He didn't want to, he tried hard not to, but he had no choice but to fail her. It would never have got by the external examiner, would in no one's eyes but his own have been worthy of a pass just because she has tried so hard and needs a break so badly. Is he doing them justice—these students who don't need theory but who, like Bayo, just need a job?

The inevitability of bad news awaits him in his office. The last round of e-mails from the dean reveal that there will be no hourly paid lecturers for next year, and class sizes will increase accordingly. Even if he keeps his job, he'll never have time to write another article. Students will consume him, making a film would be out of the question even if he could, and, fact is, without being submitted to the REF he'll never get further than the lecturer grade. He needs to make a mark in a different way, but his application for his job has been sent to Human Resources; his article on motion capture and animation has been submitted to *The Velvet Light Trap*, and he now must ensure that he doesn't botch the interview. The one for his current job is the only interview he hasn't botched in his life, except maybe the one for a stock boy position at Sainsbury's when he was sixteen, when he jabbered on about the importance of fresh milk.

Bayo spots him as she walks away, the blackened leaves of her burnt essay fluttering on the ground beside the cement wall. He nods, but she doesn't acknowledge his gesture.

Olivia paces in the corridor; a scowl, eyebrows close together. Robin slows down in his march back to his office. Bayo, Olivia: too much today. But as soon as she is in front of him at his desk, the born teacher in him, the part of him he wishes he could bottle so that he could sip it during other less resourceful moments of his day, arrives to shore them both up.

"That man who works for the council," Olivia says. She is ticking inside, something about to give. He puts his hand on the desk.

"What is it?"

She rubs her face. "I didn't tell you this before."

He waits, expecting that her bobbing will spin out meaning like cloth.

"He's my father." She looks at him with something akin to a dare.

"Oh," he says, and waits for her to explain.

"So, yes, that's why, that might be why."

He waits, giving her space, not wanting to force her to that place she was last year when she revealed more than he could rightfully handle.

"I haven't seen him for . . . like forever . . . and he . . . " She shifts in the chair. He waits for her to finish, but she shakes her head and doesn't look as though she will.

"Is there something else?" He lifts his baby finger to the bridge of his glasses and nudges them slightly.

"He just seemed so pathetic, is all." The tension in her face slackens.

"I don't understand," Robin says, but really he does, and there is something pathetic about a man who is responsible for heaps of lonely dead people who might lose his job because of budget cuts and shrinking economies and the careless, idiotic way we live.

"I just had to tell you that, is all. I just thought, oh, I didn't tell the whole story, and it wasn't fair, so I had to tell you that." Olivia picks her satchel up off the floor.

Now it all makes sense, her tortured, confusing designs disguised as research.

"Are you worried about him?"

"He's just this man; he sounds a bit foreign. I didn't use to think so, when he was my dad," she says.

The boundary that Robin is perched on is a dangerous one, he knows.

"What do you want to happen?" he says.

Her eyes are very clear as she looks up. "To do this project with him," she says, "so he can keep his job, and he can become—" she stops, her confidence spent.

If there are no rules, there is no game. But what kind of parent will he be if he doesn't respond with his truest impulse?

Afterimage: Katrin laughing uncontrollably: you want to be seen as a predator.

"I could talk to him," he says, and she is calmed. He is not promising anything; he doesn't have to commit to action just because that is her way of handling strife. Talking to Olivia's father would be like breaking the fourth wall in theatre. There might be no worse or better moment in his career to do so. Though coming up with a better way to eulogize over a communal grave will not save Olivia's father's job.

She rests the satchel on the floor again. "Will you? Oh, that's ace; you will? I'll set it up."

"Yes," he says with a firm nod. Formaldehyde is a difficult word to spell; Bayo knows this. Yes, he will do this small thing.

When Olivia has gone he looks at the sky through his office window. The beryl through the atrium's aperture confirms that the day has not yielded in its outpouring of painful sunlight. Skin, tongue, hips. God. It's palinopsia.

OLIVIA

Jasmine is wearing a cross the size of a door key. She looks like a jailer with it hanging around her neck, and Olivia can't hold back her smile. Even if Jasmine looked up now from her praying to see Olivia's face, she wouldn't get the smirk. Nah, Jaz is gone. Jaz has a dead-man-has-been-inside-me miracle of Christ's love to distract her from feeling duped, on account of finding out how many girlfriends Dario had at the time of being splattered on the road. Jasmine is straining towards Christ as a way of eliminating the competition.

"Jaz—we should go out, to the park or something, get some air, innit. It's stuffy in here. The sun is out—the birds are singing—feels nearly spring," Olivia says.

Jasmine looks up and glances out the window. "It won't last," she says, "and there's nowhere to go except to Jesus, Liv."

"You know you don't believe that. You didn't even know the guy, Jaz." Olivia stands and gets her coat on. "I'm off—got a ton of work to do. I'm danged, Jaz, but you just keep praying." And out she goes into the sunshine that says, cool it, cool it, right.

But it's week five of the term already, and she has to get down to it. All she has is an outline on the history of paupers' graves, a bit of research on poetry, ceremony, and commemorations, and some jacked-up ridiculousness from Jasmine on how souls who don't get praised don't go to heaven. She's bound to fail her degree now. This sunshine is not helping, not one bit. She wants to sprint like mad the way she used to in Parsloes Park on the March days when Miss Temple from Five Elms Primary school took her year-four class to the park and said, "Run wild," because she knew they'd tire themselves out and be better behaved for the rest of the day. Olivia could outrun Jasmine-who-was-then-Eleanor, Athina, Sally, and even Rufaro, Olu, and Beverly, who were the sporty ones with a lot of speed but too much attitude. There was nothing keeping Olivia back because she knew where to focus. She knew you didn't look at the finish line; you looked at your own two feet running. Right.

And now she has to do the same and not look up again until this dissertation is finished. Robin told her that he would meet Ed at his office; Robin is a man who will not let you down. Something will come, and the next time Ed has a funeral and reads a poem for the lonely dead, well, she'll take Catherine. That will be the moment, and all will be unveiled and all will be right. Suddenly she feels tired.

Her satchel buzzes.

She flips up the flap and reaches in for her phone.

You disappearing from me, but I still try, and hope. Nasar.

It's not anger she feels, no. If he's so determined, he will wait. What's in her fingers is more like the need to brush the curls away from her eyes.

Very busy now. How do you know me anyway? You're amping this don't you think?

She keeps walking. The bus will be quiet this time of day. She can read her printouts on participatory rights in international law on the way. Uni food is too expensive and too shite since they dumped all the real dinner ladies, so she'll get off early and get a sandwich from the shop, and—

You meet me on the cuts march at SU bus.

Nasar. That was him. Of course, on the student union march. Of course he isn't a random stalker. That dude was something different. A tall bloke, a small tingle, and just enough of a wish that this Egyptian will be around when she's finished her course work and that there will be an Arab Spring in London.

The 173 stops directly in front of her and the driver takes his sweet time opening the door. She was right, it's nearly empty, but even though she could without harm take a disabled and elderly seat at the front, she moves to the back, sits, and takes out her notes. As they make their way around corners and through intersections, she feels something in her knickers—a bit of wetness, which makes her uneasy. She looks around to make sure neither of the two women in the seats around her take any notice that there might be something going on inside her.

ROBIN

Sydney House, the offices of the Safeguarding Adults Team of the Barking and Dagenham Council, is drab and boxy, with the kitchen-sink realism of *Kes*, and overhead lighting to match, as though revealed through the lens filter of a cinematographer invoking the 1970s. Robin walks the corridor to the Protection, Funeral and Conference Officers. The door is open and a black man behind one of the three desks in the office stands up when he sees him. "You are Robin," the man says. "I'm Ed," and he smiles. His head is balding at the front, closer to a number-two trim elsewhere. "Or Wood," he adds, zipper teeth towards a laugh. The Caribbean accent is as mild, but present, as Olivia said.

Robin shakes his hand. "Wood?"

Ed comes out from behind the desk. He leads Robin to a small room along the corridor, where there is a table, chairs, a coffee machine, cups, and a kettle. A tiny *To Sir with Love* staff room.

"Wood is what people call me when they know me," Ed says. The man pulls out a chair at the table and sits, inviting Robin to do the same.

"Why Wood?"

"When my daughter—when Olivia," he raises his hand in a yes-of-course-you-know-her gesture. "A nickname she gave me. You go ahead, call me Wood. Olivia says you are very good to her." Ed's voice is higher when he talks about his daughter. His accent is less controlled. Robin feels both familiarity and freshness on the other side of the boundary he has crossed, and he sits up straight to resist getting too comfortable here. He will find out what Ed thinks of Olivia's eulogy project and see if he can offer any suggestions. That will be all.

"So, this must be a demanding job," he says, and shifts a little in his chair.

"No, no, not demanding—not in an ordinary way." Ed turns over a napkin on the table, folds it, opens it again and straightens out the edges.

"What sort of training do you need?"

Ed begins to talk quickly, as though he's being interviewed, and this uneasy dynamic is not what Robin intended.

"I have a lot of experience," and Ed rhymes off a range of courses and diplomas. "I wanted to be a teacher myself, once. Teachers are as important as parents," he says, but he laughs uncomfortably at this. Although he's fifty-nine, he says, he still thinks he can be a good parent. "Olivia is lovely, isn't she?" he says.

Robin nods, wanting to tell him how Olivia seems worried for him, but he will not breach her trust. And mostly what he is not saying is that you are a lucky man and if I get a child who cares about me like this I will be undeserving. He closes his eyes then opens them again quickly.

"And what about her idea?" Robin asks.

Ed shakes his head and smiles, big, wide. "Her dissertation, you mean? Oh, yes well, you know, I helped her a bit, but not too much, really, just told her a little about community graves and what goes on through the council . . . I'm not the best source; she needs to be doing the history, I think, and I—" He pauses and looks serious, nearly unhappy. "But it's all right, isn't it? My helping her a bit?"

Robin takes a deep breath; he has been set up. Olivia has obviously not told Ed about the poetry, and now Ed thinks he's here to check up on him. "No, no, it's great; it's fine." He shifts in his chair again. "Have you worked with academic researchers before?" Maybe he can salvage this without embarrassing either of them. If there's a real project here what's the harm?

Ed nods his head and begins to answer, his voice dedicated and professional. Directed by the Social Care Institute for Excellence, their work is pan-London, partnered by the police, the NHS, local authorities, and the fire brigade. His job is a small part of a bigger strategy, because, according to Ed, the whole world is going wrong. The things he does, day to day, don't change much, but there are always strategies for finding more partners, more money. He looks after the elderly, the mentally incapable, people who don't have family or friends to represent them and can't make their own decisions. Ed gets them the right help.

Robin sees the feathery blackened remains of Bayo's burned essay at the back of the library.

"Does it get you down?" he asks, looking around the room. The only books in sight are the paperback manuals piled on the table beside the kettle: phone books, regulations, government reports.

"Ah, no-no," Ed says, shaking his head. "Just the opposite."

That's the thing, yes; he knows this from teaching: it keeps you in the world. Afterimage: Emma's tiny mogul of a bump beneath her white T-shirt. "Hope you don't mind me asking . . . your accent, where are you from exactly?"

Ed is reluctant at first when he tells Robin about Guyana, but he slowly opens up and talks about the variety of landscape— sea, rivers, bush. He describes the swell of forest in the middle of the country making it sound like lungs for a hemisphere. Robin breathes in and holds his breath, thinking, yes, yes, there are things I could do to help. As they talk more, across random subjects, Robin finds himself at one point saying, "I fix nearly everything in my flat with duct tape," at which Ed nods, knowing exactly how important duct tape is.

"Did you learn to read from young?" Ed asks him.

"Sure, sure," Robin says, and they smile at one another, mirroring language as well as smiles. Ed fidgets, and Robin knows he must either take the conversation somewhere new or tell Ed about the poetry. Although the idea seems less absurd in this precise moment than it has all along, he doesn't have the words right now.

"Catherine is Olivia's mum," Ed says, saving Robin from raising his own random subject. He thinks of his own, Polish Catherine. There's nothing left to say.

"I'll think about possible research projects, a film, perhaps," and he makes moves to leave, but he doesn't want to return to the university; he wants to return only to the moment of standing with Katrin in the curve of the eaves in her bedsit, holding tight, only a slight, rocking movement, a dance, a silence.

"Olivia's project is good," Ed says, proud, maybe a bit defensive. They stand.

"I'm sure it is," Robin says.

He shakes Ed's hand. He doesn't mind that he has been stitched up by Olivia; he wants to be necessary, like this man.

FRANCINE

It might appear like a normal day if you didn't look too hard—students sitting in lecture halls taking notes, lecturers bitching in the staff room, coffee being drunk, cigarettes smoked out in the square—but London in March is not supposed to have snow crushing the daffodils poking up through the brittle ground, so Francine is shit sure that something is going down today. A few days ago the skies were like oh-hallelujah-it's-here! But now the skies are pewter, flecked with dandruff. This might be the day she hears that her job is kaput. She decides to call the States. "Scotttttttt . . . " she says, playing with him, in a way they never did as children. But when he doesn't rise to the invitation and instead responds matter-of-factly, asking her why she's phoning him so early on a Monday morning, she speaks plainly.

"I might need a job," she says.

Scott tries, in his way, but he is not comfortable with comforting, and when he says, "Things are tough there, I know, I've heard . . . " she understands that is the best he can do.

"I'll be fine . . . it's not really any of that . . . " And she finds herself telling Scott about the accident and how lousy she has felt—minus the menopause, minus the sex with Larry—and he is more at ease now, back in familiar territory with his sister who was always a bit of a case, and so he reverts to his favourite mantra of all:

"You need a good man," he says.

The silence between them feels the same as it did when their mother died: the size of the ocean that divides them.

—

After some progress on her job specification, and completion of the overview of QA for the last six months, which Lawrence has specifically asked her for today, Francine is ready for tea. The snow has melted, but she doesn't feel like trudging across the square, so she settles for the staff room. She struggles with the handle of the door.

"Pull it up a bit, then out."

Almost whispered, the words make the skin goosepimple on Francine's neck. Patricia is smiling when Francine turns around, at the same moment the staff room door becomes unstuck with a click. There's heat not unlike a hot flash, but she feels caught out. She knows this door, for God's sake; she isn't breaking in.

"Subsidence," Patricia says. "The whole building is tilting. It'll be in the river soon."

"What are you doing over this way?" Francine asks. That smell again. She knows now that Patricia brings the smell of France—croissants baked with lavender.

"Meeting with your lot about our MA programme," says Patricia. Her engine seems quiet, nothing Patty about her today.

"Oh?"

"Not enough students."

"Oh, I see," Francine says, and tries to think of something clever that will make them both feel more comfortable, but she can't, and ticking seconds of silence build and build.

Patricia stares at her now. "I'm not desperate, Francine."

"What?" Francine's face burns.

"Enjoy your tea . . . no, it's coffee, isn't it?" Patricia says. She places three fingers on Francine's shoulder (two, three, four seconds) then turns and walks towards the stairwell, disappearing downstairs.

The sudden lump in her throat forces Francine to put her hand there; she scratches her neck.

—

When she's composed after her coffee, she quickly finishes the QA document that she will give to Lawrence before leaving. She prints it out and doesn't bother to proof it again, satisfied that she's accomplished one major thing this week. She takes the document to Lawrence's office and leaves it on his desk. She hovers there, sniffing the air: it brings sandalwood, cheese, musk, and whisky. Larry is like a swamp. Larry is a bit of a jerk. If she tries, she can still feel him crashing against her, way up inside her, she on her hands and knees, smiling painfully at the wall. She leaves his office.

She can try to sneak out early to go home or she can sit at her desk and try to look busy. The announcement is expected in three weeks. She sits at her desk and clicks on to her Soulmates account:

Three people have viewed her profile since her last log-in.

She has one fan.

She has five favourites.

She has one new message.

Chris from Nottingham wants her to get in touch. Chris from Nottingham looks like mashed potatoes. Her throat catches again.

—

When she reaches her neighbourhood later that evening, she drives in the opposite direction of her flat. She turns down Ryan's road and parks outside his house. Lights are on in the living room, and there is movement behind the sheer curtains. She pushes the radio dial and catches the end of the news, not listening. And when a familiar tune of prancing violins begins, she recognizes *The Archers*. She can't stand the voices, the accents, the melodrama. But she finds herself listening.

When the show is over she starts the engine. This is idiotic. So she can barely believe it when the door to Ryan's house opens and out he comes, earphones in, and up goes the hood, down goes the head. He crosses the road towards her and is about to pass the car and she can't help herself. She opens the door and leaps out in front of him.

"Fucking hell!" He's scowling.

"Sorry, sorry," she says as she puts her hands out to touch his shoulders. "I didn't mean to startle you." She didn't mean to even be here, but now that she is she has to buck up, not fail him.

"What are you doing here?" His face has softened and there's room for her now to tell him that everything is going to be okay. Isn't that what her own mother would have done?

"I wanted to give you something—a book," she's not thinking fast enough, "a book that I thought you'd be interested in, but

I realized I'd left it at home. Sorry, I was just turning around to fetch it, and then I saw you." He's not listening.

"I could use a lift," he says quickly.

"Sure," she says, and hops to it, unlocking the passenger door for him.

He's fast, edgy, cagey.

"Where to?"

"Anywhere . . . "

She pulls out and does as he requests, driving slowly, anywhere. He smells like beer. There's a silence for a minute or two until he turns to her:

"The driver has pleaded guilty to a lesser sentence of careless driving causing death. He must have done some sort of deal." She wants to ask him how he knows, but he seems too agitated now. "I don't believe him," he says.

She takes a right at the lights because it gives her a moment to wait for a passing car, and to think. "Don't believe Rajit?" He nods and beer comes at her again. "What's not to believe?"

He turns towards her, his face pained. "That he forgot to renew his licence? Forgot? The car was borrowed. He could have just been taking a chance. But he said he forgot and was about to buy his own car." Ryan sniffs. When she and Scott were teenagers, living with Aunt T, Scott would do a lot of yelling. *What the hell does that guy think he's doing? Where the hell is the butter?* And when he was most afraid he would blame her and Aunt T for trying to get away with things, for putting one over on him. Ryan's nose is like Scotty's.

"Of course, his family—they need a car—his wife's mother—" She stops, knowing that she can't reveal her visit, can't mention the old woman in her wheelchair. "He would want a car . . . "

"I don't believe him," Ryan repeats. He puts his hand on the dashboard and it shimmers, dissolves, passes through it, into the body of the car.

They are somewhere deep in north London as the sky darkens, but she doesn't know exactly where. Stocky terrace houses, with rubbish bags popping out of bins, everything squashed together in the dinge. "Do you want to go somewhere in particular?"

He shakes his head and puts his hood up again; she keeps driving. (*To boldly go . . .*)

By the time she has figured out where they are, it has started to rain. Shit. Fuck. Shit. The street signs are difficult to see. Her hand shakes as she flicks the signal to turn left. She pulls the car over at the side of the road and puts the hazards on.

"You okay?" Ryan says.

"Yeah, sure."

He takes down his hood. "Let's go back," he says.

"Yep," she says, but she doesn't move a muscle.

"You're a good driver," he says.

"My memory's doing funny things," she says.

He watches her.

She checks her mirrors and blind spots, signals and pulls out, slowly finding her way back towards his neighbourhood.

KATRIN

They say the rain is like spit but it is not. Today the rain is oily. Katrin is inside her hat, hunched like a cat against this rain that wants to bring her low. Claire is right about March, but Claire is wrong about her.

At Epicure when she is dry and ready for the customers, she tries not to catch eyes with Claire. She must make herself brave to ask what is needed, and then be invisible again. Already it has been left too long taking chances with Robin that would give him two babies this year not one. Alejandro has a doctor's surgery that is taking new patients and she will get a prescription. But this appointment is tomorrow. This appointment will mean taking time from work to be doing something that really belongs in Ned Time. This is maybe a bad idea. The good choice would be to stop seeing Robin, to not believe him, to make him choose her or his baby, but she is weak and stupid, and she has never been touched like Robin touches her. Ania held a judgement in her face on Skype when Katrin told her about him. Alejandro says love is rare. Beata would like this English Robin.

"Guy's a fucking twat," Claire hisses in a whisper so that the bald man at the front does not hear. "Wants this heated up," she says and nearly throws the plate with the Danish onto the counter. "Why didn't you heat it up?"

Katrin's heart hammers as she picks up the plate. "He didn't ask me," she says and turns to the oven. How is she doing wrong? If she asks for time off to see the doctor Claire will think she is sick and will fire her. When her father got sick with *pólpasiec* and sores broke out on his one side and he could not work, his foreman punished him from then, and from then he started to drink and she started to lose him. She will tell Claire that she needs the day for her mother's papers, to arrange for her to be moving to London in just over seven weeks. Claire at least has a mother. She must understand.

"Claire," she says when she approaches the back office during her break. If you use the name you address the heart, Beata always told her. "May I come in?" Her heart starts hammering again.

"Ha! There we go. Have you seen this?" Claire points to the newspaper and Katrin does not know if this means yes to come in. "A new study using sophisticated brain scans shows that women have more intense responses to pain than men. Bloody hell. These people have obviously never seen man flu in action."

Katrin waits at the door. Claire looks up from her *Daily Mail*.

"You know my mother is coming to live, I told you, yes?" Katrin says.

Claire nods but it looks also like she is shaking her head, so Katrin is more nervous. "She comes in May." Katrin pauses. Claire does not change her face, but of course she is waiting for more. Katrin is slow; she has not practised this. "I need to go to Islington council, to make some applications and some papers, and I need to do this tomorrow in the morning." She waits.

Claire makes a face. There is a big silence. This is a mistake; she should have told the truth about the doctor.

"You know that you have to pay more if your mum is with you, don't you?" Claire says.

Katrin nods, but she didn't know this.

"More council tax."

"My room is very small," she says.

Claire's face goes sour again. "That's not how it works. Tell your landlord too; not all of them go for it." Claire twists the chain on her wrist, like it is something to help her not explode. Katrin regrets every word she has said, and her lip trembles. She tastes pastry like it lives in her throat. "And why do you need the whole day?" Claire says.

"I don't. I will come as soon as I'm finished."

"But how long?"

She waited for two hours the last time at an English doctor and was in his room for five minutes. "Two and a half hours," she says in a firm way. Claire looks to be thinking.

"It's not easy dealing with the council," she says, and Katrin has heard a softness in Claire's voice for the first time since she remembers. "I'll cover for you, but not any longer than that, or I'll have to get Rose for the whole day."

Claire has forgotten to hate her, so Katrin nods and nods before Claire can remember again. "Thank you, very much," she says in a formal tone.

—

It is like *wata cukrowa* at the fair in Gdansk during harvest time: the pink spun sugar, like cotton on a stick that she ate as a child.

This tree on the pavement outside of the doctor's surgery is like a *wata cukrowa* tree, pink with blossoms that looks like she could eat them if she bent this branch to her mouth. A cherry tree also blossoms in her grandmother's garden beside the river and a flour mill, where her father was raised. But these blossoms are different from Gdansk blossoms. Big, as though the tree has been fed too much. Swollen. Like she feels also. An extra hour to stand and look because the doctor was a fast Indian doctor and gave her a prescription without trouble. The sun is on her shoulder. Robin loves her and she will see him tonight. March is not brutal as Claire said. And soon it will be April. Her *matka* will love the promise in this month; she will find work cleaning or making clothes, because Beata has talent and is only fifty-eight and when she is not in the bed where her husband will never return she will not sleep so much.

When Robin is with her everything is in the right place. Before in England she did not always know where to put herself. He is where to put herself. Today everything is in the right place, like this *wata cukrowa* tree.

Ania says that Beata is in panic. That Gdansk is her home, but that Gdansk is impossible without her daughter. These two things are not lying well together inside Beata's heart. Katrin will make sure that London is home for Beata and that they will not need impossible Gdansk. When they are together more things will be in their right place.

—

He has her hand in both of his and rubs it in a gentle way. This rubbing makes her head feel light and maybe she is sick, or maybe she is pregnant already after taking chances before taking the pill, or maybe Beata forgot to tell her that love can feel like illness.

"If I don't get it, I'll have to move out of London," Robin says, and this stops the lightness and brings a heavy feeling. She rests her elbow on the small table that is her dining table, desk, and ironing board. Robin must reapply for his own job. At the university they are restructuring and deciding who they will keep and who they will remove, and Robin for the first time in his life is worried about money, because no matter what will happen with Katrin, Robin will be a father.

"But why?" She returns the rubbing and plays with his fingers.

"There are no academic jobs in London," he says. He stares at her. "I feel calm with you."

She can only smile, because he is being so serious and looks like a sad cartoon of himself. "You are teasing me. I am the least calm person, but I fool people because my face doesn't move much." Now he is smiling and they laugh.

"It's true, except when you sleep: your face dances around when you sleep, as though you're watching a circus," he says.

She breathes in. He watches her in her sleep, he sees her; he, more than anyone else, knows her.

"There's this student," he says, and Katrin gets nervous again. She hates this about herself. She does not want everything to feel like a threat. "She wants me to help her father." But Katrin can barely hear the rest because she wants him to help her, maybe too many people want Robin's help, maybe Robin is like an angel and she must remember that angels do not belong to one person alone. She wants to ask him about the council tax and how things work in the council and whether her mother will be allowed to live with her without telling her landlord. She will not ask him because maybe he will think she is trying to take advantage of his country. But it is not that. It is not.

She takes a sip from her vodka that he poured for her before he took her hand. His hands fall away and he leans back in his chair. Katrin wonders if it is this chair where her mother will sit when they eat dinner, or if her mother will prefer the one she is in, which faces the street and from where she can see the window boxes that now have tulips and *cyklameny*. The bedsit has room for only this table and a small dresser. She will need to buy a television for her mother to watch in the evenings. Where will she put that?

"He buries the unknown dead," Robin says. He is still talking about the student's father.

There is a feeling in her chest from his words, but it is not pain. It is like pain, though. "They do this in the councils?"

"All the people who have no families—the foreigners, or the people without friends who die in Dagenham, and who need funerals."

"And how will you help him?" She will try not to feel jealous. Try very hard. And she will not ask him about the council tax. She will not be in need like this student.

"I don't know," Robin says, and he looks down at his feet—his leather shoes have scuffs on the toes and the laces are frayed. Maybe he is thinking he needs to shine them, maybe he is not thinking about his shoes at all, but when Robin concentrates he is very beautiful. "Let's go to bed," he says.

And everything is in its right place.

BUT NOW I'M FOUND

ED

Long hair; smart-Beatle glasses: is this in truth how a professor looks these days? Robin's open face is not unlike Sammy's. Ed sits in front of Olivia and Robin in the staff room of the Safe and Sorrow office and feels proud. The first time the man was here Ed was worried he'd said something wrong, but the professor is back. And Olivia too. And his Olivia is something else. She's full of the things he was as a youth—Resistance! Revolution!—but she doesn't need to holler in the streets like he and his friends did when the ballot boxes got stuffed and boys in Tiger Bay got shot. She is a tread-softly warrior.

"Wood, maybe you could explain what you have to do, exactly," Olivia says to him. And, man, she's calling him Wood.

"Well, I was explaining last time—"

"But you didn't talk about funerals, not exactly," Olivia says, interrupting him like there is something urgent to organize. He looks at Robin to see if this is what the man really wants to hear. He stands up and clicks on the kettle, searches the rack for cups that aren't too stained, rinses them out, takes two tea bags from the box of Clipper beside the kettle, and drops them into the yellow teapot. "Busy here today," he says, and wipes his forehead, hot as rass with trying not to make a mess of this meeting. For her.

"You know, we see a lot of elderly," he says over his shoulder, then turns towards them. "Family left them long ago and they didn't know they were unwell, you see. And . . . " he looks at Olivia whose eyes prompt him to continue. "And some illegals . . . we don't know where they've come from—sometimes women, mostly men. A young woman—as young as you—" he says to Olivia, "nobody found her for a long time. She had nobody. That's bad, man." He shakes his head and places their cups in front of them. He goes to the small fridge for the milk. The open fridge is cool, and he stands there longer than he needs to. He picks up the packet of Hobnobs and places them on the table before he sits down again.

"And worst is the babies. Yeah, we've had some babies."

"Where from, though? Their mothers, surely . . . " Robin says, looking bruk-up inside.

"You don't know it, but some mothers walk away and leave them. You don't think so, but that's a fact." Olivia is looking at him like he's saying the wrong things. "Stillbirths have to be registered if they take place after twenty-four weeks . . . " What does she want him to say? The poor man's glasses are slid down towards the tip of his nose. "We had one a few weeks ago, was found in the rubbish . . . " He looks in their faces again. "The police had custody of the body and they needed to organize a cremation. Normally there's no funeral under these circum-stances, but Olivia has me," and the thing that's been there in the room all along catches him and he can't shake it, "thinking dif-ferent," he says and pours the tea.

He tells them about the mandatory autopsy. The police have to treat it as a crime and the morgue has arrangements with the crematorium for this kind of thing. He knows the coroner who signs the death certificate in this case, a good bloke who talks to him a lot about his cases, and maybe they should work together, because, as Olivia says, a life is a life after all. He burns out on this last sentence and looks to her, but she is looking at Robin who pushes his hair behind his ear, making him look like a girl.

"But what's there to say at a funeral like this? How could there be anything to say?" Robin's voice is tortured, like bacoo stuck in a bottle.

"True-true," Ed says, and he won't tell them about Keith Meyers. Five years ago it was the fact of Keith that made Ed go out more often, made him keep up with his friends better, call his mum more regularly, because he wanted to leave a trace of himself, didn't want to end up like Keith Meyers, early sixties, whose corpse was discovered only after his rent had gone unpaid for more than a year and his landlords at the Housing Society began proceedings to have him evicted. No one was going to evict Keith because he had already done so himself, thirteen months previously, dead on the sofa in front of the TV which, when the body was found, had one remaining beam of light coming from the centre, like a cataract eye.

"What do you think would make it better?" Olivia asks him, and he knows what she has in mind—this feeling she has that every human being deserves something good. He can tell this in the throng-bang-parrap of her body. She is a girl who feels so much she will bust open. Things don't always work out, he will have to tell her—part of his duty as father. Nah every crab hole get crab.

"Just something honourable," Ed says. "To give a bit of dignity."

Robin is nodding and fidgeting, like he's caught it from Olivia.

"Okay, okay, I see," Robin says. "Look . . . I don't know, I really don't. It's beyond me, really . . ."

Ed is confused by this modern education system—with the lecturer sitting beside the student while she's doing the research. Robin takes his leave—formal-like and polite—like a man whose own folks have just passed, and Ed is sorry for bringing this pain on him.

"He is the most caring teaching I ever met, Olivia." He will say her name until he dies of it.

"I haven't told you the whole thing yet," Olivia says.

"Oh?"

—

She tells him her plan, her crazy, beautiful plan, in the A13 café. He is more comfortable with her in the dull thud of the place that says, man, this is real, this is not a dream you once had. Now he needs to follow this through like a father.

"And what has poetry got to do with the law?"

"Nothing," she says. He waits, because she is a girl who has more, the way a river does after rain. "I don't always know if I'm in the right field."

"It's a good thing to know the law," he says. She nods then shakes her head. He has much to do in the shoring up of this daughter of his.

"Yeah, but the law gets changed, and I have this friend— president of the SU—and he says you don't wait, you don't sit it out; by the time there's a law it's way too late."

This he cannot argue with. What a father can do is encourage her every step of the way. He lets silence fall for a beat before he speaks again. "When you said everyone needs a poem, what about you? Someone writing you poems?"

"Noooo," Olivia says, like what a ridiculous question, but there is a puncture of relief in his chest.

"Why not?" He is pushing it now.

"Too busy, too busy," she says and that's that.

"What about your mum—she have a boyfriend?" Jeez and rice, now he's done it.

Olivia's eyes duck behind her curls. She shakes her head as if to say, man, he has no idea. He's a stupid rass. Of course Catherine's got a million boyfriends. Catherine was a beauty. Curvy, blonde, a Marilyn Monroe even though her face was not what everybody would call attractive. But she was sexy, with skin like cream. Jesus. Why she went for a man like him he can only put down to the fact that he tried so hard, while the blokes she knew treated her with no respect.

"Have you told her about us meeting?" he asks.

Olivia exhales. "No, no, she wouldn't be happy."

"But, darling"—yeah, he's allowed to say that, and Olivia doesn't flinch—"she should know. Lying is bad." He hears the hypocrite-rasshole-worthless nothing of a man he is by saying that, picturing the man in the Mazaruni river, face down in the halo of blood. But Olivia looks at him like it is right. Like, just maybe, he has said the right thing for a father to say.

KATRIN

There is a blond child hitting a plate with a spoon, and his mother does nothing. The noise is getting louder and other people in Epicure look at Katrin like she must do something instead, but she cannot and she must finish talking to Alejandro who is not teasing when he says, "You should have told me that was what you said to her." And he's right, he could not have known, and she is stupid not to have warned him. "You should have told me," he says. But it is too late and Claire knows about Katrin having gone to the doctor and not the council, and now Katrin is trying not to feel sick and not to need the Indian doctor more than before, because of the clanging spoon along with what Claire will now hold over her. Alejandro talked to Claire and by mistake said doctor and not council. And now Claire is being so friendly to her, talking in a little voice, that Katrin is more frightened than ever. Claire's tone of voice has made Katrin feel the same size as this blond boy.

"She will get me," she says to Alejandro.

"How? She cannot fire you. You don't have to tell her where you go. You asked for the time. It's not her business. You did nothing wrong."

"She will tell my landlord that my mother is coming."

"She doesn't know how to find him. And why would she do that?"

"I don't know." The clanging of the spoon on the plate finishes but the child has begun to cry. The mother is asking the child if it is okay with him if they go home now. The child is crying stronger and louder. Is it okay with him that they go home now? Why is the mother asking him? Katrin feels dizzy. "She'll find a way to get me," she says and now she must do it first; she must tell her landlord that her mother is coming to live with her before Claire tells him, and she will have to find more hours to pay the extra tax.

It's fine. It will be fine; if she can stop Claire from making it worse it will be fine.

—

She is walking too fast along the canal in the rain as the day is ending, but she can feel Robin dragging, wanting to slow down, wanting to walk like it is an hour for fun, even in this weather. But Katrin needs to walk fast. She is the opposite of Robin today, and this worries her. There is a time in all the loves she has had when one person becomes faster or slower than the other person in the way love is working in their heart. Robin has not been talking this last week about the coming of his baby. He has not talked about the mother of his baby. He has talked only about this student, Olivia, and her father Ed, whom he wants to help, but she still is not sure why this must be so.

"I can't join you for the movie," she says, and then spots drooping white blossoms that make her mouth water. The rain has made tiny rivers in between paving stones. She breathes in. "I have to look after some things."

He tugs on the hem of her jacket and this slows her so that now she is at his side. "What kind of things?" he says. And he pulls her to him and puts his arm around her shoulder. "What?" he asks.

When Katrin accepted her place at Gdansk university and told her *matka* that she would study economics, Beata was very angry. Beata wanted her to study music, to be a beautiful and free artist, but Katrin wanted to be part of the world, not separate. She wanted to be inside the things that make it go around. But she also knew one important thing that her classmates whose mothers were not sad did not know yet: that you do not rely on others.

"Things for my mother, when she will come," she says. Because it was not fine when she called her landlord Gary, who told her that she must move if her mother will be with her. She must not have two people in this bedsit; he will not allow this in his property and let it become like the Third World. Gary will come and make sure her mother isn't there. He will come every week if he has to. She will find a new flat that she and her mother can share, not too far from work or Robin. She will not make a new pressure for Robin who will have a baby and who has students asking him to help dead people.

"But that's weeks away," he says and holds her tighter, knowing that there is more than she is saying.

"And how will you help this Ed?" she asks, stepping back, making his arms fall.

They both know that the things they talk about now are not the things they need to talk about. "It's a crazy idea, but his daughter believes it will help him to keep his job. I don't know if that's true," Robin says. "Probably not. Probably it won't make any difference. But there is something that—I don't know. I feel moved by it."

"And how will you write for people that no one knows?" she says, trying again not to feel jealous of this student.

"Well . . . how do you know anyone? Maybe it doesn't matter," he says. But this does not sit right in the place of simple love and she lowers her eyes. She is so stupid to be touchy and moody and swinging from feeling to feeling.

"Come to the movie with me," he says, taking her face and holding it, like he has read her mind. "Come. You'll like it; I promise."

When will she visit the flats she has written down from Loot, which are too far out, or from the Islington *Gazette*, which she cannot afford. She cannot put this off, but standing with him like this reminds her that whatever is not possible now is possible in Ned Time.

"Okay," she says and kisses him on his lips.

FRANCINE

In the annual audit of the QAE processes in the Health and Biosciences School, Francine can't keep her eyes off Lawrence's tie: bright yellow. Like a TV news presenter sending a secret message. She wonders what Lawrence is trying to say and checks out his socks: black. Lawrence is not inventive or subversive. Larry might just be a knob.

In the corridor after the meeting, when the rest have dispersed, he catches her eye and jerks his head in the direction of his office, as if she should know this little secret signal of his; as if she should feel privileged to have secret signals with him. She follows him into his office.

"You caused me great embarrassment," he says as he sits down at his desk.

"What?" Her cheek tingles.

"Your QA document for the restructuring." Larry's eyebrows are like dirt smudged across his forehead.

"I put it on your desk."

"I know, but it was wrong."

"How?" Her cheek twitches. He sighs, annoyed at her for being so thick and stupid and not knowing what he's talking about. Larry is acting like a jerk.

"Look . . . " He walks towards his desk and takes the document from a pile near the corner. Hands it to her.

She knows at first glance what happened, what this is, and where her head was when she printed off this track-changes version with the red editing in the margins. She might even remember seeing the red ink as she put the document on his desk, thinking that red was the swamp smell in Larry's office. It's as stupid as someone could possibly be (*oh Mr. Graaaant*).

"Some of those comments would have got us both some bad attention," he says.

"Oh God." She flips through the document and sees his marginal comment at "difficult decisions" where he has added, "glad you didn't use the word hard, I'm very prone to suggestion," and she winces with more disgust than the first time she read it. There are no mistakes: isn't that what people say? Somewhere deep down, didn't she want to expose flabby Larry? She rubs her own waist, her hand coming across her tummy. Bloated and tender.

"I'd already forwarded the electronic version to printing before really having a good look. Then I called Sally and cancelled the print job. We were out of time, so I fixed it myself."

"Shit." The window behind Larry frames him and, if she squints, he is a portrait in an abstract painting.

"Luckily they didn't have it for long, and they're far too busy to read these things," he says, holding this fact of his doing her job over her like a banana over a baboon. The VC group decides who goes and who stays and there is talk everywhere. You can bet that Larry has mentioned her error to Sally and covered his own ass.

"I'm sorry. I have no idea how that happened."

"I do. You're distracted."

"I am?" The abstract portrait of Fat Larry goes into the transporter and starts to lose its solid lines.

"Do you want to talk about it?"

"No, no, I'm fine. Really. Everyone's stressed. Simon has shingles—"

Larry moves closer to her and she nearly coughs. "You shouldn't be stressed . . . " he says and reaches for her hand. She doesn't realize what he's doing in time to pull away. They stand there near his desk, his tiny purple lips like a skinny worm, his hand now on her hip. "A drink at the end of the day?" he asks, his hand not quite moving, but not quite still either. "We should have dinner, yes?"

"Oh, I . . . " she says, stalling. "I have to check . . . there's a friend, a young guy, I think I might have told you . . . we witnessed the same accident. He's been having a rough time and I told him we would meet up." She steps to the side just enough so that his hand falls from her waist.

"There's a new chef at the Crown, could be good," he says. He looks at her like he wants to eat her, and Francine remembers that she is supposed to want this, that there's this man who wants to eat her and she's somehow supposed to be grateful. And besides, he has just saved her butt. Shouldn't she be showing her gratitude?

"Thanks, Lawrence," she says formally, "thanks, that sounds really good. Dinner sounds good."

He licks his skinny lips and her tummy rumbles.

"I'll stop by at the end of the day, then. We can drive over convoy style," he says.

"Convoy style," she says and nods. Shipshape, yep, shipshape. "But I'm really sorry," it comes out more shipshape and peppy and snide than she means it to. "I mean, sorry," she says again, more gently and genuinely, "but I shouldn't let him down, I really shouldn't; we made a plan. Sorry."

Lawrence doesn't look hurt, exactly, but she notices that his face has tightened.

"Another time," he says and walks back to his office.

—

She marches out of the building in search of chocolate. She crosses the square and touches her tummy (smaller), her thighs (wow), her butt, just for a second (hey) and will buy both a Kit Kat and a Dairy Milk bar. She enters the atrium, and there is that film lecturer. She follows him to the student union shop (*When the red, red Robin comes bob, bob bobbin' along . . .*) where she watches him hover over the chocolate bars. She knows his choice will be a Kit Kat. It's destiny. Hello! Hello! She wants to yell across the aisle to him. Hello, she wants to say, really loudly, because they just look at each other this way, regularly, and neither says a word. In a village they'd be pals by now. She watches him leave as she pays for the chocolate.

In the atrium she joins the line at Starbucks, and she arrives at the same moment as a powerful waft of lavender-croissant. Patricia.

"How's it going? How are you?" she says more eagerly than sounds right for an atrium reunion, but since she's been avoiding Patricia the days have become longer and the spring light is creeping up on them.

"Not too bad. You?" Patricia has her guard up.

"Here," Francine says, and holds out her Kit Kat. "I got you one of these," and she pushes it into Patricia's hand.

"What? Why?" Patricia's unplucked eyebrows slide towards one another.

"Just did, that's all." Francine wants to tell her things. Instead she looks at the age spots on Patricia's hands. Her mouth goes dry. "I think it's hormones," she sputters.

"What is?" Patricia says. There's a loud crash at the end of the atrium and Patricia turns around, while Francine keeps looking at her hands.

"The fact that everything smells like it looks, like if something is yellow and gooey, that's how it smells, and if something smells rancid that's how it looks. Everything is flat and precisely so. Flat and also translucent. I can see through walls and under tables." She pauses, breathes in deeply, "Like superpowers."

Patricia doesn't laugh at her, and for that she will agree to whatever the woman says next. Patricia stares a little too long.

"We have that plan for Ronnie Scott's, remember—let's do that soon," Patricia says. "Call me." She is next in line at the till and pays for her cappuccino.

"See you later," Francine says. Patricia leaves and looks back at her like she's smelling blotchy skin.

—

Later is not something Francine understands at the moment. Later is the same as now is the same as then, because time is doing a stupid shuffle. She is sitting in her car with Ryan, who for the first time in the weeks since she's met him isn't wearing his hoodie. Hot today, spring nearly here even though she's only just noticed, and she looks up at the sky behind Ryan's house. At seven o'clock, twilight, it's lighter than usual for this drive through Queen's Park, up into Willesden, sometimes as far as Wembley. She opens the car window. One thing going for her these days is that she can make a statement to herself like the day smells longer and be proud of how precise it is.

"Where would you go if I weren't driving you around?" she says, looking back to Ryan's pointy head like an arrow on his neck.

"Dunno. Just need a break from the books."

"Anatomy?" A cherry tree in front of the house across the street has purple blossoms that look like a party dress she once wore.

"Pharmacology, genetics."

"Is it hard?" White blossoms like pompoms, three trees in a row. And there's a flowering yellow shrub she would like to know the name of—these are the kinds of things she once used to track in springtime.

"No. Just big."

She smells gum and looks over at Ryan, who is chewing ravenously. Does he really want to be a doctor or is he trying to replace his dad in the household? "Do you like it?" she says.

He stops chewing. "What? You don't think I'm cut out for it?" he says, and, oh what an idiot she is. Why is it she hasn't learned to speak to someone Ryan's age? She could have a kid his age.

"You'll be fantastic," she says, signals, and makes a right turn, back towards Queen's Park, where she'll drop him off before this turns into the Ryan and Francine sad-ass-losers show.

"Are you trying to be my friend?" he says, as she turns onto his street and slows down towards his house. She stops the car, puts in it park and turns off the engine. She looks at his arrow-like head. They smile at the same time.

"Tell me about the other students. Do you mingle much with them?"

"Sure, of course. Not recently."

"I'm sleepy," she says. He undoes his seatbelt, reaches over and touches her hand. He gets out of the car.

"See you tomorrow," he says before shutting the door.

KATRIN

Her mother cries like a small animal. Katrin has heard this sound all of her life, but tonight the squeal makes Katrin irritated. The sound grates, and her mother's face is frozen in pain on the screen, because Skype is slow tonight.

"Beata," she says, because she uses the name when it is her turn to be the mother. She calms Beata and tells her that in London it is not a problem, there are flats enough to rent, but that it might mean not in the centre as she has been before, and it might mean they will share a bed for a while until they can afford more, but it is nothing to be crying about. Please, *mamunia*, please don't cry. She talks to Beata about weather, about money, about the price of onions and about the Japanese film that Robin took her to see that made her want to eat noodles, so he took her to a Japanese restaurant afterwards. The food of Japan tastes clean and stops at the back of the tongue like a good wine does. In Japan they do not have gas, Katrin has decided. In Japan they have clean systems. Her mother laughs at her and disagrees with her, and the little animal sounds stop.

Her mother will not sleep tonight, Katrin knows, as she clicks on the red end-call icon and Beata's face disappears from the screen. A bedsit is big enough for them both. She could put a futon in the cove by the fireplace that does not hold fire and she could sleep there and give her mother the bed. She will have to lie to a new landlord to let her mother share with her; she does not want to move far from Islington or Epicure. Or Robin.

Katrin gets up from the table and pushes the button for her kettle to boil. But tea is not what she wants. She bends down to her fridge and opens the freezer. She takes the bottle of Wyborowa and pours a small level in a glass. This is her father's drink. She throws it back but promises herself she will not become accustomed to this, like her father. Her father was not reliable, but Robin is reliable, and if she asked him he would help her. Robin is a man whom both she and Beata could trust. This thought makes her scared.

She calls his phone. It rings and rings until his voicemail comes.

"Hello, baby," she says to his voicemail. She feels silly. She has not called anyone baby before, but this is what she hears lovers say to one another. She doesn't want to be confusing, with baby and babies and his future, but it has come out of her like this. "Hello . . . are you free tomorrow in the evening? Can you come here? I will cook a dinner. We can relax here," she says. "Please call me."

She pours another small level into the glass and takes a sip. The warmth in her throat takes away the scary feeling of almost trusting someone.

—

He is facing her, their knees up and touching. Katrin imagines that from above they look like they form a key hole. And into their perfect fit something perfect also fits. Sex with Robin is not only a place where everything is possible, but where nothing is necessary.

"Baby," she says, trying out this new word again.

"Sweetheart," he says and strokes her face.

"I think you should stay here," she says and surprises even herself.

He smiles. But then his eye twitches and she feels a jolt in her stomach.

"Wouldn't you like this every day?" she says. She looks at his chest and touches the few hairs there; she avoids his face in case there is something she doesn't want to see.

"Of course I would. I think of nothing else, I tell you," he says, and she can look up at him now. But his brow is creased like there is pain there.

"But . . . " she says and nods, yes, of course she knows what comes next.

"I dream of it," he says, "I do. But there is so much to sort out."

She lowers her knees and rolls over with her back to him. He pulls her in and his knees now touch the back of hers. Still the perfect fit.

"My mother will not be able to live with me," she says finally and closes her eyes; she could sleep now.

"I don't understand." His body is alert; she has made him worry, but she does not know how to correct it. When she explains about her landlord it is through sleepy lips. She is so tired suddenly that nothing he says will matter to her. "Please could I live with you, just for a little while," she says. If it was brave she wants a drink of vodka as a reward.

It is possible that she feels his foot twitch then. And now she is alert. She turns her head over her shoulder towards him. He strokes her hair.

"I told Emma that she could move in and deliver the baby

there. She wants a home birth. She has a midwife and she doesn't want to be alone when the baby comes."

Oh God. She sits up in the bed but does not face him yet. Oh God, she is so stupid. He has promised another woman to live with him, and Katrin has been taking this man inside her for weeks now. She has been making it easier for him to make promises to someone he does not love.

She gets out of the bed and puts on her dressing gown.

"Please go," she says very softly. So softly he has not heard. "I want you to go," she says louder, and she hears that she has said "I" very strongly, and realizes that this emphasis has been missing between them.

"Katrin," Robin says. "Please, let's talk."

Katrin ties her dressing gown tighter around her waist and does not turn around. She walks to the window and examines the *cyklameny* in the flower boxes, with their petals wide and holding on by one thread, their stamens fat and long now laid bare. All the *czekam* she did for the spring and now this is what is here. She opens the fridge. She pours some vodka in a small glass. She does not pour any for Robin.

ROBIN

Everything she does is deliberate: her washing up from their dinner in the sink, the way she places her hand flat on the plate then caresses its underside with the cloth. Katrin's movements are pointed and fluid at once, and this makes a hole in Robin's chest as black and deep as something yet undiscovered in science. He watches as she pours herself vodka, waiting for her to pour him one, their nightcap that is now routine. Afterimage: her back turned to him in her bed, curved as she hugged her knees. Please could I live with you just for a little while in the soft skin that runs across her back to her thin shoulders that all he wants to do is kiss.

"Katrin," he says.

"I want you to go," she says, her back still turned to him. He should not have succumbed to his guilt, to Emma's desire to share the birth of the baby with him. He is angry with her, and with himself. But now what?

"It will only be for a little while, until she gets on her feet. She is not my love," he says, and starts to dress so that he can stand beside her without shame.

She turns towards him but doesn't move, her certainty

locked in as she watches him put his shoes on. Her cheeks are wet with tears wiped away before he could see.

"You are," he says, composing himself. "You are." And he will find a way—he will pay for a flat for her mother, he will give his flat to Emma and will move here. He will do something.

"Please," she says.

He looks at his watch: 23:11. He gets up, stands in front of her, then turns and leaves her bedsit. His chest is like fraying rope, holding.

—

The next morning he texts her but there is no response. His sitting room is a tip—his clothes, papers, books for an article he must write on capitalism and schizophrenia in the films of Darren Aronofsky. His bedroom is no better. He throws himself on his bed and watches the clouds through his skylight. No trace of spring here, nothing about babies, nothing about future, just him under a puffy cloud that cannot speak his name. He will give Emma this room and will convert the sitting room. He can sleep and work and work and sleep and make sure he has enough money to feed everyone, to provide the baby with clothes, to send it to school, to football practice or dance rehearsal. God help. He picks up the pad from his bedside table and writes words that come, one at a time, each on its own separate page. Margins. Manure. Manufacturing. Munchies. He hadn't meant to be in the *M*s. *Bring something incomprehensible into the world!* He tosses the notepad aside. In avant-garde poetry one strategy in the method of "chance operation" is to pick a routine that would inspire one line of poetry each day, over fourteen days, to produce a sonnet.

A time of day, a name, an association that is repeated fourteen times by taking the first line from an existing work of poetry and using it in the new sonnet, whatever way it comes out. He looks over at his shelf of books. A dare. But he has only an hour before he needs to leave for the university.

At his desk he checks e-mail, sees that there is one from Olivia thanking him for meeting with her father, asking him his thoughts on the project. He has no thoughts. Afterimage: Katrin's wet cheeks.

He writes back to Olivia, suggesting she come to talk to him later today. He holds tight to the pen in his imagination; the pen that was Katrin's.

—

The atrium is quiet. Robin takes the stairs slowly, calmly, to Richard's office. Richard's e-mail had a red exclamation tag: urgent. He slows down, one step, the next.

"Your student," Richard says when Robin in seated in the comfy chair beside the desk. Richard stole this chair from the staff lounge, Robin knows. "Bayo Esima . . . " he says. Oh God. "She's lodged a complaint with the Dean."

Fucking hell. "What?" he says, keeping his cool.

"Says your marking is biased, and that you are picking on her."

"Excuse me, but this is outrageous. Her essay was double marked. Miriam agreed with me; it had to fail."

"I know, and there's nothing to be done about it, and you're not in any trouble whatsoever, but I thought I'd let you know, before you see her again. There's definitely some instability there," he says. At least Richard has confirmed that it's not he who is losing it, but Richard is also holding something back, he can tell, as though there's ammunition now which could be used against him at any moment.

—

Robin stands at the lectern waiting for the lecture hall to fill up. No sign of Bayo. Not in the front row, nor in the back. Miles comes to the front of the room. Miles, his DJ demeanour in full force, holds up the phantom microphone in his hand, dips his chin and turns his nearly black eyes up towards Robin. "I missed the last lecture—and I don't understand the slides on the website. Can I book a tutorial?"

"Of course, of course. Let's talk after class."

"Great, Robin, thanks." Miles is all bones and bad skin. A decent bloke who is a relief to talk to when he comes to his office, even with the phantom mic. A decent bloke who wants to know things, to do well, to pull his weight. Robin checks his notes and starts the powerpoint.

"On the day the world ends, a bee circles a clover . . . " He pauses. This hasn't worked; he hasn't got their attention. He looks up and sees Bayo, snuck in by the back door. He has to pull this off, has to rehearse his presence and power so that next week's interview will not be a complete shambles. "The depiction of the process of art within another work of art—a film for our purposes—liberates the event for all time." He needs confidence, deliberateness. Afterimage: the look on Katrin's face when he said snake.

ED

Resistance? For some mad reason the light in this Great Court of the British Museum makes him feel a child again, playing games in the yard: Dog and de bone, One Two Tree Red Light, and Bun Down House. He is running wild and one of the mothers of his playmates is cussing them for pulling the sheets off the clothesline and telling them not to tek they eye and pass she. Crisscross lines from the skylight in the Great Court make a shadow on the wall of the reading room that catches them in all the clotheslines of all the childhoods of all the world. Resistance has no force here.

Ed hasn't been to the British Museum since before there was a Great Court. It is like morning in the Iwokrama Forest—without the screeches from howler monkeys, and except for the fact that it's still rass cold as far as he is concerned, never mind how others are saying it's spring. He will tell Olivia about the forest, about the trees as big as this reading room, about the cock-of-the-rock bird, the macaws and the electric-blue butterflies.

"You want to get a drink?" he asks her. He doesn't want to break the mood of this special outing—he has not thought to ask about Catherine, and Olivia has not talked much about her project, the reason they have come here in the first place. They have floated along beside one another, through China, India, Egypt, like real father and daughter on an adventure. But she has to leave by four o'clock, and there is so much to say. She nods and touches his arm to guide him to the café at the edge of Enlightenment.

"I like this," he says, when they are sitting with their tea. She smiles, the museum her idea after the nearly two weeks since she brought Robin to his office. She is different today, not electric, not treading-threading, not crease-up in her face, just smooth-like. Something has changed.

"I can't believe you never come here," she says.

"Not for a long time, no."

"Mum said you used to like museums and stuff."

"When did she say that?"

"A few days ago."

In her face is something like defiance more than resistance—a little smirk as if she has done something bad. She has talked to her mother about him, and from what he can tell it seems that whatever Catherine said has not fouled the image of Wood in the girl's eyes.

"And does she know you're here?"

She shakes her head, no. He rubs his hand across the top of his head in search of a part of himself. Catherine has said his name, Catherine has told their daughter about the museums that he liked to take her to when they first met. Catherine has probably mentioned how bad his learning was, how he didn't read books. He hopes she also told her how he taught himself and made himself better.

"We aren't telling each other things at the moment." Her thrumming has been given a poke and resumes while she sips her tea.

"Why not?"

She looks up into the canopy of the Great Court. "We had a giant row the other day because I want us to move," and she looks back into his face.

Jesus. "But you mustn't fight with your mum," he says. Feeble.

"It's fine, happens all the time. She thinks the world is against her."

Of course, this is what it feels like to her. Catherine was happy before she met him.

"Listen, darling," but this time it doesn't sound right. "Did she ever tell you about my brother, about Geoffrey?"

Olivia frowns. "Not that I can recall, no."

And so here goes. Olivia is too clever for the slowly-slowly approach. "My brother, Geoffrey, he is in jail for killing a man." It's not so bad. It doesn't sound so echoey in this hall as a man might think, and doesn't make him feel corrupt and small in his own skin; it just is. Olivia nods her head as if she has known all along.

The details come out at a good pace—how everyone suffered, especially his daddy, how his mummy still watches out for Geoffrey along the road every day, how Ed sends his brother letters and packages once in a while.

Olivia is quiet through the details, but suddenly she sits forward, then back, then forward again, her face a balloon. "She's insane!"

"Well, darling," he says, only after realizing she's talking about her mum.

"Did you do something too? Did you help him? Did you kill anyone?" She is angry at them both now.

"Of course not," he says, slumping back into his chair the way he slumped into the sand by the river, frightened now, as he was then, by what to do with death lying before him like that and a brother running, running, running in the distance.

"Well, that's crump . . . " Olivia says, but he doesn't know whether to agree or disagree. "Didn't she love you?"

Now here's a question. This one and what is a brother to do? Both of them buzzing like a marabunta, for the last eighteen years. Ed and Olivia look into the continental exhibits—Africa, China, South America—of each other's faces. The answers lie somewhere there. They stay silent.

"Will you ask her if she'll meet me?" he says, finally, taking strength now from her face, because he has to know once and for all—needs to know why.

"I will," Olivia says, with pepper in her tone.

They throw away the rubbish—tea bags, napkins, a part-eaten brownie, a piece of lemon cake—put their trays in the rack, and walk through the Great Court towards the exit, passing by an exhibition about the horse: in stone reliefs, gold and clay models, horse tack, paintings, trophies. The thoroughbreds that his daddy looked after at the racetrack in Berbice were Arabians, but skinny for so: hungry horses that raced too much, that foamed at the bit out of vexation. By the time they leave he is nearly used to not telling her the things he really wants her to know: how dredging for gold does make you hungry all the time, how the Mazaruni River drops like a waterfall, how black electric eels, piry, haimara, and baiara fish in the Mazaruni don't measure up to anything like the lau-lau, the half-ton fish which is the next thing down the scary scale from the kamundi snake. But even with all of that, the Mazaruni does bear diamonds like a pawpaw does bear seeds.

OLIVIA

At the buzz in her pocket, Olivia puts down her fork to slip the phone out and read the text, even though she knows this is mega rude at the dinner table. Jasmine watches her with a sly smile.

In media lect showed film of chomsky. You see it?

For two weeks he has been texting her and receiving one word answers in response. It's now a little game they have set up. He asks her questions—*what is name of your mother? where is your favorit place for dancing? do you think government will bring EMA back if there is rioting?*—and she writes back simple answers: *Catherine. Nowhere. Never.*

For two weeks she has eaten crisps, Maltesers, with granola bars to keep things balanced, while she stayed late at the library and did everything her studies demanded of her, and more, even taking Ed to the British Museum to check out death in other times, burials and rituals throughout civilizations. She felt more at ease with Ed. Having a brother who killed a man is surely not enough of a reason for Catherine to refuse to see him. She will find the right moment and find out the real story.

She is at Jasmine's for dinner because, turns out, Jasmine is not as religious as she thought she could be, on account of it meaning you can't be letting new boys put their hands in you up so far that you become their ventriloquist dummy.

"How is your granddad, then?" Jasmine's mother asks as she spoons a tiny bit of mash onto Olivia's plate and then a ton on Jasmine's like she wants her daughter to get fat. The sausages in the centre of the plate spin and slide left, making room.

He's the same old bastard he was the last time you asked a month ago, but Olivia doesn't need to say this, because Jasmine's mother is being polite and all Christian-like, all the while knowing that Granddad hates her and her Christian ways as much as he hates the rubbish bin thieves.

So, "Same old, you know," is all she says, and now that everyone's plate is full they can eat.

"Bless," Jasmine's mother says.

"Mum, I'll say grace and then Liv and me are going to take our plates up to my room, 'cos we have so much, like so much reading to do we don't have time to take a break, really, really," Jasmine says.

Her mother looks at her as though Jasmine has told her that the next man she's going to shag is the devil himself.

"Olivia, I'm sure you are very respectful of your mum," she says.

Olivia isn't fast enough with the right words to slip in here between mother and daughter. Jasmine's mother bows her head.

"Peak," Olivia says quietly, but only Jasmine hears, and in any case, Jasmine's mum wouldn't understand their language and how there're some really fucking sad times going on here. Jasmine's mum bows her head, not giving over that bit, at least, to her gnarly daughter. She mumbles a little prayer over the bounty they are about to receive. Amen.

—

"Liv, when a bloke says he wants to get to know you, means he doesn't fancy you," Jasmine says, with her head upside down, dangling off the bed, so that she really does look like a puppet. "Means maybe he wants help with his coursework but not that he wants anything romantic." Jasmine smacks her lips because she still thinks she's got big ones and her new boy is from Grenada and even if she did shag a dead dude she's back into trying to be West Indian. From this angle her mouth does look mega. "And you can get who you like, don't need no Arab who can't spell," she says.

"Shut the fuck up, Jaz. Shut your ugly lips." Olivia picks up her satchel and makes a show of putting books back into it so that she can walk out of this hellhole of a house where mother and daughter are God and the Devil playing draughts. Jasmine's upside-down eyes go wide and she sits up, then stands, furiously, like she has heard what Olivia was thinking, and shit, what's happening? Is Olivia in some freaky place now where absolutely nothing is kept inside?

"Right," she says as she too stands.

"What's the matter with you?" Jasmine says.

When Olivia is silent for too long, Jasmine walks over to her, holds her hand and pulls her down gently to sit with her on the floor. Olivia follows like it's a dance, and they sit face to face at the foot of the bed. Olivia can smell Jasmine's breath and it is sweet like she has been chewing on fruity Mentos. Jasmine touches Olivia's shoulder and the sweetness and the little tickle of fingers cause a lump to form in Olivia's throat. She can see why blokes get all gooey over Jasmine; she understands that now.

"Filigree . . . " she whispers.

"What?"

"Nothing. I'm sorry, Jaz, didn't mean to snap before."

"Your dad is just your dad, you know. It's mums who do all the work and mums who get left, even if she did turf him out—you found out why yet?"

Olivia shakes her head and then takes Jaz's hand off her shoulder and folds her fingers into Jasmine's—doughy, smooth. Jasmine's fingers rub hers, and there is calm.

"I'm a virgin," Olivia says softly.

Jasmine's fingers stop their rubbing and go all alert and stiff.

"Hoooo!" Jasmine's laugh is long and pigeon-like. She can't control herself now. "Ah! Whh . . . " she holds her tummy . . . "What, they making born-again virgins these days?" Jasmine manages to squeeze out in her fake West Indian accent. "You think Nasar wants a virgin, is that it? Some Arab shite you're riffing on?" Olivia's fingers fly-away-home from Jasmine's, who pigeon-laughs again and it must be her new boyfriend who has taught her this. Her new hench hubz who is a garage house DJ in some basement off Romford Road. What would Ed think about Jasmine?

"Flipping," slips out, but Jasmine doesn't react; she's still hooooing.

ED

The boombox speaker is scratchy; embarrassing, man. Borrowed from Ed's neighbour who plays music too loud, the sound is raunch but at least he has tried. Olivia is the only one in the pew of the Rippleside chapel, so for her alone he plays this hymn he found on a CD of greatest hymns in the check-out queue at Tesco. He tried out a few others—"Abide with Me," "There Is a Green Hill Far Away," "The Lord Is My Shepherd, I'll Not Want"—but this one has the best melody, and the words, well . . . *now I'm found.*

He sings along with the recording of "Amazing Grace." This feels good, and he sees in Olivia's face that it is. He is one step closer today to losing his job, now that the council has outlined what the new Safe and Sorrow office will look like, so he sings a little louder than he normally would. He is singing for Jonathan Henley. Jonathan was sixty-three years old, lived at 29 Fanshawe Crescent, alone in a garden flat where he'd been for twenty-two years. Notice of the death came on the day that Ed's foot ached so badly in the joints where his arthritis flared that it was difficult to put the foot down on the floor when he got out of bed. He cursed that pain, despised it so. By the time he reached work the pain had lessened, but he remembers it now, remembers it with gratitude as he sings for Jonathan who has no pain. The man's flat from the outside looked fine enough, but inside—oh man. The place was littered with newspapers as though Jonathan had kept every edition of the *Times,* the *Sunday Times,* the *Times Literary Supplement*—a whole lotta *times* for Jon—that he'd read since he moved in. The paint was peeling off walls and the banister; books filled their cases and lay piled high on the floors. The man had some fine learning. According to the neighbour who stood at the door while Ed did his work, Jonathan's learning was the thing that kept him apart from his neighbours, kept him to himself. "A friendly enough man," said the woman whose alluvial voice gave Ed goosebumps, "but we always thought he didn't like to talk, only liked to think, so we didn't really try—when he was away we assumed it was with family. How wrong we can be sometimes." The woman was in her fifties and trim, and she looked to him for more talk, but Ed silently noted the pain in his foot, thanked her, and left with plans to return with the removals team. Why for rass' sake was he always running away? He's seen a few women over the years, had sex if he could get it, but whenever there's a woman who seems like she could actually know him: not a chance. Surely Catherine is waiting for him to come home.

Jonathan Henley will be buried, not cremated, so Ed has had to arrange the pallbearers and hearse to drive the few yards to the communal grave—a half dozen in this one already. He and Olivia follow the hearse towards the far east corner of Rippleside Cemetery. Olivia is quiet, contemplating, and Ed is hush-hush in the spell of this young woman.

The coffin is lowered, the priest says his words of dust, of ashes, and just like that it starts to rain.

"Jonathan might like this," Olivia says.

Ed looks at his puzzle of a daughter. "Why do you say that?"

"I don't know, you never know—some people like rain." And he sees now. She doesn't care what it is that they know about Jonathan, as long as they have wondered, for even one moment, what he might have been like.

And the man with his face in the Mazaruni River, his arms splayed, and his legs floating like dry branches? The least Ed could have done was stop long enough to wonder.

At the A13, after the funeral, Olivia is calm, and even though there is so much they will never get back, there is something better between them, the way intentions are more solid than dreams.

"And the job?" Olivia asks after their tea has arrived.

He doesn't want to worry her, but a shake of his head has her bobbing again. "It's fine, fine . . . I know how to find work," he says to reassure her.

"You need to invite them to one of these—I'll talk to Robin again," she says, and her voice is macaw-pitch, her breath quick.

He looks up at her. "You think I'm a joke, right?"

"What? No . . . " And she sits forward in the brown vinyl chair. A clang comes from the kitchen. Ed listens for the comforting bright hiss of something frying, but he can't hear a sound.

"I think it's time you and Catherine talked," Olivia says. This is not what he's been angling for; still, his shoulders rise.

"Is that what she wants?" Ed says, trying to shush the hope from his voice.

"Yeah," she says, and oh man, oh man.

"Good-good. That's good," says Ed.

"I will set that up then."

And now it is he who is bobbing, and the sounds of the A13 turn buzzy, and it's all he can do not to stand up and pull her across the table to him. Silly rasshole. He calms himself.

"Well," he says.

She gathers up the things around her, puts them in her satchel.

KATRIN

Each of Robin's voicemail messages tastes like sand. She cannot understand how this is so, because she has never experienced the taste of words before now. From working at Epicure her taste has become more sensitive. She knows the taste of every ingredient in the chocolate hazelnut ganache. And she knows how they make gianduja curls for the top.

In Robin's message he tells her that they must talk, that he loves her, that they will find a way to help her mother. Maybe his colleague will let Beata stay in her home for very little, or in exchange for some housework because his colleague's children have grown up and many rooms have been left free. Perhaps there will be room for both Beata and Katrin. There are arrangements that can be made. But in the days since she last saw him, her back turned towards the door as he left, her eyes on the dirty dishes from their dinner in the sink, she has not heard what she has wanted in his voice. There is no sound of changing his mind about Emma in his voice.

She is so stupid.

"Katrin, you are dreaming," Alejandro says over her shoulder. "You must make coffee while you dream." Epicure is busy, but she cannot concentrate or remember the orders or make enough coffee.

"Al, I am tired, will you take over for me, just a minute?"

Alejandro stares at her like she has sworn at him. "Tired?" His face has no sympathy. "Maybe you should sleep not shag on the nights before work." He uses his elbow to push her a little to the side, and he opens a bag of espresso. Katrin hates him. But just for one minute until she remembers that he is on her side.

"I'm very sorry," she says and takes the bag from him and continues her job. "I'm sorry." She looks at him and nods, to make certain he believes her. He leaves the counter to serve a customer.

Not all landlords will stop two people living in a bedsit. If she takes the flat in Walthamstow she will need another job along with Epicure to pay the rent. Or her mother must find a job as soon as she arrives. If they move even farther away from the centre the travel will be expensive and she will still need more money. She could take more work from Claire. She could work at the new Epicure in Soho. Katrin washes her hands. The buzz against her thigh tells her there is a text message. She has forgotten to leave her phone in the back room with her coat. She reaches into her pocket.

You don't have to respond, but I wanted you to know I'm thinking about you constantly, and that I am holding you in my heart.

No, don't hold me in your heart, Katrin wants to tell him. Don't think about me. She reads the message again and wonders why he does not say that he will tell Emma that he loves Katrin who will be living with him. It is because Emma demands to be primary with the father of her child, and Katrin has for a long time—with her father, mother, lovers, Ania—been secondary in her own life. This thought brings the weight of a boulder onto her chest.

"For fuck's sake, this is basic . . . you are not on a break, we are busy. What are you playing at?" Claire's voice has made the boulder move from chest to stomach. Claire has money in her hands. Rolls of notes and bags of coins that she is bringing to the till where she has stopped to find Katrin staring at her phone. Katrin who has no words again. This has all been coming. All the hours of working with Claire have been coming to this when she will feel the smallest she has felt in her life and it will be her own fault. "Al is taking all the tables; you are checking your phone—is there any part of this picture that I shouldn't fire your arse over?"

Katrin's eyes fall closed for only one second but she would like to keep them closed. She turns to face Claire. "I'm having trouble now. It will not last; it is just for now," she tells her.

Claire shakes her head and turns towards the cash register. She pours the coins from the bag. She flips open the trap for the notes and fills tens and twenties in the slots. Her face does not change. Katrin has stood up to the snake and there is a small twinge of pleasure in her chest. She is learning how to be in England.

—

Robin has sent two more texts by the time she wakes the next day. These make her weak because he has said things that only they know the meaning of. He has repeated their secrets and their words of love in the night and the words of songs they have sung together. These texts are not helping. They confuse how she feels with what she must do. She must take the flat in Walthamstow today and she must ask Claire for hours at Epicure Soho. And she must not think in the second person. She must think with I in every thought. I have remembered to do everything for this week, she says to herself, and there is toilet paper, dish soap and milk in the fridge.

It is grey but warm outside. It will be Easter soon. On the 38 bus there are no schoolchildren today. Next week will be the days of Crucifixion and Resurrection. Beata will be on her knees at church and not thinking about London, so that is good. Beata loves the Holy St. Mary church in Gdansk as much as she loves her daughter, so this week Mary will look after her.

"It will be dead today," Alejandro says when Katrin arrives at Epicure. Claire is not yet in, and this feels like a bad omen.

"There are reasons to thank Christ," Katrin says and he gives her a thumb up. She loves Alejandro when they are like this. "And maybe Claire is one of the dead," she adds but feels guilty; she doesn't mean this.

"She's at the Soho branch. She'll be in later."

The landlord from Walthamstow needs to know by noon if she will take his tiny flat for seventy pounds more per week than she is paying now. Katrin's phone is in the back room and Claire is not. The regular cappuccino-and-Danish man is in the front seat; a young mother and her daughter have ordered tea and hot chocolate from Alejandro. This is her chance. She goes to the back room.

Her handbag is not organized. This is the next thing that needs attention. Her phone is difficult to find at the bottom of it. She sees another text from Robin: *Please don't treat me like this.* This stabs her heart. She doesn't mean to hurt him. She will call him on her break. The landlord's number is her last dialled so she will call him now.

"Katrin." Claire's voice is over Katrin's shoulder and the blood is cold in Katrin's arms. She turns around to see that Claire has no snake in her throat. Claire does not look angry. Claire looks like she is happy, and this is the worst look so far that Katrin has seen.

"I thought you were in Soho," she says.

"And so you could piss around."

No, she wants to say, no, please.

"Please get back to work," Claire says, and the quiet calm tone makes the flesh inside Katrin's cheek feel like it has been bitten.

ROBIN

At least there's no sun today, despite the warm weather. Pathetic fallacy. And if it rains, so much the better. A jet flies low above and the noise is comforting. Kurosawa would use the noise and the pending rain. He would begin this scene with a long, wide-angled exposition—water, concrete, a lid of clouds—and then move to the contracted theatrical space to focus on the unknown woman. Robin looks around him, and, of course, there she is. Bayo is sitting at her spot behind the library, writing furiously in a notebook. Her hair has come undone from its clips and some of her extensions hang loose from her head as though she's been clawed at. He makes himself small, afraid that movement will alert her. Has he begun to fail his most needy students, now? Who else has Bayo complained to? Formaldehyde. Timber. Mannequin. Puncture. Words that are nowhere near a poem. He misses Katrin so much he can barely breathe.

Bayo is mad; he is not. God, surely not. He has had no word from Katrin in four days. One more hour like this, this clawing from inside and he and Bayo might as well make a life of it together.

He takes out his phone and checks it again. Maybe the texts haven't gone through. They don't; the network fucks up.

Are you okay? Please ring me.

He sends it. He could ring her if he wanted. So, why doesn't he? Nothing is fixed yet; he doesn't want to mislead her.

Firefly. Butter. Pig's breath.

He dials. "Hi, hi. How are you doing? Just checking in," he says to Emma's voice on the other end of the line. "I thought maybe we should have dinner."

—

From behind, Emma is sexy, her hips, the curve of her shoulder: great proportions. The mother of his child. A surge of hope. He can do this. Maybe they can be a family. He watches Emma walk around his flat as though she's never been before, and a tinge of resentment surfaces when she stands at his bedroom door, sizing it up, wondering where the cot will go, where her clothes will go—those heavy hiking boots she wears when she trudges across the Lizard Peninsula to Kynance Cove, where just above the rocks at the highest point the choughs fledge and fly.

"I've made dinner," he says and when she turns around he goes cold. She's cross, put off; he clearly doesn't have enough space. "Something healthy," he says.

The chicken stir-fry over rice is his best meal. Emma sits down. Afterimage: Katrin laughing until she can't stand up, tears rolling, when he'd tried to do a Polish accent and it came out Indian.

"I'd forgotten that you're a good cook," Emma says.

"You're much better," he says. He can do this. They are good to one another, always polite, always friends.

"What will you do for Easter?" she asks. She wants him to go with her to Cornwall, maybe to his parents', to start this little family thing off with a good holiday.

"Don't know. Lots to think about. You?" There's a silence as Emma touches her ear.

"I'm sorry," she says. She has blue eyes that have always looked bigger than they really are, because her head is small, her black hair a frame. Audrey Tatou. Emma is a broad, stocky Amélie.

"I don't know what you're sorry for, but you don't need to be," he says. He can do this. His mother and father talk like this. His mother and father have been married for almost forty years.

"It's a lot of pressure on you, I know." See, she's kind. "But it's an adventure." This is not helpful. He doesn't want an adventure with her.

"My interview is day after tomorrow," he says because he wants her to know that if he doesn't get the job they're done for—they won't even be able to afford this place let alone a place for when she moves out. And what about her work? Will she go back to being a dental hygienist? Wasn't that what she was going to do in Truro before all this happened? Pays well. Recession-proof. People's teeth are always dirty.

"You're not good at interviews, are you," she says. And this is how the forty years will go?

—

He hugs her goodnight at his door and tells her that it was great to see her, that they are doing well, that this is all going to be fine. And when he closes the door his stomach hurts so badly that he has to sit straight down on the floor. He remembers the chance-operation poetic strategy. He will rise from the floor only when his clock says 23:11.

FRANCINE

When people say heads will roll, they don't really mean that. What they mean is heads will drop. Eyes will dart to the floor as you pass your colleagues in the corridor. Doors will stay closed during lunchtime breaks as everyone decides to eat at their desks. There will be no water-cooler chatter. Francine is sure something is going down today.

She walks past Lawrence's office but stops, turns and knocks on his door.

"Hi," she says, as she opens it without waiting for an invitation.

"Hi." Wary; cold, even.

"Just saying hi, really."

"Great."

"Is there something going on today?" She had vowed never to do this again, didn't want him to have anything to hold over her.

His face suggests that he knows she's breaking her own vow.

"No, not particularly, not today, but next week, before Easter break," he says and seems nearly to smile, which makes her feel sick.

"Okay then, thanks—sorry to bother you," she says, and closes the door.

The hallway smells of fear. She returns to her office and closes her door, clicks on Guardian Soulmates. She types in ReallyYouandMe, and her password: Isoam.

CharlesNW8 has sent her a message:

I like your cheeks. They look like they hold a lot of love. Have a look at mine and let's meet up.

You're a fatface but so am I is what this message is really saying, but when she checks Charles's profile she's shocked. He's young-looking, maybe in his thirties, but his profile says forty-five. Handsome, with a smile that reminds her of John Clarke's, but a little less crooked.

This is a ruse. If this is really Charles then there's something wrong with him, or he's cheating and has put up an old photo. She wants to punch that face.

She picks up the phone and dials.

"It's me," is all she says, not even wondering if Patricia will recognize her voice. "Want to see a movie?"

—

"I'm pretty sure I'm going to be made redundant," Francine says, within seconds of Patricia arriving.

"What? How do you know that?" She puts a hand on Francine's arm. Francine doesn't move from under it, but feels queasy.

She turns and starts to walk towards the Prince Charles Cinema. The sky is big and boozy, the moon like a fat, squat egg over the buildings in Soho. Patricia catches up to her and keeps looking over, examining Francine's face.

As they sit in the cinema Francine regrets that she's chosen the film this time, and that it's a silent film, the one she missed after it won an Oscar. She's nervous about breathing too loudly. The opera was at least something to hide behind.

"You know, Francine," Patricia says. Francine turns towards her and feels a warmth in Patricia's croissant breath.

"There's a veil . . . "

A veil? She looks up at the curtain over the screen that is parting. Yep, guess that could be a veil, bit thick . . .

" . . . between us and death, most of the time."

Oh. She feels like burping, but she holds it back because Patricia's trying to say something and how is it that this woman is both far away and close up at the same time? Too far. Too close.

"But when we witness it, or when someone we love dies . . . "

It's like Patricia is on the inside of her brain and not beside her in this cinema where the lights go down and the screen comes alive like daybreak.

" . . . that veil drops away . . . and we see it, and it's . . . " Music starts. Strings. Horns. "Frightening," Patricia whispers the last word.

Francine tries not to breathe too loudly.

—

The film has had its light-hearted effect. She stays silent, but she is dancing inside like the actors in the last scene, and she's making silent plans to lose weight and to dance on the outside too. This is good. And here is Patricia beside her on the tube, just letting her sit with the silence.

"What you said before the film," Francine says, finally. Patricia turns towards her. "About the veil."

Patricia nods.

"That's for kids . . . that's the kind of thing you say to a child."

"Well—" Patricia starts.

"It is, and I get you, sure, but it's not true. Not now. I know, I feel it. There's no veil, and there never will be again." There's relief, and nothing else to say.

Patricia looks around the tube carriage, back at Francine and gives her a smile that Francine doesn't get the meaning of.

"The film was good," Francine says.

"Yes, it really was. Charming."

"I never get it when English people say charming, if they mean it was kind of creepy or not. In the States charming isn't always a good thing."

"It's a good thing," Patricia says. "You're charming too."

Francine squirms. "Then I understand the word even less now," she says.

COLD BLUE STEEL

OLIVIA

"Please," slips from Olivia's lips, but Catherine is still asleep. Olivia slides her legs alongside her mother's and feels how hot Catherine's skin is. Her mother is hot a lot these days—throws the duvet off violently in the morning, tugs off jumpers and scarves like they are strangling her. Catherine won't admit that it's the menopause, and Olivia sometimes feels embarrassed watching the sweat pour down her mother's forehead, but there's no doubt there's something going on. "I don't want the summer to come," Catherine said to her last week, "The summer will kill me." But Olivia doesn't want the summer for completely different reasons: her dissertation project will have to be finished before that; she will still be a virgin; and, worse, she will have had the conversation she's about to tackle with her sweating mum. "Mistakes," she whispers, but it is intentional. "Mistakes, Mum . . . everybody makes 'em." She presses her face into her mother's back and rubs her cheek along the moist skin, smelling Catherine's tanginess and stale Calvin Klein, Obsession. "Mum," she says again, into the skin, "Mum," and hears the catch in her own throat.

Catherine turns over gently. "Baby, what is it?"

"I've found my dad." Right.

Catherine's jolting shoulder is almost like a punch to Olivia's jaw. "Ow," she says, and lifts her head. "Ow!"

Catherine sits up and takes Olivia's head in her hands. "Sorry, baby, sorry . . . What are you talking about?"

Olivia rubs her chin, and bloody hell she could just haul off on one at Catherine right now, but she has to handle this carefully; she can't blow it.

"Wood. I've met him; we've met. Again." She looks into Catherine's face to see the effect.

"Where?"

"At the council office, where he works."

"And what were you doing there?"

She should have rehearsed this, should have made him the knight coming to the rescue, should have known her mother would need it to be mighty-like.

"My project. I was doing research; he was there." Simple.

"You remembered him?" Catherine is sitting up straight now, the duvet pulled up around her like she's suddenly cold.

"Not exactly," Olivia says and takes hold of the duvet where Catherine is clutching it and slides closer, slipping down beneath the cover, her head resting on Catherine's forearm. "I figured it out."

Olivia runs her tongue along the roof of her mouth and feels the canker where she burned herself on a microwaved pizza pocket. She uses her tongue to count the teeth along the upper row and to steady her breathing. There's no talking about Wood. No seeing, no hearing from. She's broken all the rules. She waits inside their breath, which is now in tandem. Catherine's skin is not powdery now, but more like steel, hardened but hot, like the hot-water pipe. "Mummy," she says to soften things, but nothing yields in Catherine's adamant arm.

"What have you done?" Catherine says.

Olivia sits up. "I haven't done anything. We talk, he's helping me with my project—"

"He's doing what?"

"My research . . . he's giving me information." But it's hot as shite under this duvet and Olivia kicks it off now. "We talk. And he wants to meet up with you."

Catherine leaps out of bed and puts on the blue Scottie-dog dressing gown that the twelve-year-old Olivia gave her for Christmas, which she still wears, faithfully, every day.

"You don't know what you've got yourself into," Catherine says.

"I do so."

"No, you don't . . . you really don't. Why didn't you tell me about this before?"

Olivia gets up and is standing beside Catherine, but Catherine doesn't want to be standing at all; she wants to be getting out of here. She closes the bedroom door so that there's no chance her mother will leave.

"I knew you had your shite with it all, that's why," Olivia says. Catherine begins to pace.

"You just have no right—"

"Excuse me?" Now it's so fucking hot in here. Olivia's voice makes Catherine stand still. "*You* have no right to keep me from him." Olivia is amazed by her own swagging. "For years you lied to me; you told me you didn't know where he was—"

"I didn't!"

"But you made it sound like he was in Afghanistan or some shite like that, not like he was just around the fucking corner, Catherine."

Her tongue goes back to her teeth, this time the bottom row: three, four, five. Catherine's green Kat Slater eyes get smaller as her breath gets quicker, and she's like a kettle on boil; she takes off her fleecy Scottie-dog dressing gown and it falls to the floor, leaving her all fleshy in her nightie.

"Edward is not your dad," Catherine says.

Olivia laughs because this is what Catherine has been trying to get at for all these years, this fact that if a dad is a dad he would actually be there, raising you, and not off somewhere else with maybe a whole other family or maybe not even knowing that every morning you wake up and it hurts in your stomach because he's gone. Catherine has been trying to drive this point home, gently, since Olivia was thirteen, but it's not going to work now. There is biology. End of.

"Catherine, all your shite about a man not being a father if he's not around—what, like Granddad is such a shining example?"

"You're not his . . . you're someone else's." Catherine's eyes are wide now, gone all glassy-like.

And it takes a few more taps of the teeth with her tongue before Olivia actually hears what it was that Catherine said. Like there is a lip-synch problem in this movie and the sound comes after the movement of the mouth. Catherine steps closer to Olivia and puts her arms around her. And everything is there in her skin. Not powdery. No longer hot. There's only one sensation, like cold blue steel.

ROBIN

He arrives at the door of Epicure and sees her standing at the counter beside Alejandro as though in an afterglow—of sex, or jokes, or just spring air. He hesitates, then enters; Katrin sees him, is jolted out of her reverie, rushes towards him.

"I can't talk now," she says, blocking his way, and a bolt of shame passes through him. "I'm sorry," she says. "Just not now." Oh God, what a fool he is.

"When?" Now she will pity him; he will see it on her face.

"Come," she says and takes his arm.

Her hand. Her hair. The perfect rhythm of the way they walk beside one another. She tugs him harder, then moves slightly ahead.

"I love you," she says. But she's crying. He pulls her sleeve.

"And I love you," he says, but she doesn't stop. It hasn't been enough to make her stop, and he scrambles to find what will be. "Where are we going?"

She keeps walking quickly, but slows in front of a furniture shop. She stops to stare through the glass. Eames chairs, Cornell desks, Mondrian coffee tables. This is the kind of home he'd make for her. How did he get to this place where furniture tortures him?

"What will you do?"

He doesn't understand. He follows her eyes to a white Eames chair. Then he realizes.

"I can't do anything. Not yet. I promise I will, though, after the baby is born."

Katrin moves off from the shop window to the next one. Within her, though, she's not budging. Her deliberateness is set in gear. The thing you love someone for is the same thing that will kill you in the end. The next shop has clothing. He wants furniture: a loft; he will build her a loft in his flat. This will work, if he gets the job. When the baby . . .

"You can't do anything yet," she says and nods. "You tell me when you can," and thank God, she has given him some reprieve. There is possibility here, even if he knows of no way to manage it. Possibility and madness are not the same.

KATRIN

Epicure is quiet, the sun has come out, and something has changed today in London. The feeling of wanting Robin is in her chest, her stomach, her arms, her legs, and between them. There is not a part of her that does not miss him. The day is too slow. She will apologize for hurting him with her silence.

"Claire says we can clean the freezer because it is so slow today." Alejandro has come out from the back room and he stands beside her at the counter. Like her he does not want to do this work. They stare out into the sunlight and Katrin notices particles darting between them. She wants to tell him how frightened she is about Claire's calm face in the last two days, and how she has lost the flat in Walthamstow, but she does not want to pierce this moment.

But suddenly it is pierced, and he is there.

"I can't talk now," she says to Robin and hurries to the door of the shop to stop him from coming in. His smile disappears. "I'm sorry. Just not now."

"When?" His face looks like she has hit him.

She cannot stop her throat from being tight, her tears from rolling. "Come," she says, and she leaves the shop and takes his arm to pull him with her. "I love you," she says beneath the rolling tears. And she is stupid for letting him see that she is weak.

"And I love you," Robin says, and tries to stop her from walking fast, but she keeps going. "Where are we going?"

She does not have a destination.

They pass the furniture shop with a chair that is one piece of moulded fibreglass, the arms curving out from the seat like wings of a gull. She has wished she could buy this chair for months, but now this wish is pointless.

"What will you do?" she asks.

He looks puzzled for a moment. "I can't do anything. Not yet. I promise I will, though, after the baby is born."

She stops in front of the next shop that has shoes and vintage clothing. There is a hat that has embroidery that would make it camouflage among butterflies. It is difficult to breathe now on Upper Street. It is difficult to breath anywhere in this England. There is nothing here that makes her free.

"You can't do anything, yet," she says, nodding, and she hears how so quickly she has forgotten to live in the first person. "You will tell me when you can," she adds, but she is really saying, I was wrong. She has been doing English all wrong.

She turns around and heads back to Epicure. Robin follows her, but at the door she tells him he cannot enter or she will be in trouble. "Later," she tells him. But as soon as she walks through the door and sees Claire she knows about where she will be later. Orange blossom marmalade, bittersweet chocolate flurries, sweetened cream-cheese frosting—these she knows in the present participle: spreading, stirring, pouring, baking, working. The verbs are in the continuous form, but too they are verbs of movement and position. Katrin sees in Claire's face what she must do. She walks to the back room, collects her coat and bag and makes a signal to Alejandro that she will call him. She is steady as she walks through the coffee shop and out the door.

She is Katrin from Gdansk again, because to be from nowhere is impossible. "I" . . . she says, as she walks to the 38 bus, "I," to remind herself that this is correct . . . I am coming home, *mamunia.* I will not make you worry.

FRANCINE

The next time Francine is outside of Ryan's house it's 7 p.m. and darkness is more than an hour away, spring having come, the clocks moved forward, making the day feel like it's got some heft.

"Hey." She waves out of the open window of her car. "Hey." More friendly the second time. Spring. She's wary of feeling happy just yet.

Francine and Ryan drive with the windows down.

"Rajit gets sentenced soon . . . Thursday—they might . . . "

"They might?" She looks over, fast and stern. This is not the way a young man should be thinking. A young man should have more resilience than Ryan has been showing in wanting another man to suffer. Thursday is also when she'll know if she's sacked or not.

"Then we'll see," Ryan says.

"See what?"

He puts his hood up, like on a colder day. "Just see . . . " Anger like mud. She sits back and concentrates on the road.

"So, nearly finished your term? An Easter break coming . . . " she says as she decides to take a different route. She heads towards Finchley Road.

"Yep, yep." He's nodding inside his hoodie. "Where are we going?"

"No idea," she says but is thinking of maybe driving up and around Hampstead Heath. She wants the smell of spring.

"What, we on a date now?"

She laughs.

He smiles.

She would never have made a kid as good as Ryan.

OLIVIA

A coat, some makeup, a twenty-quid note. She rushes down the stairs with everything she needs, and what she needs most is to get out of here. The television is blaring with *Deal or No Deal* and there is TV drum rolling and TV telephone ringing and her head is going to bust open if she has to hear another second of it.

"Livi!" Eric shouts from the sitting room. Christ no. She pokes her head in the door of the sitting room. The contestant has said "No deal," and there's loud applause.

"Idiot!" Granddad says to the contestant.

"Which way you headed?" Eric asks her.

Way far away, but she merely shrugs.

"Pick us up a Chinese for tea, will ya? Dad . . . give her dosh," Eric says. And there's a one-, two-, three-second wait while Noel Edmonds says we'll find out after this break, and Olivia turns, runs back up the stairs and fetches her satchel. Running back down the stairs she's not-soon-enough out of there.

—

"I want to party," she says, and Jaz's face lights up like Olivia is her very own brand new baby.

"Well-sick!" Jasmine squeals and launches into how her Grenada DJ hubz is doing a gig in that basement on Romford Road and they will go there tonight. Jaz is talking at a wicked speed and asking her what they should wear but Olivia doesn't want to talk, or think, for fuck's sake. She just wants to be out.

Jasmine goes out to pick up things she says she needs, and Olivia circles Jasmine's bed for nearly an hour before it takes her down, and she falls asleep there. Two hours later when Jaz returns she can't remember where she is or why, but she's told that it's late enough to start getting ready.

She puts makeup around her eyes, following the outline of her lids with charcoal liner, slowly, trying not to poke herself in the eye, 'cause she's not used to this shite that most girls do on a daily basis. But this shading, this bandit mask, feels right because: fuck.

"You look hot," Jaz says when Olivia appears in the hallway ready to go, and Olivia wants to scratch Jasmine's eyes out. "Here . . . " Jaz adds, and hands Olivia a small white capsule. Oh.

"Meow meow," Jaz says, "my treat."

Olivia knows that Jaz is new to this, that she tried "MDMA-zing" once last year which made her in love with her media studies buddies for a whole week but that Mcat is cheap and nearly the same and easy as shite to get and why not. Why not?

"Not sure," Olivia says, but takes the pill and slips it into her coat pocket. "Let's get going." Her body is already humming, thumping, twitching, and she needs to dance.

—

The dubstep is in her chest. And she is strapped up like a suicide bomber with this bass beat between her breasts. She bounces on the spot, then moves through the bodies. Jaz is chomping on her teeth like there's something she should be eating but can't find, and she smells like fish. Jas is in meow-meow heaven and has her hands all over the boy wearing the wife-beater who smells less like fish and more like a dead whale. Olivia has the meow meow in her hand and could take it now if she wanted, could take it and touch the dead whale, touch herself, touch the sky, because there's nowhere else to touch when everything is a lie.

"Errybody hands up, errybody hands up . . . "

She does as she's told by the thumping singer in the speakers, fisting her right hand with the meow meow, the left hand open like a hallelujah and errybody hands up, errybody hands up, she bops to the centre of the dance floor.

An arm comes from behind her and wraps around her waist. The whale smell comes too, and she looks over her shoulder, around his smooth sculpted arm, to where Jaz is standing, waving, all gift-giving and full of promises, having sent the cornrows dude in the wife-beater over to her.

The bomb strapped to Olivia's chest beats harder as the music gets louder, speeds up, and *jump, jump ya, jump, come on na*, and the whale dude has his other hand on her arse and it's like he's propping her up from tummy to bum, like he's trying to hold her all in, the way she's doing too, so she lets go a little and they jump like they are told to, and then move over to the wall, and he holds her in some more and then puts her back to the wall, and she opens her eyes and his face is right there, all sweaty and lippy, his bulgy eyes closed, his hands moving over her hips and bum now, but her hands are still in the air, one clutching the meow meow, so she lowers this one and opens her palm, pokes his shoulder with her fingers, his eyes open and move fast-like to the capsule in her hand, and his smile is bright white, and the bomb at her chest ticks louder while she fingers the capsule and holds it up, knocks on his big white teeth to be let into the tongue that is as dark as a plum, a thick-wide disc that laps up the capsule like a starving mollusc, and while he's swallowing he is pressing his chest into hers and moving his hands between her legs and farther up, up, his hand, just there, is still, like the second before a bomb goes off, then she moves, just an inch forward, which says sure, yes, and he goes to the top of her jeans and down with his whole big hand, flicking away the top of her pants and passing through the bush, all matted with sweat, and then his finger makes a j and up he goes, and the other one too, both way up and she is barely breathing, and now that he has swallowed the pill the purple tongue presses her lips and she opens up and the mollusc dives in, but it does not taste good, does not feel good, but the breathing and the fingers and the oh way up higher in her than is possible and there's nowhere she can go now, nowhere that isn't into the dynamite strapped to her chest. . . .

But still no.

Olivia turns her head, shoving the whale dude's mouth out of the way. She pushes on his chest and grabs his arm, lifting with all her might to drag his hand out of her pants. He is strong, doesn't let her, but she pushes him, lifts her knee and presses him back with it. He takes his hand back, smells his fingers, licks them, and she ducks under his arm and hauls her arse out of the basement without her coat, into the iron-orange wind on Romford Road.

—

When she opens her eyes the next morning to the sound of a knock, she looks to her left and she is in the bed alone. Jasmine isn't home. When Jasmine's mum opens the door she closes her eyes again and deep-breathes so that she won't have to tell her that she has no fucking idea where her daughter is. The door closes with a creak, or maybe a cry.

She checks her phone. There are text messages, but none from Jasmine.

Again you disappear. SU demonstration Fri. Will you meet me? *Nasar*

There's a fire in her face and she wants to aim it at him and set him and everyone else alight so that they burn, burn, burn. The whole world should fuck off right about now.

Stop contacting me. I will never meet you. Leave me alone.

That ought to do it.

A similar one goes to her mother who is oh so worried she doesn't know what to do. Well, should have thought about what to do at the beginning of all the fucking lies.

Jaz, where the fuck are you? Can I live at yours for a while?

She throws her phone to the bottom of the bed and curls up under the duvet that is not hers, in the bed that is not hers, in the house with a mother that is not hers, in the city where she is nothing.

When she wakes up again Jasmine is sleeping beside her, smelling from Mcat, bloody hell, like Billingsgate market. She gets up, puts on Unkle's "Sunday Song," loud as shite because she knows Jasmine won't hear it and that her mum will be at church.

She stands at the foot of Jasmine's bed and feels that thing like dynamite in her chest again, as Unkle sing *You can be so imaginary, nobody knows or seems to see, I've reason enough to keep from you, the consequences I can't undo.*

It's one of those moments when someone like Robin would say she has choices, would tell her she could make something of it or she could let it all take her down. Fuck, she could burn them all, him too.

The next tune is "Only the Lonely." Dub version. She rushes to the iPod deck and switches off the player. There's nothing to be done. She picks up her satchel and heads out, with a remaining shred of gratitude for the university library that is open 24/7.

FRANCINE

It's like being in a damn projector, that's it. As the tube leaves
Baker Street station, she nearly has it, is on the brink of figuring
it out—this thing that is going on with the smells, with the veins
and bones behind people's skin: the suited guy's hand on the top
rail; the skinny leather-pants woman shaking her foot up and
down and around as she chews gum; the seventy-year-old
woman that no one has given their seat to, Francine included,
because she feels fat and pinned sitting, as the carriage lurches
along the Bakerloo line towards home. This way of seeing things
is like being the projector itself, like life has a movie and she's
showing it. All these people and their bodies: celluloid. And
when life checks out, when it clicks off, it stays in other places,
like in her hand, like in her finger. Like in her jaw. Sayonara!

She doesn't leave the tube at her normal stop. She stays to
watch a woman with a small makeup mirror putting on her mas-
cara, and she wonders how the woman hasn't poked herself in the
eye. The woman stops, having found a zit, which she squeezes, and
Francine will never get over the things people do on the tube not
knowing or caring if anyone watches. Two more stops and
Francine gets off at Willesden Junction. Outside she walks quickly

because she knows there is a window between six and seven that might work: Rajit's wife will be busy making supper, and Rajit will answer the door, will talk to her, and she will . . . what?

—

Flowers—big puffy hydrangea. Blue flowers are only a little bit ridiculous. They say something strong. She holds these behind her back.

"What do you want with us?" Rajit's wife says in the doorway, the door wide open, not as an invitation, more like a gesture of defeat: take all of this now; you want it too? Francine looks through to the kitchen and sees Rajit at the stove. She got this all wrong.

"I just wanted to give you my support," she says but holds the flowers by her side, tilted down to the steps; blue is ridiculous.

"Support? You are a funny lady," Rajit's wife says. "You want to support us. He has no licence to go to his job every day. You will support us now?" She doesn't quite laugh but very nearly. Francine sees Rajit put down a large ladle. He turns and shuffles towards the front door. He looks old, his hair matted, and still in his pyjamas like a ward patient.

"Who is this?" he asks his wife.

"She came before, remember?" his wife says.

Francine has never seen a less dangerous-looking man.

"I was there," she says.

Rajit looks accused, not at all what she meant.

"I was right behind you." What an idiot. Rajit starts to turn and walk away. Mrs. Mahadeo comes closer like she's going to hit her.

"He's a very proud man, Miss," Rajit's wife whispers as she bends towards her. The woman's thin shoulder touches hers, and

Francine wants to have been more proud in her life. *Don't ever spit, baby.* Her mother had been proud, but it has bypassed her.

"I know the sentencing is soon—Thursday, right?" she says, and Rajit turns back towards her. "I just wanted to wish you . . . " What is it that you wish a guy who might go to jail? " . . . fairness." But that's as stupid as the blue flowers.

Rajit stares at her and in his stare she sees legs, arms, a crushed face, a broken helmet: the recurring content of his thoughts—and these comfort her for being like her own, and for a split second they dissolve together in the transporter, beamed up by Scotty.

"I'm sorry," she says and turns, only hoping that they don't despise her.

ROBIN

There are three on the hiring panel; he sits before them like a felon in front of a parole board: the dean, the head of health sciences as the external, and his line manager, Richard, who looks sheepish. Has he told them about the Bayo business, and will they take into account her complaint? To have passed her because she has paid fees, because she will carry debt, because she is a young person who needs to be encouraged: is this what the world demands of him now?

"Robin, welcome. Do you have any questions about the process or the post before we begin?" The dean has opened the meeting and it's too late to back out now.

"No, no thank you," he says, clearing his mind of everything but what he rehearsed: the stinging, precise rhetoric of form over function; the knife-edge of reason over intuition. If he stays in the place he can trust—the place where minutiae create kingdoms, where the facts he possesses can be trained onto the subject of film like a dazzler in the green electromagnetic spectrum—if he can have no after- or future-images, he will get through this.

The interview commences and he tells them about his research, about the notion that contemporary independent cinema can be analyzed alongside avant-garde poetry by inter-rogating the idea that all motion produces space, produces the time-image, and the time-image presents movement as a multi-plicity of relations. Cinema, like poetry, wants to create the finite that restores the infinite.

He finishes and realizes he has barely taken a breath. He launches back in. "And these are the same principles I apply to teaching, that this teaching in turn feeds back, via student response, to concepts and ideas, making an interplay between theory and practice that is crucial in contemporary culture." Each week he is renewed by his interaction with the students; the results he has helped them to achieve in their coursework confirm this crucial exchange. Since his arrival at Thames Gateway University, over twenty of his students have achieved first-class honours degrees. He takes a second breath and looks at the faces of his parole board. He can read nothing, but he has done all he can.

The interview ends after he tactfully answers questions about how he would approach teaching larger groups of students. Richard thanks him for his cooperation in this round of restruc-turing and assures him of their intention to be among the finest film departments in London. Afterimage: the white shadow of bones like tiny pins, translucent fingernails, baby fingers.

—

He has had a dreamless, undisturbed night. No images, sounds, sensations of any sort. Outside: sun for Easter weekend. Friday is a holiday, he has finished classes for this week, and all he has to do now is wait. Christ.

He orders an espresso from a young man, twenty-two at best, whose hair has been cut in a number two, his stud earrings tiny diamante, making a trophy of the shape of his head. If he doesn't get the job, Robin will get a number two. He will not go as far as the earring, but the hair will have to go.

This café has nothing on Epicure, a few streets up Upper Street. But it's safe here, while he has nothing constructive to say to Katrin. His hand wants her. His mouth hallucinates her taste. He is like a man away at war, deprived of everything that feels like home.

His phone rings. Richard. He doesn't even bother to take a breath, like you're supposed to do on the verge of bad news.

"Richard." Robin is calm. He asked a barber for a number two, years ago, when he thought he would fail his PhD viva, but the barber told him to be optimistic and come back only if he had. He listens to Richard's voice at a remove, as though Richard, or he—one of them—is under water and the other is above it. The way Richard tells him that he has the job makes Robin feel like he's sinking—a backwards elation that he wasn't expecting. The job allows him the responsibility he must take on in any case. There's no turning back.

"We wanted to invest in your position as an early career researcher," Richard says. Robin knows enough about the finances of the university and budget cuts to translate this as, *You're the cheapest of the lot.*

"Thank you, Richard. Yes. Have a good holiday," he says and hangs up.

He pays for his coffee and walks up Upper Street. He takes out his phone, to call Emma, but rings off, and continues north. By the time he's at the door of Epicure, the sun is so hot on his forehead that he is seeing spots before his eyes. He will tell her that with the job he can give Emma money to live elsewhere with the baby. They will find a solution for her mother. Aren't all solutions as obvious as the feeling of this sun?

He doesn't see her at first, but never mind, she must be in the back. He sits at a table near the counter, not the window, ready to resist if she asks him to leave. He doesn't want to disrupt, just to tell her there is hope.

Alejandro comes to his table. He's not as tall as he remembers him and this is another good moment in the day. He pushes his glasses up higher on his nose.

"Is Katrin here?"

"No, she's not," Alejandro says.

The man has sideburns but seems harmless, so what has Robin been all in a knot about? "Ah, I was hoping—I thought her day off was Sunday."

"She's not here any more," Alejandro says, and his eyes show some sort of compassion. Robin senses a throbbing in his shin.

"Since when?" It was only a little over a week ago that he was here. They walked; she said *you tell me when.*

"Last week," Alejandro says. Too many thoughts to have them here. He thanks the man, stands up and leaves the café.

The 38 bus takes forever to bring him to Katrin's bedsit. He rings the buzzer. Again. One last time. She might have found another job. He didn't even think to ask. Fool.

FRANCINE

Thursdays smell like pickles. Francine takes her sweet time to walk from the parking lot through the atrium, past Starbucks, the student union shop, the main reception, out the door to the university square, across the square with a little wave at the river, then to the Watson Building, past the Costa's, up the lift, slow, slow, slow, no rush on this day that will be her last. If they give her a few months' notice will she bother coming in again at all? Nah, a few long weeks of sleeping in and eating chocolate until she smells of it is more likely.

"Hello, Simon," she says when the elevator opens and he moves towards her, looking like the marked man he is, depleted and thinner thanks to the shingles.

"Francine," he says, nodding. Simon is the kind of guy you could stand in the elevator with and not notice.

The day ticks over as she sorts out things on her desk, in the shelves, in her files. Years of files to clean out. Sayonara. She starts a pile for shredding; she will destroy each and every report so that no one can follow the trail of six years of her not giving a shit, of her pushing papers around for the real academics, of sitting on her

butt growing fat on slice after slice of cheap pizza. What is the
sound of one hand clapping? It's a riddle she learned in eighth
grade from Mr. Sullivan when they studied World Religions. The
smell of melting snow in spring, earth and dog shit rising from
beneath it. Nail polish on the nails she'd bitten down far below her
finger's soft pads. Ivory soap wafting up from the crook of her arm
as she slouched at her classroom desk, listening to Mr. Sullivan but
staring at Trice Hopkins' chin. She's not until now understood the
answer to the riddle, which is "yes." Yes, she says, yes, to nothing,
to all of this nothing, to the fact that living on air was never a possibility; the airless creases in Dario's twisted trouser legs. Nothing.

Yes.

Towards 5 p.m. her stomach rumbles, not with hunger, not
even with fear. There's a light knock at her door. Lawrence is
there, looking as pale as she feels.

"We're in the clear," he says, his face expressionless.

Larry, you're a fat ass, she thinks, and has not taken in his
words. Larry, Larry, you need to get off your fat ass.

"All of us?" she finally says, her stomach churning.

"All of us," he says, but without a smile, as though he regrets
that this is the news he has for her. When he closes the door she
is aware that the curdling in her stomach has not subsided, that
her stomach is, in fact, a little disappointed about the outcome
of the day.

———

Spittle on the windshield is not something she's taking personally
tonight. No, it doesn't all happen to her. Someone got fired and she
didn't. Someone teaching history or a non-viable foreign language,

or maybe even anthropology. She didn't wait for Lawrence to give her names. And now Ryan is running towards her car, hoodie up through the rain. He opens the door and throws himself into the passenger seat like cargo into a hull. He is jittery, can't settle.

"He got thirty-six days plus community service for the rest . . . lost his licence permanently." He says it all through his teeth, hot spittle hissing.

"His family will suffer," she says.

He looks at her and snorts, shakes his head. Looks back at his hands, where he's picked at the cuticles around his nails. He shakes his head again but doesn't say anything yet.

"You shouldn't have left the scene before giving all your evidence," is what finally comes out. There's a scalding, like steam, on her skin. His fingers picking, picking.

"You couldn't have saved him," she says. He shakes his head again.

"You need to leave me alone now," he says to the dashboard, not daring to turn his head. His hand reaches for the door handle.

What is the sound of one hand clapping?

She drives down Salusbury Road past the mosque. The sky mewls. The rain in Spain falls mainly on the plane. On the plain? She has never known which. She pulls over in front of the Sainsbury's, parks, goes in.

The self-service check-out voice tells her to take her items and thanks her. The flowers are shabby and predictable, but she is pleased with them. Tulips and freesia: two bunches. She walks up Salusbury Road in the spitting rain; the smell of wet asphalt is like cake. She crosses the road to the middle, waits for a northbound lorry to pass and heads towards the other side, where dried bunches of roses, lilies, and a few fresh tulips hang from a rope around the oak tree a few inches from where Dario's head lay face down. She wonders who it is that keeps replenishing this shrine, but likes the fact that they've both thought of tulips. She slides the freesia in the string ring and stands back to examine their effect. Just right. She walks to the other side of the tree where there are no bouquets. She pulls on the string to slide in the tulips.

"These are from Rajit," she says.

ED

Catherine never liked a pub. Nor any other public places to eat or drink; she did all her drinking and eating in their tiny house in Bow. And things don't change in all of the years you think it tek to change a woman. The thought of her was in his head like paper close to fire, day in and out since Olivia put it there, causing him to do sit-ups and push-ups in his flat, stopping the grog for two weeks. Then Catherine called him. She wanted things in broad daylight, where everything is real and true, she said. So they are in Parsloes park, on a bench like old people in the afternoon and this is exactly how he used to imagine them—sitting and watching people walk past, knowing Olivia was good and in school. Except that now in front of them is a wall with a painting of a head like a mad hatter, grey streak in black hair, and letters that spell something about the mad-ass graffiti artist who made it with a can of paint. Above it is another drawing—a green man, the Incredible Hulk, busting out of his clothes. Not romantic, but not dull either.

Catherine looks old for a woman not yet fifty, but he's not looking there, he's looking into her eyes that are not looking at him, and he's trying to find the tiny Marilyn Monroe in her and to get those years back. She has talked, breathless-like, filling in every silence with something that means nothing. She always did that, always the one to guide him towards the feelings they were both having, and it seems today, according to her talk of nothing—about the work she does, the place she lives, and the state of things now that things are tight all round—he thinks that the feelings she is having have something to do with money. But, true-true, the looks of the pudding is not the taste.

"Olivia is coming up good," he says, to give them something they can share, but Catherine's face goes sour and he is sorry he said it because he can't take any credit for that.

"You helping with her project?" Catherine is holding back now, he can tell.

"As much as I can, of course."

She stands and begins to walk; he leaps up to follow her. "I know you sent money," she says. So she is admitting now that she opened the envelopes before marking them Return to Sender. "Whose money was that?" she asks.

Jesus.

"My money; I worked hard for it," he says. She stops and looks at him. "I wanted Olivia to grow up good, to have everything she needed."

Catherine tosses her head back, turns and walks faster; they pass the playground at a pace before she stops again and looks at him.

"You never knew what you needed, didn't know whether to be here or there, always wanting things to be different," she says.

How to mash-up a heart is easy. "You do any better?"

She starts to walk again, slowly, as they reach the tall trees near the end of the park. "My dad was sure you were involved with Geoffrey."

"Of course he was," because Catherine's father is an ignorant rass and they both know it.

"So was he right?"

"No, no, he wasn't right." But there is no way of telling the story that doesn't make him look bad somehow. "I wasn't involved in anything that Geoffrey did," he says, and this seems to calm her if not convince her. And then he is vex. "You just went along with what your dad thought?"

Catherine squints and keeps walking. He knows this is the thing that will bruk them up, right here, once again, but he has no choice. "Why wouldn't you let me see you?"

"I couldn't trust you any more," she says—hard-hard, like she is holding stone in her teeth.

"You didn't even give me a chance, not a one," he says.

"It wouldn't have been good for Olivia."

"I'm her father."

There's a look on her face like she's sucking a tamarind. Catherine turns to him beneath the branches of the smallest of the oaks in the row. "No," she says.

He looks in her face, the Marilyn Monroe eyes and pout that have gone droopy with age and probably too much drink, there with her father and brother in front of the television. He waits for her to continue.

"No, you're not."

There is a bird making a racket above them in the oak tree. A cawing like it has been set on fire and it's trapped among the leaves that each catch-a-fire, and it's like the whole tree is going to burn down. He looks up at the cawing but can't see the bird. What he can see is the place she lived, the flat on Romford Road where she told him she was pregnant.

"She looks like me." The fire in the tree is hissing. Catherine shuffles her feet.

"You're much better looking than he was," she says.

And now he knows. The man before him, the one from St. Kitts; the one whose photo he saw in her purse: wide-faced, big hands, for so. The one who, three weeks into Ed's courting of Catherine like she was the last queen of England, was going back to St. Kitts and asked to see her one last time.

When a couple months later she said she was pregnant it wasn't with a thrill in her voice the way a woman expecting a baby should be. It was him who was chuffed, looking around Catherine's flat, declaring it was unfit for bringing up a child, and securing them a council house.

"Catherine." The sound of her name is flat and treacherous. *You knew all this time?* But that is just a waste of words, because of course she knew. A mother knows these things.

"What about Olivia?" he says.

Catherine eases herself down to sit on the grass. "She knows now."

"Since when?"

"A couple weeks."

The last time he saw her was at Jonathan Henley's funeral where she watched Ed sing "Amazing Grace" like a fool.

Christ. The damn bird keeps cawing like a rass. A mad good-fa-nothin' bird. Not tiyoooh, yooh-yoooh of a toucan; not yeeh, yeeeh of a kiskadee. This bird is caw-caw like it sick.

"You're the one she remembers—to her you are her father," Catherine says.

What does someone remember from four years old? His legs are boneless beneath him and he slips down to the grass beside her, not to sitting, just perched on one knee like a man proposing to a tree.

He's nobody's father.

Saltfish, tamarind balls, metagee: he doesn't need to remember the taste of these now, or to rhyme them off for Olivia. His mother's bangle in the top drawer of his dresser—her pulling it over her hand and wrist the last time he saw her on the steps of her sister's house in Rose Hall Town: this too can wait. His auntie Margaret has children who pay attention to mum, but for twenty-two years she has wanted to see her granddaughter. For eighteen years she has been sending small gifts for her, the gold bangle the most precious. Every Guyanese girl must have a bangle, and most fitting if the bangle is from the grandmother whose middle name the child will bear her entire life. Olivia.

Niggeritus, backoo, obeyah, piknee: he need not mention these. If you eat labba and drink creek water you will return to Guyana. None of this matters now.

Catherine does not move or say a word. Sitting, kneeling, the two of them under the tree on fire. He's surprised by how quickly it seems that the light has gone dimmer and there is a pain in his knee. He gets up and Catherine does the same. They walk together, slowly, to the exit of the park. She wants to say something, he can tell, but no, please don't. He catches her eye and then turns to walk away to the bus.

OLIVIA

Good Friday, flip the bird to you, Jesus, and all she needs is more Maltesers, more coffee from one of those chains, she doesn't mind which, 'cos principles and politics and parental units are the fuck-up of the tiny bit of herself that once thought she had something significant, special, banging, to be sharing and making a difference with, but all that's holy in this weekend is the fact that the library is still open. She is the fuck-you-I'm-going-to-crack-it-and-make-something-of-herself Olivia who never did a single thing but look out for everyone else, never had a thought that was solely her own and never did like she's doing now which is writing with her head trained on the page like it is in a brace, and writing a word at a time, building to a sentence, not looking further than a sentence or thinking about the whole of the sum of the sentences; she's writing one word like it's one foot in front of the other, out, out, out of here.

Another ping from the mobile at the bottom of her satchel. These are regular-like now, one every few hours. Pleading. From Jaz. From Catherine. But nothing from Nasar, the most obedient of the lot. She pulls her phone from the satchel.

I saw Wood. Told him everything. Please come home now.

Her heart goes all dented for Wood but not for Catherine, because a mother who lies to you your whole life will have to do a whole lot more than ask please. She holds tight onto herself in that clench she has perfected. In four thousand more words, one after the other, she will examine legislation that needs to go beyond current rights issues: beyond the disposal of bodies; beyond crimes committed against dead bodies in which there is a tangle of competing rights pitting survivors against the deceased, or the deceased against the police or the powers of the state; beyond cases of harvesting sperm from a corpse; beyond the definition of sex with a dead body as rape; beyond the ana- tomical gift act that regulates organ donation and follows the wishes of the deceased unless the family vetoes them and gets the last word. And if she gets beyond all these, she will have arrived at something resembling an original idea. There is a case to be made for rights that take into account a proper goodbye.

ROBIN

His side hurts, his calf, his right hand, and there's a feeling in his ear like someone is twisting the tip. He stands up. If he stays perfectly still he can feel his insides churning, his body's organs at work as though against one another. He lies back down on the bed. The ceiling of Robin's bedroom has a brown stain left over from a leak of many years ago, a stain he's not got round to painting over. He will have to do that, soon, before Emma moves in, before things get crammed with baby paraphernalia, before he forgets that these small things make a difference to a life, that aesthetics are important. These are the kinds of things that people with children forget. The stain looks like the figure of a giraffe. Perhaps he should keep it.

He has been lying on his back now for over twelve hours, the light on throughout the night while he dozed and woke, not sleeping deeply enough, not having changed out of his clothes.

Emma is thrilled with the news of his job. She is planning on bringing him an Easter Sunday lunch to celebrate, to share as a family.

The fact that he waited outside Katrin's bedsit for an hour until he realized how futile that was, the fact that he returned to

Epicure and Alejandro was able to confirm that she had not left for another job, that Alejandro had received a few texts from her about the possibility of leaving London but nothing more, the fact that Robin's calls to her phone were answered by the woman who tells you that the number has not been recognized, the fact of Katrin as only an afterimage: his head is somewhere else entirely from his legs, feet, fingernails, groin, heart. The only thing to do is to keep staring at the giraffe.

He looks at the clock and waits until 23:11 before he closes his eyes again.

—

Emma's Easter lunch is roast lamb, potatoes and green beans. She is gentle, careful, trying to help him feel better because he's told her he is ill, has some sort of Asian flu probably, some ghastly thing from his students, not well at all.

"Any old excuse not to wash up," she said at first, but she must have then taken seriously the anguish in his face, because now she's clearing up and making the flat comfortable for him. This will be his life. Surely not a bad thing.

"Maybe we should go to Cornwall—you could use a break, and you have two weeks before teaching starts again. The sea, some walking, check in on your folks," she suggests. But he would be too tempted to slip down one of those cliffs. Too tempted to tell his folks that he doesn't love this woman and that they should not go thinking it's all just one big happy family now—that it's not as simple as that. He will look after his child. He will. He will love, provide for, play with, challenge, educate and be a good, honest role model. But before he can do that he needs to drag all the pieces of himself together in one spot, to pull in his insides, to gather up his fingers and the strands of his hair. Together.

He goes back to bed when Emma leaves. The giraffe holds its head up high as Robin's body litters the room. Deleuze: The shadow escapes from the body like an animal we had been shelter-ing . . . It is not the slumber of reason that engenders monsters, but vigilant and insomniac rationality.

What kind of success is it to have saved himself a job where he does nothing but think? He sits, picks up the journal on his bedside table: L=A=N=G=U=A=G=E. He flips through, but then tosses it aside. He lies back down and stares again at the ceiling. He tries to focus on the feeling of being a dad, but nothing comes but terror. Fact is, fear might just create a new stain. Deleuze: If you're trapped in the dream of the Other, you're fucked.

He picks up the list tucked into the journal. On it are Bernadette Mayer's suggestions for poetry experiments:

• Write the same poem over and over again, in different forms, until you are weary. Another experiment: Set yourself the task of writing for four hours at a time, perhaps once, twice or seven times a week. Don't stop until hunger and/or fatigue take over. At the very least, always set aside a four-hour period once a month in which to write. This is always possible and will result in one book of poems or prose writing for each year. Then we begin to know something.
• Attempt as a writer to win the Nobel Prize in science by finding out how thought becomes language, or does not.
• Take a traditional text like the pledge of allegiance to the flag. For every noun, replace it with one that is seventh or

ninth down from the original one in the dictionary. For instance, the word "honesty" would be replaced by "honey dew melon." Investigate what happens; different dictionaries will produce different results.

None of these is as structured as chance-operation. He looks at the clock, watches it until 23:11. The first book of poetry he takes from his shelf is *White Egrets*.

"The chess men are rigid on their chess board." Okay, line one. He turns out the light and tries to sleep.

ED AND ROBIN

The stapler is his—he must remember to take it. They give you rass-hole staplers in the council and this one he bought himself, top of the line. Sammy steals it at least once a day, but it's Ed's.

"This place," Sammy says as he opens the office for the day. "This place," again, and Ed isn't sure if Sammy means the Safe and Sorrow office or if he's talking about the local authority, or London, or the whole damn world. It doesn't matter, because all of them feel like a head-shaking mess to Sammy today, and this you can see in the man's shoulders, which have gone hunch-up. But what's to be hunch-up for? When water throw away ah ground yuh can't pick am up.

"You know, it's not me they've booted out only because they'd have to give me more severance, don't you? Longer-term service, uninterrupted. You know that, right?" Sammy says. They both look over at Ralph, who looks straight ahead, filling out of a form on his computer.

Poor Sammy is feeling sad, but this shaking-head is the only way he knows to show it. He hasn't looked Ed in the eye since they heard the news.

"Sammy," Ed says, calm fa so. He pauses so that Sammy will stop and turn around, but he doesn't, just keeps tidying up, putting paper in the shredder. "Sammy, I'm fine, you hear?" And Sammy does hear, but that doesn't make him stop tidying, and Ed can tell from how Sammy sits down at this desk that his heart is mash-up. Ed will remember to get Sammy a raisin Danish on his break.

He's not the first one in, but Robin is standing at the door of the Safe and Sorrow office as soon as Ed opens it. He knows him only by the glasses that look bigger on the man's face now.

"You cut off all your hair!" Ed says, in a tease, but in fact Robin looks better this way, more grown-up, dignified-like. He doesn't bother to take Robin to the staff room. Sammy and Ralph can overhear anything they want at this point.

"How's Olivia's project going then?" he asks. "Haven't seen her since before Easter. She tried to reach me, but I've been busy-busy," he tells Robin because when guilt is so big, lies come fast and easy. He will ring her back, he will, but what to say? Almost-dad. Not good enough.

"I would like to contribute, to her project, your funerals," Robin says.

"Doesn't matter, not now," Ed says.

"Oh," Robin says, yet sees nothing like sadness in Ed's face. Only some small trace of Olivia. "I'm sorry," he says. He touches his pocket and feels the crunch of the paper there, the ridiculous, irrelevant game of the past fourteen days.

Wood's face opens up to a smile. "Sorry? What you have to be sorry for?" The man's accent is strong today. Robin nods.

"I thought I would try, in any case—Olivia's idea, it might bring some good," he says.

"Well, it might, but who knows when the next one will be—we can't predict these things. Maybe Sammy will work with you." Ed looks over at his friend, who is listening but making a show of ignoring the whole damn scene, probably wondering what the rass is going on over here. These two men like surra and durra on the stage, both wishing they could do a little something, both just sorry-sorry to one another. Olivia missing in between them. The St. Kitts man must have been something. Who gave the girl her sense of right and wrong? Is that something you are born with?

They sit in silence until it becomes uncomfortable. Robin pulls the piece of paper out of his pocket, unfolding it. He reads over it, quickly. Crap, not a poem, but deliberate, like lightning. He gives it to Wood, who takes it but doesn't look at it. There's a gritty irritation in Robin's eyes, as though sand is caught on the underside of his eyelid. His eyes water and he wipes them. In cinema a flash burn is named after the effect of snow blindness, which is akin to a sunburn of the cornea. But a flash-burn effect is too obvious, too simple for now.

Wood holds the piece of paper, still just looking at him. Robin imagines Wood at the head of a coffin, reading his plagiarized nonsense.

"Well, it was good to meet you," he says.

"And you," Ed says. Robin stands up and shakes his hand. This man is something good, true-true.

Then Robin has the opposite of an afterimage: a time image that produces space, the finite restoring the infinite; it's the house where Katrin's grandmother grew up, beside the river, and his finger on the tiny buzzer alerts its occupants to a visitor. Fact is, Gdansk is only a city. Gdansk cannot be that big.

OLIVIA AND ED

"An examination of civil rights in death," Olivia says, and keeps her knee from moving. Holds it there, stone-like, 'cos this is how it's going to be from now on, steady, like steel, but knowing, like silk. She will not be tricked again by Catherine or anyone else. "My supervisor said I needed something historical, not practical—it's not practice-based research," she says. Ed nods, but maybe he's disappointed that she abandoned the lonely dead. She hasn't, really, it's only the appearance of stone there in her leg; there's no stillness in her heart.

The A13 feels different. Same emptiness, same salt, pepper and brown sauce, but today it looks sparkly bright, as though Mary has been scrubbing and buffing and picking out the grime with a cotton-tipped swab.

"Sounds good," Ed says, and man, oh man, the girl is clever-for-so, but where once he thought he had something to do with it, now he feels like a rasshole fool. There's no one here but Mary to see him cry if it comes to that.

"It was possible all on account of you," she says, and it's true, even if it was for all the wrong reasons. Catherine is the lifetime liar, and Olivia is taking her sweet time to talk to her mother again, but Wood—Wood is solid fam.

She's humouring him, of course, he thinks, because he is laughable, lonely, nearly dead himself. He takes a sip of his tea and sneaks a quick look at the evidence of her face, and maybe there is a trace of the St. Kitts man there in the wideness, when all along he thought it was like Auntie Margaret's face.

While Ed is staring at her Olivia knows there's stuff for him to get used to, expectations he has to stop having, so she lets him. She lets his eyes wander over her ears, her nose, her chin, like he's looking to see if maybe Catherine was wrong after all. Olivia hasn't even wondered what the other bloke might have looked like, doesn't want to know, doesn't want to have another face or another voice in her head to haunt her. Once she thought she would ask Ed to sing the song again, of the brown girl in the ring, but, hell, no. She doesn't want any more incantations or ghosts.

"But I still want to do the project with you—it's still right, still good," she says. With her dissertation finished, she's confident of a 2.1, at least, and if she doesn't get a first, well, she'll still become a lawyer, will still train further, will still make enough to move out—alone—but there's no giving up; this she accepts. The questions change. Who will _____ these people? Fill in the blank. Living with Catherine, Nan, Granddad and Eric won't be as bad, for a while, if she knows at least this much about herself.

"Look, Olivia," Ed says, and meets her eye. There is no denying that she is beautiful and of course she is nothing like Geoffrey. He pulls apart the paper napkin that came with his tea. "The man Geoffrey killed . . . " the napkin looks like snowflakes . . . "I wanted to say . . . " and there's a tinkle-like sound from Mary's bracelets as she wipes the table next to them . . . "I arrived at the spot where Geoffrey killed him—minutes too late—and he was there, his face in the river. He was dead, I was sure of it, but I could have done something, maybe. I could have called someone; I could have turned him over. I could even have said something like I was sorry, but I didn't. I did nothing. I watched Geoffrey run through the bush and I didn't tell anyone what I saw. I went back to the camp farther down river and I pretended I saw nothing, and no one asked me, and no one expected me to know, so I kept it to myself. I had gone to find Geoffrey, to give him the money he needed, to make sure he wouldn't get into trouble, and found a whole lot worse." He looks back at her. Olivia has questions in her face the way some women have desire. She nods. "It's what I thought you did for family, for a brother."

"You thought?" she says.

"I don't know, now. I don't think so, no," Ed says. The real story was so much easier than he had imagined for so long.

"So, you'll let me know when the next one is?" Olivia says, and for a second he thinks she's referring to Geoffrey, before he realizes.

"I might not have a funeral again before I go—you can't plan these things. I have only three months."

"It would be a good thing if you got none in three months, wouldn't it?" she says. Olivia is mash-up for anyone's heart. "But if you do, you'll tell me, right?"

"Yes, I will," Ed says.

"We could go to the museum again. Or I was thinking, I've always wanted to go to the Carnival."

"Oh?" She's never jump-up, never played Mas or ever wind-up and fete so. He nods, and his heart is doing a j'ouvert jump-up of its own. "I was doing some research, too—there's a Guyanese poet . . . it might be good."

"Oh?" Same intonation as his, but she is not mocking him.

"Death must not find us thinking that we die."

"That's good!" she says with a flourish. They both pick up their teacups at the same time. They sip.

"Wood," she says, and she sees where the word has landed in how his shoulders relax. This man was the only one who ever picked her up and held her.

FRANCINE

At the door to Ronnie Scott's Patricia doesn't look unhappy, doesn't look like a woman whose whole department has been shut down—"Who needs a degree in anthropology when you could get one in marketing?" Patricia said flatly to Francine on the phone. It was Francine's idea to come out tonight. "It's fine," Patricia says to her as they walk up the stairs to the salsa room.

"What will you do?" Francine says.

"Never write a book again," Patricia says, and Francine is surprised by her equanimity, not believing that she could be as fine as she professes. Upstairs Francine checks their coats, gets them a drink and then the feeling of being in the transporter is back.

Diaphanous men in their twenties: African, Latino, tight jeans. Very tight jeans. Their skin is translucent in Francine's X-ray vision.

There is a dark Latino dancing salsa with a tiny woman with straight, brown hair whose short flounce skirt splays like a sail when he turns her. The man's arms are as sculpted as an Oscar trophy.

Patricia raises her glass and sips from a straw. Francine looks at the pad of lines on the skin of Patricia's knuckles, there like ancient footprints or dinosaur knees. They are the oldest women in the room. There are one or two middle-aged men, but the rest are in their twenties or thirties, not English. How is it that Patricia has no self-consciousness here?

"You look good," Patricia shouts over the horns, conga drums, the singer and his repeated *galenga, galenga, galenga*. But Francine is sure she looks like shit and that to see through her you'd have to penetrate her puffy, ricotta-cheese cheeks. But maybe Patricia has seen through her all along.

The instructor turns down the music and she notices for the first time that the men here are checking them both out. When she looks through them, she sees them in a sandbox: dump trucks and spades and diapers full of poo hanging down from their backsides. If she looks harder, she sees them fifty years in the future: their skin loose and iguana-neck-like, their butts gone soft and droopy; their penises bulbous but flopping. What is the sound of one hand clapping?

"Line up, line up. Girls on one side, boys on the other—but some of you will be acting the part of boys," says the instructor, who is taking into account that the females outnumber the males. Francine does as she's told and is face to face with the Latino with the Oscar-trophy arms, who couldn't be older than thirty.

"Now face your partner—girls, stretch out your arms; and boys, take her waist. Girls, hand on shoulders."

He starts the music again and shouts instructions at them while doing the moves himself, his hand on his tummy, his hips swinging side to side. He does the steps, shouts the ins and outs, the hand holding, the spinning, and Francine follows along with trophy man without a foot wrong. She looks up at him, sees him smiling at her, and he pulls her close, suddenly: "Manuel," he says in her ear. She looks down at her feet. His hot breath on her cheek makes her nervous and she misses a step. When he releases her she looks up and says, quietly, "Francine," but he's not looking at her any more and will never know her name.

"Now change—cha cha!" the instructor shouts and Manuel moves her forward and back, one-two-three. She searches for Patricia and sees her with one of the middle-aged men. She's not smiling, but not unhappy either as she concentrates on her steps.

"Rum makes me stupid," Francine says to Patricia in passing, after they are instructed to switch partners. They dance for hours, and the beat will not give up. When she stops for a rest, Manuel takes the rum and Coke from her hand, places it down on the table and leads her again to the dance floor.

"You are good," he says, after he twirls her as the music changes, goes slow and thumpy. He brings her in close, and, yep, there it is, his hand on her giant ass like a butcher with a prime cut. She holds her breath. "You are very sexy," he says in her ear. This is not happening. She says nothing. He pushes her back and holds her at arm's length, looking her up and down.

She laughs, which he seems to like, and he pulls her close again and gives her a peck on her cheek that feels nearly like a lick. A tingle at her neck, along her arm, to the tips of her fingers and she squeezes his hand. Oh shit. She didn't mean to do that. She is the opposite of a thirteen-year old, but feels exactly the same. Maybe the thing that love comes with is seasons. She sees Patricia smiling proudly at her from the side of the room.

They close the place, are the last ones out, even after Manuel and the women he gravitated towards at the end of the night, who are young but do not have Francine's life raft of a butt, of which she is a tiny bit proud.

"Let's get something to eat," Patricia says, and out they head and turn onto Old Compton Street, where Francine smells urine and is convinced she hears bones clacking. She stops and stands on the spot to watch. The black cast-steel bollard, the warped brick of the corner building, the corrugated iron that covers the shop window: she is small and soft beside these.

"That was special, no?" Patricia says, coming close.

Francine tries to smell her but the familiar butter and lavender are lost amongst the piss and beer on the pavement. Iron, rust, fried onions, exhaust fumes, tobacco. She smiles but doesn't answer, doesn't say heck, yeah Patty! Because she's wondering how much a landscape gardening programme might cost her, wondering if she'll make more than minimum wage in any future job, and she doesn't want Patricia to look at her with horror when she tells her that she's quitting her job in QA and going to tell Larry he's fat. She doesn't want to worry Patricia or for her to think it's false solidarity in the face of her redundancy. Instead, she leans in towards Dancefloor Patty and kisses her on the lips, and holds her mouth there. Patricia doesn't pull back, not first in any case, and when Francine is again aware of how she feels, well, she's certain it's only a hot flash.

OLIVIA

Oi. She flicks away the wasp on her wrist. It's hot even in the thick-as-paint shade of the yew tree outside the crematorium at the Rippleside Cemetery. Holy, holy, holy, like a beat girl poet, 'cos Olivia is now down with ceremonies as though they are the new #Demo. Though there's no knowing the religion of Diyanat Bayar, who Ed thinks is Turkish, or maybe Armenian, which would change things, the service is about making praise, even though it's not in the chapel. Diyanat's UK passport might even have been stolen, forged, and so the truth is that no one knows a thing about this body that is about to be burned and disposed of. The twenty-seven-year-old Diyanat, if that is his name, has no family in the UK. The Turkish consulate is busy with Turkish nationals, the coroner told Ed, and haven't been able to trace anyone yet. The coroner who registered the death also told Ed that Diyanat has a tattoo on his arm of an anchor, but there's no link to Diyanat being a sailor, because Diyanat's last job was in the bakery where he'd been hired only a few months ago. Holy, holy, holy.

Olivia watches as Ed arranges the bouquet of lilies on the top of the cardboard casket. This is his last funeral. Ed wanted her to be here, saying he had something to show her, something that he thought would make her happy, and something that was on account of her.

When Olivia was still researching her dissertation, way back in May, which was the last time it was hot like this and the last time she saw Ed, she read about three people of the same family discovered dead by the police in their apartment in the northern district of Tokyo. Electricity and gas had been cut off; there was no food in the house and just a few one-yen coins on the table. The grotesquely thin bodies belonged to a couple in their sixties and their son in his thirties, and they had all died of starvation. The management property reported getting no rent, and the newspaper said that the family had asked a neighbour for help. The neighbour told them to go on welfare, which they didn't do, on account of losing face. The report went on to say how lonely deaths are increasing in Japan. In the winter two sisters in their forties were found dead in their freezing apartment on snowbound Hokkaido.

"Thank you for coming," Ed says to Olivia, as she is the only mourner in attendance. The funeral director and his assistant stand off to the side, looking like they're daydreaming about the cold pint they'll have as soon as this is finished.

"We are here to pay our last respects to Diyanat Bayar, who was too young to be leaving us, really," Ed says and then looks down at the casket. The breeze around them is soft and she feels gooseflesh rise on her arms despite the heat.

Ed looks older. Not so much in wrinkles or greying or geezer-like stuff, but just in the way his mouth falls when at rest. Right. She will not worry; she is working on this part of herself in relation to everyone else. He will find another job. Just look at him. Wood is strong, worthy, a man with a good head. He takes a piece of paper out his pocket and unfolds it, catching her eye with a look that says: *This is it, here, now.*

"I would like to read something for Diyanat—something that was written by a friend of ours, a while back. He gave it to me and asked me to read it the next time I had the opportunity, and this is that opportunity, so please allow me," Ed says, and gives her a nod.

Olivia feels the gooseflesh grow and spread up towards her neck.

Ed looks down at the paper and begins.

"The chessmen are rigid on their chess board,
I can hear little clicks inside my dream,
Auntie stands by the kettle, looking at the kettle,
If I were a cinnamon peeler,
That strength, mother: dug out. Hammered, chained.
What can I say about the storms?
An eagle does not know who he is,
Who modelled your head of terracotta?
Chalk and beaches. The winter sea,
I wonder at your witchcraft
One morning Don Miguel got out of bed,
Let us go then, you and I,
Not a tent of blue but a peak of gold,
No getting up from the bed in this grand hotel."

Ed looks up proudly at her. But Olivia doesn't think she caught it right. There's nothing she understands about the poem and what it means. She wants him to read it again, to take his time, because what is Robin saying here?

The funeral director and his assistant make their way to the casket, looking annoyed, as though their time is being wasted in this boiling July heat for this man and his daughter to work out some puzzle between them. They wheel the casket towards the back door of the crematorium and Ed watches as Diyanat takes his leave. Olivia leaves the shade of the yew, headed towards Ed, practising her one-foot-in-front-of-the-other strategy. Since her last exams she's been calmer, been spending days sleeping when she wants to, nights with Jaz who is single once more, and she is slowly starting to allow Catherine to talk to her again. She has a paid internship with the Citizens Advice Bureau starting in August and she's had the time not to feel panicked.

"What did you think?" Ed says.

"Yes, yes," she says. "I'd like to hear it again."

Ed holds the page up to her. "You take it," he says.

"No, it's yours," she says and pushes his hand back.

There'll be no more use for this poem, she knows, but she's afraid to read it for herself now. And maybe she doesn't need to.

"I should get going," she says. She doesn't want to go to the A13 today; she wants to stay out in the sun.

"Okay," Ed says, and she has to resist the dented feeling in her chest. Wood is proper nang. Wood is going to be all right. This is not where she's from, but this is more like who she is.

She kisses his cheek and stands back, turns and walks towards the gates of the cemetery. The sun is wicked and makes the back of her neck ping like there's a message for her. If Nasar still has the same number, it will be in her phone.

Right.

ACKNOWLEDGEMENTS

This book was possible thanks to the insight and inspiration I gained from my students and colleagues; the quiet writing space graciously provided by friends; and the generous feedback from special readers. My thanks to — among other students, too many to be named here — Danielle Jawando, Joe Pierson, Samantha Dodd, Jo Berouche, Joe Caesar, James Moore, Annette Kamara, Sandra Majchrowska, Erica Masserano, and Naida Redgrave, who inspired the fighting spirit of the students in this novel.

Thanks to my colleagues at the University of East London for their support, resilience, and good spirits during difficult times: particularly to Stephen Maddison, Marianne Wells, Kate Hodgkin, and especially to Tim Atkins for poetry, humour, and Zen. I am grateful to the University of East London for research support and leave that enabled me to finish this book.

Thanks to the green mamba for Ned Time, to Danielle Jawando for the Rubik's Cube moment, to Sandra Majchrowska for help with Polish, to Andrew Ruhemann and Jennifer Nadel for Paris, to Mike Perry for Ffynnonofi, and to the Morris family for kindness and Wood. I'm indebted to Marko Jobst and David Friend for crucial feedback on an early draft; to Fides Krucker for writing companionship, banana bread, and voice insight; and to Stephanie Young for being there, reading fast, and knowing what a first draft is. Eternal gratitude to John Berger for his wisdom and generosity.

Thanks to Andrew Kidd for belief, rigour, telepathy; to Anne Collins and Philip Gwyn Jones for courage, enthusiasm and invaluable support; and to the kind people at Random House Canada and Scribe UK for making this book happen.

"I'm the pen your lover writes with" is from a poem by Bernadette Mayer; her poetry experiments inspired Robin's poem, which is formed by the first lines of the following poems:

Derek Wallcott, "White Egrets"; Anne Carson, "The Glass Essay"; Jo Shapcott, "Somewhat Unravelled"; Michael Ondaatje, "The Cinnamon Peeler's Wife"; Anne Carson, "That Strength in Decreation"; Dionne Brand, "Ossuary IX"; Al Purdy, "Man Without a Country"; Ted Hughes, "The Earthenware Head"; Anne Michaels, "Fontanelles"; Daniel Wideman, "Glass Eater"; Don Paterson, "Two Trees"; T. S. Eliot, "The Love Song of J. Alfred Prufrock"; Seamus Heaney, "Death of a Painter"; and Carol Anne Duffy, "Cuba."

"Death must not find us thinking that we die" is from the poem "Death of a Comrade," by Martin Carter. Quotations attributed to Gilles Deleuze are from Deleuze and Guattari, *Capitalism and Schizophrenia: Anti-Oedipus* (1972) and *A Thousand Plateaus* (1980).